# Blast FROM THE Past

## TONI L. P. KELNER

BERKLEY PRIME CRIME, NEW YORK

**THE BERKLEY PUBLISHING GROUP**
**Published by the Penguin Group**
**Penguin Group (USA) Inc.**
**375 Hudson Street, New York, New York 10014, USA**

Penguin Group (Canada), 90 Eglinton Avenue East, Suite 700, Toronto, Ontario M4P 2Y3, Canada
(a division of Pearson Penguin Canada Inc.)
Penguin Books Ltd., 80 Strand, London WC2R 0RL, England
Penguin Group Ireland, 25 St. Stephen's Green, Dublin 2, Ireland (a division of Penguin Books Ltd.)
Penguin Group (Australia), 250 Camberwell Road, Camberwell, Victoria 3124, Australia
(a division of Pearson Australia Group Pty. Ltd.)
Penguin Books India Pvt. Ltd., 11 Community Centre, Panchsheel Park, New Delhi—110 017, India
Penguin Group (NZ), 67 Apollo Drive, Rosedale, North Shore 0632, New Zealand
(a division of Pearson New Zealand Ltd.)
Penguin Books (South Africa) (Pty.) Ltd., 24 Sturdee Avenue, Rosebank, Johannesburg 2196,
South Africa

Penguin Books Ltd., Registered Offices: 80 Strand, London WC2R 0RL, England

This is a work of fiction. Names, characters, places, and incidents either are the product of the author's imagination or are used fictitiously, and any resemblance to actual persons, living or dead, business establishments, events, or locales is entirely coincidental. The publisher does not have any control over and does not assume any responsibility for author or third-party websites or their content.

BLAST FROM THE PAST

A Berkley Prime Crime Book / published by arrangement with the author

PRINTING HISTORY
Berkley Prime Crime mass-market edition / February 2011

Copyright © 2011 by Toni L. P. Kelner.
Cover design by Annette Fiore DeFex.
Cover illustration by Julia Green.
Interior text design by Kristin del Rosario.

ISBN: 978-0-425-23990-2

BERKLEY® PRIME CRIME
Berkley Prime Crime Books are published by The Berkley Publishing Group,
a division of Penguin Group (USA) Inc.,
375 Hudson Street, New York, New York 10014.
BERKLEY® PRIME CRIME and the PRIME CRIME logo are trademarks of Penguin Group (USA) Inc.

PRINTED IN THE UNITED STATES OF AMERICA

10  9  8  7  6  5  4  3  2  1

*continued . . .*

# Acknowledgments

I want to thank:

Stephen P. Kelner, Jr., who reads drafts while on planes to far-away lands.

Charlaine Harris and Dana Cameron, who take time away from their own work to help with mine.

My daughters, Maggie and Valerie, for their patience.

Joan Brandt, who got me this far.

Joni Langervoort, who donated actual money to charity so I would name a character after her.

Jerry Frazee, creator of *Nazrat*, for sharing his experiences in the world of comic books.

# Chapter 1

**flash-forward** *n* Simply put, the opposite of flashback; a filmic technique that depicts a scene, event, or shot taking place (or imagined) or expected that is projected into a future time beyond the present time of the film, or it can be a flash-forward from the past to the present.

—TIM DIRKS, WWW.FILMSITE.ORG

IT was a perfect night for romance. The moon was full, the temperature cool enough to make hand-holding desirable, and the only sounds were seabirds calling and the lap of the ocean waves. All that was missing was for Dylan O'Taine to leave the sanctuary of Pharos, his mystic lighthouse, to share some of his magic.

Unfortunately, Tilda was alone except for a cell phone, and though she was talking to a man, he was quite happily married.

The man in question, Tilda's friend Cooper, asked, "How much longer are you going to be on the Cape?"

"As long as I can get away with. Did I tell you what Dianne brought home last week? A snake!" Dianne was Tilda's latest roommate.

"Don't tell me you have a snake phobia. Do you know how Freudian that is?"

"Of course I know. My sister is a psychologist. But I

don't have a snake phobia. As pets go, snakes aren't too bad. Except that she put it in the living room, and she was going to feed it in there."

"I'm guessing that it doesn't eat Purina Snake Chow."

"Try mice. Cute little white mice who squeal when the snake starts swallowing them."

"That is gross. You have terrible luck in roommates."

"Tell me about it." Tilda was apparently incapable of finding a roomie she could put up with for longer than a year. Only three months into the lease with Dianne and she was already poised to toss the woman and her never-ending pet parade into the street. It made the Cape Cod stay, even without a nice bit of arm candy to walk with in the moonlight, all the more enjoyable.

"Gotta head out," Cooper said. "Let me know how it's going."

"Will do." She hung up the phone, and once she'd put it into her pocket, realized she could hear voices. Up ahead, she saw two people walking along the other side of the road, probably heading for the building where she'd just had dinner.

The Glenham Bars Inn was on Shoreline Road, the unimaginatively named seaside road in the town of Glenham. The main inn building and cottages of varying sizes and levels of luxury were scattered on both sides of the road. With lights strung in the trees, it looked like a nicer brand of carnival, though the brochure described it as a fairy-tale setting.

From behind, Tilda heard the sound of a car engine, and stepped several more feet away from the edge of the road. The graveled path was plenty far enough from the roadway to be safe, but after an unfortunate incident some months back, being around cars tended to make her skittish.

The vehicle was going considerably faster than it should have on the curved road, and Tilda flipped him a bird as he zoomed past her. She opened her mouth to add a description of his parentage, but it turned into a gasp as the car veered into the other lane and straight at the people walking toward her. There were screams, flying gravel, and a thunk. Then the car swerved back onto the road and sped up as it went past the inn.

Tilda started running. Both the people struck were down on the ground, and only one was moving. As she reached them she realized she knew who they were—it was John Laryea and his assistant Foster. Then she realized something else. She'd recognized the vehicle, too. It hadn't been just any car. In fact, it hadn't been a car at all. It had been a black stretch limo, one with a very recognizable license plate. And she'd been in that limo just three days before.

# Chapter 2

*The Blastoffs*, a live action Saturday morning show of the early eighties, featured a musical pair of brothers—Sid and Marty Blastoff—who toured the galaxy with their alien babysitter/manager, Posit, spreading "love and groovy tunes." Only eighteen episodes were filmed, and the show would probably have disappeared into obscurity like its contemporaries, *Laverne & Shirley in the Army* and *Turbo Teen*, had the show not introduced John Laryea.

—*SATURDAY MORNING SPREE* BY CHARLES M. LUCE

TILDA and Pete Ellis could have waited inside the limo that day, but had agreed that the unseasonably warm October weather was too nice to waste, so instead were leaning against the side of the glossy black vehicle enjoying the sun when Tilda's cell phone broke into the opening bars of the theme from *Buffy the Vampire Slayer*.

"This is Tilda."

"What was your favorite Saturday morning show?" a familiar voice demanded to know.

"Forget it, Cooper. I told you, no more polls."

"Come on, Tilda, I have to get a dozen more people."

"Then you shouldn't have laughed your ass off when I answered your questions about the shows that make me cry."

"I couldn't help it. I mean, you cry at *A Pinky & the Brain Christmas Special*."

"Which everybody on Facebook now knows, thanks to you. They also get to mock me for my favorite romantic heroes."

"Jonny Quest was a romantic hero?"

"Good-bye, Cooper."

"Please, please, please. I swear, I'm on my knees. I can take a picture right now and send it to you."

"It wouldn't help."

"Ten minutes. I just need ten minutes."

"I don't have ten minutes. I'm at the airport and John Laryea is going to be out in five."

Pete Ellis, the limo driver, cleared his throat. "Actually, I just got word from Dom. There's been a slight delay with the flight, and Mr. Laryea won't be deplaning for another twenty minutes. Then they'll have to get his luggage, and . . ."

"Thanks a lot," Tilda said. Then inspiration struck. "Cooper, you need some fresh blood. I'm handing the phone to my new friend Pete. I know he'll love answering your questions."

Ignoring the look of panic on Pete's face, she pressed her phone into his hand, and leaned back to drink a Dr Pepper from the limo's refrigerator while he admitted to Cooper that he'd always been a fan of *Scooby-Doo*, *Thundarr the Barbarian*, and *The SuperFriends*. She'd halfway expected him to mention *The Blastoffs*, since they were waiting for the star who'd made his first foray into show business singing his way across the universe in that show, but it didn't happen.

After Pete was finished with the survey, he handed the phone back to Tilda.

"Now it's your turn," Cooper said.

"I don't want a turn. What I want is for you to deliver a message to Jillian for me. Tell her I've got a fresh lead on the last guy from *Power Pets*—I think I'll be able to track him down within the week."

"Oh, about that . . ."

"Don't tell me she's spiking the article!"

"No, she still wants it, but you don't need to find that guy anymore. We found him."

"What do you mean you found him? I've spent the last three weeks looking for him. Nobody knows where he is."

"We do now. He heard from one of his costars that we wanted to talk to him, and he got in touch with us. Nicole did a phone interview with him this morning."

"You have got to be kidding me! Which costar? They all swore that they didn't know where he was!"

"Joy something. The one who did Clueless Cub."

"Joy Baird? That bitch!" Tilda had known the woman hadn't liked her because she'd been honest when naming her favorite character on the show—and it hadn't been Clueless Cub. She'd thought Baird might be holding out on her, but hadn't expected her to pull an end run. "What am I supposed to do with the interviews I've already done?"

"Nicole is going to send you her notes so you can integrate the material with your stuff."

She took a deep breath. "Fine, I can do that."

"Um, Jillian says she's going to dock your pay a little, too."

"Of course she is. Why would she pay for my epic fail?"

"It's not epic," Cooper objected. "Everybody has an off day."

"This is my second off day in a month."

"Hey, that other guy wasn't your fault. How were you supposed to know he'd had a sex-change operation and moved to Denmark?"

"Whatever."

"Tilda . . ."

"Sorry, can't talk. Here comes Laryea! Bye!"

Pete was straightening up to greet the arriving star until he realized Tilda was blowing off Cooper.

"Sorry," she said. "I needed to get off the phone."

"Anything wrong?"

"I just found out I screwed up an assignment."

"It happens."

"I guess." Except that finding the formerly famous was supposed to be her specialty, and missing two targets in less than a month wasn't going to instill confidence in the editors from whom she was soliciting work. *Entertain Me!* was one of her best markets, and if Jillian, the editor in chief, decided they didn't need her, there went a large slice of her income.

Pete waggled a finger at her. "No brooding. It's too nice a day for it. Take a deep breath, and let it go."

It sounded a little touchy-feely, but Tilda did so, just to be polite. And it did help a little. There would be plenty of time to brood later.

They resumed their lounging, and Tilda found it oddly comfortable for being with a man she'd just met. She took a sidewise look at Pete. He was in his midforties, with a long, angular face, a wiry build, and thick hair that either nature or nurture kept nut-brown. And damned if he didn't look familiar!

"Pete, have we met before?"

"I don't think so. I've only been in Boston for a few months."

"Where were you before that?"

"Dallas—that's where I met Dom, and he talked me into coming here to work for him."

"You're not originally from Texas are you? Not with that accent."

He chuckled. "No, I bounced around quite a bit. I grew up in Colorado."

"Oh well," she said, mystified. "You sure look familiar."

"Just that kind of a face, I guess." Then Pete put his hand to his earpiece and listened for a few seconds. "Dom says he's got Laryea and his group, and they've got the luggage. They'll be on the way out in a few."

He tossed away the Coke he'd been drinking and went to stand at attention by the door.

"What's the etiquette here? Do I wait inside the limo or greet them outside?" Tilda had interviewed plenty of celebrities, but never in a stretch limo.

She'd been surprised when Dom Tolomeo of Tolomeo Personal Protection had called the day before to offer her a private interview with Laryea. The idea was for her to ride along on the trip from Boston's Logan Airport to Glenham, the town on the Cape where Laryea was headed to film location shots for his new movie. Dom had sent Pete Ellis, a combination limo driver and bodyguard, to pick her up that morning.

"Have you met Laryea before?" Pete asked.

She shook her head.

"Then you probably want to let Dom introduce him and his crew out here, and then let Mr. Laryea decide where he wants everybody to sit."

"Fair enough." That meant she was standing next to Pete when she saw Dom, Laryea, and the rest of the party come out of the terminal. They were at a dead run.

She heard squawks from Pete's earpiece, and he said, "Forget what I said before—GET IN!"

Tilda threw herself back into the limo, staying as far away from the door as possible as a confusion of people tossed massive amounts of luggage into the trunk. As Pete jumped into the front seat, with Dom taking shotgun, three men and two women flung themselves into the back with Tilda, with one of the men ending up with his head in her lap.

Tilda caught a glimpse of a redheaded guy in jeans running toward them like a bat out of hell. He looked as if he wanted to get in front of the limo to block them, and Tilda heard Pete mutter, "Blasting off!" as he revved the engine and peeled out. The guy jumped back onto the sidewalk, but Tilda was no longer paying attention. Instead, she'd realized why it was Pete Ellis looked familiar.

He might be driving a limo, but unless she'd completely lost her touch, at one point he'd piloted a fictional spaceship. Pete Ellis was Spencer Marshall, the man who'd costarred in *The Blastoffs* with John Laryea.

# Chapter 3

*The Blastoffs* was half adventure show and half music video, much like *The Bugaloos*. The Blastoff brothers rescued space princesses and saved orphans from certain death, while still making it to their concerts on time. Elder brother Sid (Spencer Marshall) was the brains and played guitar, while Marty (John Laryea) was the romantic dreamer and keyboardist. Comic relief was provided by Posit ("Himself"), the wise-cracking Twizzle who played the drums.
—*SATURDAY MORNING SPREE* BY CHARLES M. LUCE

TILDA would have liked to have spent more time thinking about her discovery, but she was distracted by the man whose head was in her lap.

He was a dark-haired Italian stallion. Not that Tilda could identify his nationality just by looking at him. She'd been told about it when they first met, a few days before their first date. It was Nick Tolomeo, her ex-boyfriend. Not coincidentally, he was Dom's son and favorite employee.

Now she knew why Dom had invited her to come along.

The blond man Tilda recognized as John Laryea said, "Did we lose him?"

"Dad, did we shake him?" Nick asked as he tried to untangle himself from Tilda.

Dom was looking behind them in the rearview mirror. "Yeah, we're clear. By the time he gets to his car, we'll be long gone."

Laryea and the other members of his party sank back into their seats in relief, Nick finally got himself situated, and to give him credit, he looked as taken aback to see Tilda as she was to see him. After a moment of staring at each other, they both turned to glare at Dom, who was carefully not looking in their direction.

Then Nick lifted one eyebrow quizzically, and glanced at his father. Tilda and Nick had dated long enough for her to interpret his expressions. He'd had no idea she was going to be in the limo, but obviously his father was up to something. She shrugged in response, knowing he'd realize that she was just as much Dom's hapless pawn as he was.

Then they both nodded, agreeing that it wasn't the time to discuss it.

Out loud Tilda asked, "Who did we shake?"

"A stalker," Nick said. "The guy was waiting by baggage claim, may have known we were coming."

"What did he do?"

"He followed me into the john," Laryea said indignantly, "and pulled out a camera while I was pissing!"

"Geez! Did he get a picture?"

"Nope," Nick said. "I went in to let Mr. Laryea know we had the luggage and got the camera just in time. The guy started squawking, but I held on to it until Dad got Mr. Laryea away, and when he grabbed at it, it slipped into the toilet. It'll still work if he got it out in time. Probably."

"Excuse me," a man Tilda didn't know said, "but who are you?"

"Sorry," Dom said from the front seat. "There hasn't exactly been time to make introductions. John, this is Tilda Harper, the reporter I told you about. She's going to be interviewing you during the drive to the Cape."

Tilda offered the star her hand, which he took in a manly but sensitive grasp. Laryea was famous for manly yet sensitive roles, an everyman rising to the occasion when caught up in bigger events—a kind of low-grade Harrison Ford. In his last three pictures, he'd played a man whose wife and kids had been kidnapped by drug dealers, an accountant who unknowingly uncovered an international conspiracy, and a researcher who'd realized that his chemical discoveries were being misused by arms merchants. He'd risen to the occasions successfully enough that he was now counted on to open pictures.

"A pleasure," Laryea said.

Nick took over the introductions. "This is Francis Foster, John's personal assistant."

Foster, a slight man with tight lips, took her hand in a much less impressive clasp, and said sharply, "The story about the restroom stalker is off the record."

"No problem," Tilda said. It was more of a tabloid story, anyway, which meant that she wasn't professionally interested.

Nick went on. "This is Joni Langevoort, who is directing *Pharos*, and Edwina Hudson, who is producing."

"Pleased to meet you," Tilda said. Langevoort was an attractive blonde with a petite figure, blue eyes, and a friendly smile. Hudson was taller, darker, and, though she smiled, too, looked considerably more reserved. Tilda knew from her advance research that the pair made movies together. Langevoort was known to be the creative half of the team while Hudson was the practical one. Most of their previous work had been smaller films—well-reviewed with modest box office numbers—but casting Laryea to play Dylan O'Taine in the adaptation of the cult comic book *Pharos* could put them into the big leagues.

Nick continued in his role as host by making sure everybody was comfortable and then dispensing drinks all around. Tilda really wasn't sure what had happened to her Dr Pepper in all the excitement, but turned down a replacement so she could have her hands free to take notes. As she pulled out her pad and tape recorder, Nick said, "Should we rearrange so that Mr. Laryea and Tilda are sitting closer?"

"I don't know why this couldn't wait until later," Foster said with a sniff. "Mr. Laryea deserves a moment to relax."

"If Mr. Laryea would prefer that, I'm fine with it," Tilda said. She'd rather not conduct an interview as a spectator sport anyway.

But Laryea said, "No, this is perfect. It's a long drive, and I can't think of anything that would be more pleasant than chatting with a lovely young lady. And please, call me John."

Joni and Edwina shared an indulgent look which told Tilda that maybe it was just as well she wasn't interviewing the man on her own, while Foster just pursed his lips and reluctantly switched places with Tilda.

After she took care of the preliminaries—asking if it was okay to record the interview and so forth—Tilda said, "I'd like to start with some of your early experiences in the business, working on *The Blastoffs*." She couldn't help looking toward the front seat, but there was no reaction from Pete. Could she have been wrong about him?

Laryea said, "*The Blastoffs* . . . Wow, I was just a kid then."

In fact, Laryea had been nineteen when that show was filmed, but Tilda knew that most actors preferred to shave a year or three off their ages whenever possible. To be fair, it wasn't purely vanity. Hollywood was known for its bias against older actors, particularly in action hero roles. So she just said, "That was your first big break, wasn't it?"

"Yes and no. It was a start, but it was my work on *More Bitter than Death* that really got the industry's attention." He went on to describe how wonderful it had been to work with Emma Thompson and Mark Wahlberg in that film. That led him to talk about how wonderful it was to work with the people in his next few movies—in fact, how wonderful the entire industry was to work with and how each new project was a virtual Eden of a working environment.

Tilda dutifully wrote down every ecstatic quote, not because they were particularly interesting or insightful, but because she was pretty sure that's all she was going to get. Laryea was, after all, trying to promote himself and *Pharos*, in that order. That meant he wasn't going to admit that he hated the script for last year's movie—he was still trying to sell DVDs of that movie and the rumored sequel. And he wasn't going to say he hated the other actors cast in *Pharos*—he was going to be working with them for the better part of a year. Besides, his director and producer were sitting right there. Naturally he was going to put a positive spin on everything.

Tilda understood completely. She was just a little bit bored with it all.

Laryea got his flirt on halfway through the interview, but for three reasons, Tilda ignored it. One, she wasn't particularly attracted to the guy. Two, even if she had been, she wasn't willing to provide drive time entertainment for the other people in the car, especially not an ex-boyfriend and the ex-boyfriend's father. And three, experience had taught her that if she remained aloof, Laryea would keep answering her questions in hopes of winning her over, whereas if she flirted back, he'd lose all interest in the interview, which would give her nothing for her article but lame double entendres.

By the time they reached the Sagamore Bridge, which carried them across the Cape Cod Canal and onto the Cape itself, Tilda was so bored that she was thinking that maybe she should have gone for the double entendres. Despite a tsunami of name-dropping, Laryea wasn't open enough for a stellar interview.

When Foster insisted that Laryea take a phone call, Tilda was more than ready to conclude the interview, and was satisfied to watch the scenery go by for the rest of the drive.

# Chapter 4

Local cartoon hosts loom large in the memories of their fans, no matter how cheesy their costumes or goofy their dialogue, and former viewers are just as excited about meeting Rex Trailer or Sonic Man as they ever were. Hugh Wilder, more commonly known as Quasit to Cape Cod's former cartoon viewers, recently headlined a family festival in Glenham, and fans waited for an hour or more for autographs.

—"HEY KIDS! IT'S CARTOON TIME!"
BY TILDA HARPER IN *ENTERTAIN ME!*

ABOUT half an hour later, Pete pulled the limo into the circular driveway in front of the Glenham Bars Inn, a gorgeous white clapboard hotel straight out of the Gilded Age. Tilda had been part of an extremely fancy wedding there a few years before, and knew the basic layout. The inn itself was the biggest building, and contained the dining room, bar, and a selection of rooms ranging from deluxe to more deluxe to obscenely deluxe. It was situated high enough up that there was a breathtaking view of the Atlantic Ocean from the veranda and dining room. Shoreline Road, which naturally enough paralleled the shore, ran in front of it, and across the road were more of the inn's facilities: the tennis courts and shop, boathouse, and pool, which was usually much nicer to swim in than the ocean itself. In case guests preferred more privacy or space than the main building provided, there were two dozen or more cottages clustered behind the Inn and along Shoreline, on both sides of the road.

The place reeked of old New England money, the kind of people for whom *summer* was a verb instead of a noun. Tilda had shared a cottage with four other bridesmaids for that wedding, and had been relieved that she hadn't had to pay for it herself. Even a fifth of the cost would have devastated her budget for months afterward.

As the limo slowed smoothly to a stop, Tilda made a quick check to make sure that she'd gathered all her stuff, so she didn't see what John Laryea was seeing. All she knew was that the previously genial star had suddenly burst into a string of profanities.

When she looked out the window, it was all she could do to keep from laughing. Standing on the veranda, waving merrily, was a neon green fuzzy alien with a rotund tummy, big googly eyes, and three shaky antennae.

"What the hell is that?" Joni asked.

"It's Posit, the wisecracking Twizzle from *The Blast-offs*," Tilda explained. The wisecracks hadn't been particularly good ones, but certainly funny enough for the demographic at which the show was aimed.

"I am not going out there!" Laryea said.

"Dom, get rid of him!" Edwina said, and though Dom looked as if there were nothing he'd less rather do, he climbed out of the limo, pulled up his khakis, and went into battle. Tilda could see that it must have been nearly impossible for Dom to get tough with a guy in a green fur suit. In fact, she didn't think a color change would have helped—any furry suit would have made it hard to get macho. At any rate, the discussion stretched into minutes.

"Why is he still here?" Laryea asked angrily.

"I think he's hoping for a photo op with his former costar," Tilda said, since there was a photographer snapping photos of Dom and Posit.

"Hell, no!"

Dom seemed to be making some progress. Posit removed his head. Or rather, the person inside removed the big fur headpiece, revealing a somewhat wilted-looking older man with bright blue eyes and a cherubic grin.

"That's not . . ." Pete started to say.

"I know, technically, it's not Posit," Tilda said. "After *The Blastoffs* went off the air, Hugh Wilder there got hired to host a kids' cartoon show here on the Cape. He wanted to use the Posit character, but the studio's lawyers objected, so he altered the costume just enough to keep from violating the copyright or trademark or whatever." As Tilda recalled, Posit had two antennae while Quasit had three, and Quasit was a brighter green and didn't wear a shiny vest like Posit. Plus Wilder got rid of the tail because it was a pain to work with. "He doesn't do the cartoon show anymore, but he's still enough of a public figure to show up at parades and kids' festivals around here."

"How do you know this?" Nick asked.

"I interviewed Wilder a couple of years ago. I was doing a piece on former cartoon show hosts: Bozo the Clown from Boston, Sonic Man from North Carolina, and of course, Posit. Or Quasit. He's a sweet old guy, really."

"I don't care if he's Mother Teresa—I want him out of here!" Laryea snapped.

Dom wasn't having any luck, and Tilda could hear Joni and Edwina muttering about the bad press resulting if Laryea snubbed Posit/Quasit or, worse still, indulged in a star-power temper tantrum. Though Tilda didn't particularly care if Laryea made an ass of himself publicly, she did care about Dom getting into trouble. And of course, doing a pair of powerful moviemakers a favor could only help an entertainment reporter.

"I've got an idea," Tilda said, "but it'll mean a slight bit of pretense."

"Lie through your teeth if you have to, just keep him away from me," Laryea said.

"Nick, is there a back door into the hotel?"

He nodded.

"Good. I'm going to get out of the limo in a minute, and when I do, drive around to the back and take Mr. Laryea in that way."

"Won't Posit just follow us?" Nick asked.

"I think I can distract him."

She opened the door just enough to slip out, and as soon as she slammed the door behind her, the limo took off.

As Nick had predicted, Posit started down the stairs and toward the limo.

"Mr. Wilder!" Tilda said cheerily. "Remember me? Tilda Harper." She stuck out her hand, which he automatically took to shake. "I am so glad I ran into you. I had a computer meltdown a few months ago, and lost your contact information, and I wasn't sure how to get in touch with you to arrange an interview."

*Interview* was the magic word. Unsurprisingly for a man who routinely ran around in a fur alien suit, Wilder liked nothing better than to meet with the press. He straightened up and gave her a big smile. "An interview with me? About my work with sick children?"

"That might be a good sidebar, but I was really hoping to talk to you about your work on *The Blastoffs.* Maybe a bit about what John Laryea was like to work with as a kid?"

"Wouldn't it be better to talk with both of us at the same time?" he said, looking in the direction the limo had gone.

"I wanted to get the background from you first." She lowered her voice. "Besides, John is feeling a bit under the weather. He's not sure if it's a stomach bug or something they fed him on the plane, and he would have come out to see you himself, but his assistant Foster insisted he go get some rest. I don't have to tell you what a mess it would be if production was slowed up by illness. When we spoke before, didn't you mention something about the time both of the Blastoff brothers got chicken pox right before filming?" He had, in fact, told her about it in excruciating detail, pox-by-pox, but he couldn't wait to tell her again. They found a couple of wicker chairs on the veranda to sit on, and once Tilda pulled out her notebook and tape recorder, he happily launched into it.

In the meantime, Dom scooted into the inn and the bored photographer took a few shots before trudging away.

Unfortunately for Tilda, the interview with Wilder

was even less interesting than the one with Laryea had been.

After the chicken pox story, he started gushing. "It was like a family on that show, a big happy family. The boys were just amazing to work with, too. John had this spark in him from day one. You could see the greatness there." And so on, and so on, and so on.

Not that Tilda had expected a lot of dirt about Laryea since Wilder wanted to play up his great friendship with the star, but she'd have been happy with something human. Surely Laryea must have flubbed a shot or played a prank on the director or tried to sneak a girl into his trailer or drank too much—anything that normal teenaged boys did. But according to Posit, it was like working with a real-life Brady Bunch, without the punch lines.

After forty-five minutes of rah-rahs, she figured she'd given Laryea plenty of time to make his escape, and was ready to wind it up. She let Wilder finish the story about Laryea's amazingly generous presents for the crew members when the show wrapped, then said, "This has been great. I really appreciate your candor, Mr. Wilder."

"Call me Hugh!" he said. "Or Quasit." He looked around and winked conspiratorially. "If the lawyers aren't listening, you can even call me Posit."

"You bet."

"Did you want to get some pictures?"

"Absolutely," she lied, and took more shots of him than she would ever want, with and without the Quasit head. Then she accepted the hug Wilder was determined to give her.

"Maybe I should go inside and check in on Johnny," Wilder said.

"I got the idea he was going to go straight to bed, and keep quiet for the rest of the evening. He's got some prep work for tomorrow."

"That's Johnny," Wilder said fondly. "Always a professional. I'll call him tomorrow."

He headed out to the parking lot while Tilda packed her notebook and other odds and ends into the black leather messenger bag she used to carry far too much stuff. Then she pulled out her phone to make a quick e-mail check, and replied to a couple of messages.

She was about to go inside when she saw that Wilder was still in the parking lot, talking to somebody. She moved close enough to recognize the other person as Pete, the limo driver.

"Curiouser and curiouser," she murmured to herself, and on a whim, snapped a couple of pictures of the two men. Of course, if Pete really was Spencer Marshall, it made all kinds of sense. But the fact that he'd waited for Wilder out there rather than joining them on the veranda made for a bit of a mystery, and an intriguing one at that.

# Chapter 5

In Issue 4, the mermaid Melusine is washed up on the shore near the lighthouse. While nursing her back to health, Dylan O'Taine falls in love with her, but while she seems to return his feelings, she reveals that her father is the chieftain of his enemies, the Blue Men of the Minch. Melusine refuses to choose between them, and instead goes to live alone in an underwater cavern, halfway between her father and her lover, and maintains relationships with both.

—*TEENAGE MUTANT NINJA ARTISTS:*
*THE BEST OF INDIE COMICS* BY JERRY FRAZEE

SINCE it was off-season, Tilda had expected the inn's lobby to be relatively quiet, but she'd forgotten just how many bodies a film unit required. The place was hopping with people who looked as if they'd be more comfortable in a Days Inn than a refined New England hotel, and the staff members had a slightly dazed look. Perhaps the managers hadn't known just what they were getting themselves into.

As Tilda walked in the door, she was approached by a man with an earpiece wearing a royal blue polo shirt with *TOLOMEO PERSONAL PROTECTION* and the name *Hoover* embroidered in white thread. "Excuse me, ma'am, are you a guest here at the hotel?"

"No, but I came in from Boston with Mr. Laryea's

party." Hoover looked doubtful until she added, "Either Dom or Nick can vouch for me."

He immediately mumbled into his mouthpiece, waited a few seconds, then replied.

"Mr. Tolomeo will be here in a moment."

Tilda expected him to go about his business, but instead he stayed on alert until Dom showed up and said, "Tilda! You are a lifesaver!" Only then did Hoover discreetly step away and go back to guarding the door.

Dom went on. "The way you handled that guy in the costume was brilliant. Joni and Edwina told me to tell you that they would like to pay for your dinner here at the inn, and if you've got time, they'd like to talk to you a little later. Pete is going to hang around until we're done, and then he'll drive you back home. How's that sound?"

"It sounds great, but what do they—?"

"They'll explain it themselves." He bustled her toward the dining room, and after he had a quiet word with the hostess, Tilda found herself at a table with a menu in front of her. "Order anything you want," Dom said. "They know to put it on the *Pharos* tab. I'll come back down to get you after you eat." He was gone before she could question him further.

Now that she had a chance to notice it, Tilda realized she was starving. The prices on the menu were about what she'd expected, which is to say that she was glad she wouldn't be paying the bill. She ordered a green salad and the pan-seared haddock and, since she wasn't going to be driving, let the waitress talk her into a glass of wine to accompany it. Then she leaned back to raid the bread basket and people-watch.

Normally Tilda wasn't overly fond of eating alone in a restaurant, but the film crew milling and swilling provided enough of a floor show that this time she didn't mind. Presumably the lower echelons were eating in town or at the hotel bar, but there were still plenty of people around spending their per diems. The folks at the table nearest her were apparently stuntmen and special effects people. Either that or they were kind of freaky because they were describing stunts gone wrong in loving detail.

When her salad came, she decided bleeding wounds no longer appealed, and switched her attention to the trio on her other side. From their analysis of the local weather and light quality, she guessed they were cinematographers or something along those lines. Eavesdropping on their concerns about a predicted rainstorm later in the week got her through that course.

She'd planned to discreetly change seats before the haddock arrived to try to guess what a foursome of well-dressed men did on the set, but then somebody stepped into her line of sight.

"Hey, Nick," she said.

"Mind if I join you?"

"I've already ordered."

"I'll catch up." He waved the waitress over and ordered scallops and a Coke.

Once the waitress left, Nick said, "So how've you been?"

"Since when? Since we last saw each other? Or since you broke up with me by e-mail?" She took a certain pleasure in watching him squirm.

"Yeah, that was a pretty shitty thing to do."

"Kind of pointless, too. I mean we weren't exclusive, were we? I assumed you were seeing other people—I was."

"I know, but it was getting serious with Cynthia, and I thought I should tell you. It seemed like the decent thing to do."

"Sure, that's why you told me by e-mail. That gave it that personal touch."

"You're right, I should have called, and I would have, but I was still in Prague and with the time difference . . ."

"According to the time stamp, you sent that message at noon my time."

"Really? I never can keep that straight."

Tilda waved it away. "Don't sweat it. It's just as well you didn't call. You would have caught me in bed and that would have been awkward."

"At noon?"

"I didn't say I was alone. Like I said, I was seeing other people, too." She knew it was incredibly petty of her to enjoy the expression on his face, but it almost made being dumped by e-mail worthwhile. But since she'd had her fun, she was willing to let it go. "Anyway, we can still be friends, right? Sans benefits, of course."

"You bet." He offered his hand, and they shook on it.

The waitress, who must have been specially trained for perfect timing, showed up with their entrees, which gave them a moment to catch their breaths.

After a few bites, Tilda said, "So what's your father got against your new gal pal?"

"You made that connection, too?"

"Please. He calls me up out of the blue, offers me a

sweet opportunity to interview a high-profile star, and forgets to mention that you're going to be here?"

"Not big on subtlety, is he? Funny thing is, he hasn't even met Cynthia. He usually needs to spend at least a little time with a person before deciding if it's thumbs-up or thumbs-down."

Dom had an uncanny, almost scary knack for judging people, which was part of what made his personal security business so successful. Within minutes of meeting Tilda, he'd decided she would be perfect for Nick, and current circumstances suggested that he hadn't given up.

"I'm surprised you haven't brought her home for him to vet," she said.

"There hasn't been time. As soon as we wrapped in Prague, she had to head back to LA for postproduction. Did I tell you what she does?"

"Nope, and I'm good with that. I just wanted to know if she was going to be showing up anytime soon."

"No, she's not coming. What about your guy?"

"The guy from when you Dear John-ed me? Old news." In fact, he'd been old news almost before she even read the e-mail from Nick. Being dumped by Nick and then dumping the other guy had not made for a gold star weekend—a day of videos and several shared pints of Toscanini's ice cream with Cooper and his husband Jean-Paul had been required to cheer her up.

"Sorry to hear that. Should I throw out a few platitudes about there being plenty more fish in the sea?"

"I really wish you wouldn't. Though now that you mention it . . ." She realized this might be a good opportunity to discreetly check on Pete Ellis and see if she was right about him. "What's the story on the new limo driver?"

"Pete? Dad met him on a job in Texas, I think. Five minutes afterward, he decided he would be great for us, and offered him a job. I haven't spent much time with him, but if Dad trusts him, that's good enough for me." He took a bite of his scallops. "A little old for you, isn't he?"

"I don't know—older guys have a certain appeal," she said. "But if it makes you uncomfortable, let's talk about the movie instead. How's Laryea to work with?"

"Who's asking? Tilda my friend or Tilda the reporter?"

"I'd say this is Tilda the incurably nosy movie fan. But I trust you remember the magic words."

He looked blank for a moment, then said, "Can we keep this off the record?"

"Done."

"In that case, it's not bad. I only met him last week, but he seems like a decent enough guy. The only unusual security problem has been that dude in the bathroom this afternoon."

"No tantrums?"

"On the low end of the bell curve for a star of his stature. No more than one a day, and you already saw today's."

"He really didn't want to see that Posit guy, did he? It reminds me of why I like to work with the *formerly* famous. They're a lot more mellow."

"Putting up with tantrums is part of my job."

As they finished up their meals, Nick went on to describe more severe tantrums from other stars, including stories Tilda might have been tempted to use had it not been for the "off the record" rule. Dishing dirt wasn't her usual thing, but she had to admit that it would be nice to have something to peddle to offset the loss of income from not being able to find two of her recent targets.

They'd just decided to pass on dessert when Nick's cell phone rang. He took a look at the screen and said, "It's Pop. Do you mind if I answer?"

"No problem."

"Hi, Pop. . . . We're just finishing dinner. . . . Yeah, I'll bring her on up." He put the phone back in his pocket and said, "Pop says they want to talk to you upstairs."

"That's what he told me before dinner. Any idea what that's about?"

"Not a clue."

They were nearly at the elevator in the lobby when Nick glanced toward the front door and said, "Son of a bitch!"

"What?"

"It's that stalker!" He took off at a dead run, somehow managing not to mow anybody down.

Tilda hesitated, not sure if she should follow or not.

"Head up to the third floor," Nick yelled over his shoulder. Tilda saw the inn's front door open and somebody scoot out, and Nick was right on the guy's tail. Then they both disappeared into the night.

# Chapter 6

A comic book artist has to tell the story with the right empha-
sis and yet as efficiently as possible, because you only have
so many frames on a page. That's really intriguing to me
because the director of a film also has the same problem. But
a comic artist has to get everyone in the frame, as well as the
dialogue and have there be a kind of logic to it all. It's complex and I find it fascinating.

—WILLIAM SHATNER, WIZARDUNIVERSE.COM

NOT feeling a pressing need to watch Nick chase after a
stalker, she left him to do what he did best and followed
his instructions. Nobody had told her which room to go
to, but when the elevator opened, Dom was standing
outside an open door.

"Where's Nick?"

"Pursuing a stalker—he thinks it's that guy from the
airport."

"Persistent son of a gun," Dom said. He spoke into
his headset, and then said, "Gave us the slip again."

"Both persistent and swift."

"Nick and a couple of the men are going to make a
circuit of the grounds and make sure he's really gone.
Come on in." He courteously stepped aside to wave her
into the room.

Correction, not a room. It was a suite, and a well-appointed one at that. Even the room the bride had used at that long-ago wedding hadn't been as large as this one. The combined living room/dining room was as big as many Boston apartments, and there were two open doors leading to bedrooms that were comparably spacious. Maybe the nautical motif was a bit overdone for Tilda's taste, but she wouldn't have turned the room down just because of a few excess decorative anchors.

Joni and Edwina were seated on the couch in front of a coffee table they'd managed to completely cover with papers in the short time since they'd checked in. She saw two laptops, too, but they were nearly swallowed by the detritus.

A third woman was in one of the armchairs across from them, typing furiously on an iPad while Edwina read aloud from a piece of paper.

They were so involved that Tilda didn't think they even noticed her and Dom standing there until he cleared his throat. "Here's Tilda, ladies."

Joni came over immediately to take her hand. "Thanks so much for helping us with that costumed character this evening," she said. "We really owe you one."

"You're certainly welcome, but dinner was more than enough of a thank-you."

"I don't think so, but it's a start. Come on in and sit down. Would you like something to drink?"

"No, thank you, I'm good."

Joni waved Tilda to a second armchair, covered with a delicate pattern of knots and of course more anchors, while Dom pulled over a chair from the dining room set.

"Tilda," Joni said, "this is Dolores Goldin. She's writing the screenplay for *Pharos*."

"Yeah, right," Dolores grumbled. "Me and anybody else who has ideas for me to stick in. Which is everybody." She was a buxom woman with close-cropped flaming red curls and such fair skin that living in California must have been torture for her. "Pleased to meet you."

Dom said, "Tilda, I guess you must have figured out that I had an ulterior motive for calling you to join us in the limo, right?"

"I'm not one for looking a gift horse in the mouth, but I did wonder," Tilda said.

"The fact is, the ladies here could use your help."

"Dolores," Joni said, "can you show Tilda the blogs?"

"Oh yeah, I can't wait to look at that crap again." She fiddled with the iPad a moment, then shoved it in Tilda's direction. "Read 'em while I weep."

Dolores had brought up a bulletin board for comic book fans, and the top post was a screed about how horrible the adaptation of *Pharos* was bound to be. The next post was more of the same, with a tad more profanity. Ditto the third, and so on and so on. Apparently they were all convinced that Dolores's screenplay was going to bring about the end of comic books and civilization, in that order.

"How did they get a copy of the script?" Tilda asked.

"Somebody leaked an early draft," Joni said. "Dom is checking into that. The problem is that this early negative buzz is spreading all across the Web, on dozens of sites and blogs. And it's not just comic book fans. Movie news sites are picking up on the story, too, and I don't have to tell you how much that can hurt the film, even this long before it's released."

"They'll be quiet once the movie comes out, right?"

"I hope so, but we need fan support before then. Part of the way we got backing was convincing the studio that *Pharos* has a cult following that will guarantee a good opening. We're going to have a dog and pony show at Comic-Con next summer, which should help, but in the meantime, we want the bloggers on our side."

Dolores grimaced. "As if we didn't have enough people to suck up to already. Now we have to suck up to the bloggers. Once Peter Jackson let bloggers onto the set of *Lord of the Rings*, they realized they had clout."

"So you want me to do what exactly?" Tilda asked. "Write positive comments about the screenplay and start spreading them around?" She was trying not to sound insulted, but if they wanted a PR flack, they needed to look elsewhere.

Fortunately Joni was shaking her head. "No, we've got people to do that—they're already tweeting and blogging their fingers off. But I had another idea." She tapped the iPad screen. "This stuff claims that we're subverting the original text of *Pharos*, which we most definitely are not. I fell in love with that comic the first time I read it, and there's no way I'd let it be ruined."

From the conglomeration on the table, the director pulled out a book Tilda recognized as the graphic novel version of *Pharos*. "Not only have I worn out half a dozen copies of this, I have the original comic sealed in Mylar plus half a dozen reading copies of each issue."

"Not to mention some of the original pages that we

had to lug with us all the way from California," Dolores grumbled. Sure enough, there was a stack of matted pages leaned up against one of the walls.

Joni ignored her. "I had to do a lot of work to get this movie green-lit—it took us three successful films to give us enough points to pick our own project. After all that, do you really think I'm going to screw it up?"

Tilda nodded as if she hadn't heard other directors make that same claim about work they adored. In one noted example, Francis Ford Coppola had so worshiped the source material that he called his movie *Bram Stoker's Dracula*. It would have been more impressive if he hadn't later admitted that he'd never actually finished reading Stoker's novel. Still, Tilda was willing to believe that Joni had made it through at least a few issues of the *Pharos* comic book.

"So couldn't you leak a later, more faithful version of the script?" she asked.

Dolores threw up her hands in apparent disgust. "If it could only be that easy! They're too focused on the changes to appreciate how I've maintained the spirit of the comic book. 'It was set in the 1980s—how can they move it to the present?' 'Dylan O'Taine was way younger than John Laryea.' 'Melusine was always barebreasted.' 'The Asrai would never have worked with the Blue Men of the Minch.'"

"I thought we decided not to have the Asrai working with the Blue Men," Edwina interjected.

"Fine, whatever," the writer said, rolling her eyes. "The fact is the great unwashed aren't going to be satisfied no matter what we do."

"Yes, they are," Joni insisted. "All we have to do is get Leviathan to read the script and tell the fans he approves of it. I'm sure he'll be okay with the small changes we've made."

Tilda said, "Leviathan? The author of the comic book?"

Joni nodded. "We'll even bring him out to the set if he's interested, whatever it takes to get his seal of approval."

"That sounds like a good plan."

"It sounds like a waste of time and effort," Edwina said. "And money, which we don't have to throw away."

Joni ignored her, too. "The problem is, we don't know where he is. Or who he is. All we've got to go on is the pen name."

Dom nudged Tilda. "That's where you come in."

"Dom tells us that you're good at finding people," Joni said.

"I'm not a PI," Tilda said, "but I've managed to track down some people in the past."

"Some people!" Dom said. "Don't listen to her, Joni. She's the best. She found every one of the Cartwright brides from *Bonanza*! If anybody can find your comic book writer, it's Tilda Harper."

Tilda appreciated the recommendation, though it made her suspicious all over again. Why had Dom been following her career so thoroughly if he wasn't still trying to fix her up with Nick? "I'd be willing to give it a shot," she said.

"Fantastic!" Joni said, though Tilda noticed Edwina didn't look particularly pleased.

"But what if I find Leviathan, and he doesn't approve

of your movie?" Tilda said, remembering how Alan Moore had publicly washed his hands of the film version of *The League of Extraordinary Gentlemen.*

"Then we'll change it until he does!" Joni said emphatically.

Tilda wasn't completely convinced that Joni would stick to that once money was on the line, but the director honestly sounded as if she wanted to do right by the book. So she said, "All right, I'll see what I can do." She was about to bring up the delicate and detested subject of money when Dom jumped in again.

"Now don't think she's doing this for free," he said. "You know how much it costs to hire a PI? You have to do right by this girl."

"Absolutely," Joni said.

"I told you this would happen!" Edwina said. "You know there's no flex in the budget for something like this."

Tilda tried not to roll her eyes at such a clumsy attempt at bargaining. Anything she asked for would be trivial compared to what the film crew had already spent at the inn's restaurant, not to mention the inevitable bar bill. But since she had her own idea of a good deal, she wasn't concerned.

"Actually," she said, "I don't want money, other than for expenses. What I'd really like is a chance to come back to the Cape and embed myself in your production to produce some in-depth articles."

Edwina frowned. "I suppose you'd want us to pay for your hotel room."

But Joni said, "We can do that."

"An interview with the two of you would be great,

too." There weren't that many women in producing or directing, even in the modern world, and Tilda knew she could rewrite a profile piece like that for a dozen different markets and collect a dozen checks.

"Time permitting, you've got it."

It was almost too easy, so Tilda figured she'd take it a little higher. "One other thing. Can you help arrange a press pass for me for Comic-Con?"

Joni smiled. "Consider it done."

"Then it's a deal." Tilda could tell that Edwina still wasn't happy and that Dolores was probably never happy, but Joni was delighted and Dom was beaming like a proud uncle.

There were a few minutes of arranging details before hands were shaken all around and Dom escorted Tilda downstairs to the bar, where Pete was drinking a ginger ale and watching something sports-related on TV. Then he walked the two of them out to the limo, and gave Tilda a quick hug before telling Pete he'd see him back on the Cape the next day.

# Chapter 7

**Episode 1**
Marty decides that he wants a turn piloting the Blastoffs' rocket ship and takes the controls while Sid is napping. When they end up way off course, Sid is furious, but thanks to the detour, they run across a malfunctioning ship filled with orphans and rescue them before the ship falls into the nearby sun.
—*SATURDAY MORNING SPREE* BY CHARLES M. LUCE

"YOU want to ride up front with me or in the back?" Pete asked.

"Up front, if that's okay."

"Sure." He even opened the door for her, which was a nice touch.

As they pulled out onto the road, Tilda said, "Long day for you, isn't it? And you've got to drive back tomorrow?"

"It's not so bad. I like driving."

"Even in Massachusetts traffic and weather?"

"That does make it interesting sometimes. It's not bad now."

He was right. The sky was clear, the moon was bright, and traffic was light. It was an unusual enough combination to be savored.

"How was your day?" he asked.

Tilda thought it over. The interviews with Laryea and

Wilder had been snoozers, but she'd likely be able to salvage both of them, and hunting down Leviathan could potentially be a lot of fun. Plus she'd gotten back at Nick for his shabby behavior, and had still been able to renew the friendship. Then there was the question of Pete himself, and this golden opportunity to explore it further. "All in all, not bad. It looks like I'll be coming back to the Cape, too, but I'll be driving myself down next time, so you're off the hook."

"I don't mind the company." He made the turn onto U.S. 6, the main road that bisected Cape Cod. "Are you going to be interviewing Mr. Laryea again?"

"Not exactly." She explained what Joni wanted her to do, and why Dom had recommended her for the job.

"So that's what you do? You track down people?"

"Not all the time, but the 'where are they now?' stories are the ones I like most. They're more of a challenge."

"That's kind of creepy, isn't it? I mean, isn't it like stalking?"

"Not at all," Tilda said, offended. "Most people want to be found. They like knowing they haven't been forgotten, and that people still enjoy their work. Look at Hugh Wilder. He loves talking about *The Blastoffs*. Wouldn't you want to be remembered if you'd done something like that?"

He dodged the bait. "Mr. Laryea didn't want to talk about the show so much."

"True, and I've run into a few people like that." She looked pointedly at him. "I think Laryea would rather not be remembered for that when he's done other work he's more proud of."

"But you'll put something about the show in your article anyway," he said, almost accusingly.

"Just a mention. It's not like it's a deep, dark secret. There have been other times I've run into people who really did have things they didn't want the world to know." Again, she looked at him.

"Yeah?"

She nodded. "A former pinup queen who didn't want people to find out that she'd posed nude, for one, and an actress who was afraid she'd be in danger if I said anything about where she was."

"What did you do?"

"Duh! What do you think? I didn't print anything about them."

"Doesn't that go against journalistic ethics or the public's right to know or something?"

"Oh please! The public does not need to know where some old TV star ended up. Now if I caught a conservative gay-basher swapping spit with a male prostitute, I'd break that story in a heartbeat, but if a former public figure prefers to keep to the shadows, it's no skin off my nose."

"Seriously?"

"Seriously. There are plenty of formerly famous people out there for me to interview."

Pete nodded and relaxed visibly, and Tilda figured that was all she was going to get for the time being. Either she was completely wrong about the man, or he just didn't want to talk about his work on *The Blastoffs*. Considering the magazines that had printed pictures of Gary Coleman on his deathbed, she supposed she shouldn't be surprised if people thought the worst of entertainment reporters.

The rest of the trip back to town went pleasantly enough, and Tilda got a kick out of stopping along the way to get drinks and hit the restroom. There was something wonderfully decadent about going to McDonald's in a stretch limo.

She only wished her roomie could have been outside to see Pete drop her at her latest address, a small house just off East Border Road in Malden. He even got out to open the door for her and walked her to the front door. It was enough to make her wish she'd asked Joni for a driver along with her other perks.

# *Chapter 8*

**Episode 14**
Sid and Marty encounter a space-age version of Noah's Ark, a stranded starship on its way to a colony world. The crew of cute girls at first refuses their help, but when it turns out that one of the animals is a saboteur in disguise, Sid and Marty are suddenly needed.
—*SATURDAY MORNING SPREE* BY CHARLES M. LUCE

TILDA steeled herself before unlocking the door to the house. Seconds after stepping inside, she heard the clicking of tiny nails on the hardwood floor and the heavier sound of much bigger paws coming toward her. Then the yapping from Calvin the Yorkie began, followed by deeper woofing from Honeypaw, the Newfoundland.

"It's just me," she said, knowing it was useless. Only after three minutes and forty-five seconds of overly personal sniffing did her roommate's dogs decide that she was authorized to come in.

Lights were on all through the house, even though Dianne's car was missing from the driveway, meaning that she wasn't even home. She usually left them on all day long, no matter how their electric bill suffered, because "the animals needed it." Tilda's arguments that creatures in the wild were completely acclimated to

darkness made no difference, any more than her suggestion that they only light part of the house. Then again,
Dianne might have a point when she said the whole
place needed light. As time went on, there wasn't a room
left that didn't have pets.

When she and Dianne moved in together, Dianne
just had Honeypaw and two guinea pigs named Tama
and Hershey. Those three had been enough to give Tilda
some qualms. Not so much the piggies, since they lived
in a cage in Dianne's room, but Honeypaw was a different story. Newfoundlands are large, and they drool frequently and copiously. Still, Honeypaw was extremely
good-natured, and the idea of a guard dog had a certain appeal, so she agreed as long as Dianne signed an
addendum to the lease guaranteeing that she would pay
for any pet-related damage.

It was only while they were both unpacking their
worldly goods that Tilda saw the cat toys and found out
that Dianne had unexpectedly inherited Fluffy, a cat her
mother could no longer keep. In the following weeks,
Dianne unexpectedly inherited a wide variety of pets:
a noisy cockatiel; two cranky turtles; and a tank filled
with pale, nearly motionless frogs. With Calvin, Dianne
hadn't even pretended—she'd seen the dog at the animal shelter and couldn't resist bringing him home and
announcing, "Honeypaw needed company." The way
Tilda saw it, Honeypaw had more company than the
Gosselin kids.

The snake Tilda had complained to Cooper about
had been the last straw, and after its arrival, she had
extracted Dianne's heartfelt promise that she would add

no more creatures of any kind, not even if the floods came and the future of any given species depended on members of said species moving in.

When Tilda stopped by the kitchen to get herself a drink, Honeypaw and Calvin were waiting by their empty water dishes looking mournful and accusatory, respectively. Tilda sighed and filled the bowls at the sink. Supposedly, Dianne was solely responsible for animal care, but she couldn't let the dogs go thirsty. She filled up Fluffy's bowl, too.

She then took her own drink and headed to her bedroom. At least that was the plan, but when she got upstairs, she heard guinea pigs vocalizing. That wasn't particularly unusual—the piggies frequently let their presence be known. The difference was that the sounds were coming from the spare bedroom.

Fearing the worst, that the pigs had escaped their cage, Tilda should have been relieved to see that the pigs were safely contained. Except that the cage wasn't supposed to be in the spare room. She was going to have yet another talk with her roommate.

When she finally got to her room, she booted up her computer and went straight to the Internet Movie Database (IMDb) to see if she could find any pictures from *The Blastoffs*. There wasn't a lot of information about the show, which didn't surprise her, but there was one clear publicity still of the Blastoff brothers with Posit. She zoomed in on it and took a good long look at Sid Blastoff. The eye color was right, and the general shape of the face, but of course the hair was different. It sure looked like Pete Ellis. She couldn't be positive, but she was 80 percent sure.

Then she checked the entry for Marshall, but there wasn't much there: a birth date that fit well enough for Pete and a few credits starting a few years after *The Blastoffs*. A brief Web surf didn't give her anything more. The guy had either given up acting, or it had given up on him.

Other than the sad irony of Pete working as a driver and bodyguard for his former costar, given the obscurity of *The Blastoffs* it wasn't much of a story. Tilda doubted she could sell it anywhere, and it was moot anyway, since obviously Pete didn't want to talk about it. Besides, wouldn't Laryea have recognized him?

Tilda heard the front door open and close, and since Honeypaw didn't bark, she figured it was Dianne. That meant it was confrontation time.

"Hi, Tilda!" Dianne said brightly. Tanned and fit from all the dog-walking, her roommate kept her brown hair in a long, thick braid down her back to keep the guinea pigs from chewing on it.

"Dianne, why are Hershey and Tama in the guest room?"

"I took Ka out of the dining room like you asked, but he made the piggies nervous, so I had to move them."

"Didn't we agree to keep that room for company?" It had been a strain for Tilda, too, who would love to have had the extra space, especially since Dianne had won the larger of the other two bedrooms in the traditional coin toss.

"Who would mind sharing a room with them? They're so cute."

"That's not the point. We agreed to keep that room clear, and they strew litter and droppings like crazy."

"I'll clean it up whenever we need to use the room."

"They can also be pretty noisy."

"I thought you liked them. They like you." As if to confirm Tilda's irresistible charms to four-legged creatures, Honeypaw padded over to rub against her leg, leaving a loving trail of slobber behind.

"I do like them. I like the dogs. I like the cat. The bird's not bad, and the rest of them are at least innocuous. Any one of them would be a joy unto me. But I feel as if I'm living in a zoo."

"I already promised, no more."

"You promised that before the snake."

"I really mean it this time. No more."

"Okay, fine. But if you keep the guinea pigs in there, I get the closet."

"I was going to use it for the piggies' supplies."

Tilda glared at her.

"Okay, you can have the closet."

"Fine." Tilda extracted herself from Honeypaw and started to go back upstairs.

"By the way, I'm thinking about going out of town this weekend. Do you think you could take care of the animals?"

It gave Tilda enormous pleasure to say, "Sorry, but I'm leaving the day after tomorrow for a job on the Cape. I'll be gone a week at least."

# *Chapter 9*

*Pharos* was among the best of the independent black-and-white comics produced in the eighties. Leviathan, its pseudonymous creator, had a strong graphic sense and deftly portrayed the emotions of protagonist Dylan O'Taine—a kind of mash-up of Doctor Fate and Namor the Sub-Mariner. It's no surprise that the ten-issue run continues to attract a cult following.

—*Teenage Mutant Ninja Artists: The Best of Indie Comics* by Jerry Frazee

THE next morning, Tilda was ready to play Ahab and seek out the Leviathan, but there was old business to attend to. First off, she gritted her teeth and finished up the article about voice actors who'd worked on the 1980s cartoon *Power Pets*, incorporating the notes Nicole had e-mailed her. She did not incorporate the snide comments that had accompanied the notes. Knowing that Nicole would sift for faults like a mother gorilla grooming her young, she forced herself to do as good a job as she could. The only bone she allowed herself was neglecting to include a plug for Joy Baird's latest project—it was petty, but satisfying.

Tilda shot the completed article off to the magazine, and then wrote up her interview with John Laryea. It wasn't particularly fun since Laryea hadn't told her a whole lot worth writing about, but she scraped up a few decent quotes from her tape, and when she added in some background about the *Pharos* comic book, it was fairly solid. That one she sent to *Entertain Me!* on spec, but she was reasonably sure they'd take it. If not, she had a list of lower-paying markets to try next.

She still had the notes from her talk with Hugh Wilder, but decided not to write them up until she knew what angle she was going to take. Instead she sent out half a dozen queries to noncompeting magazines, offering to write an article geared to each. With luck, she'd sell six versions of the piece, but as long as she got one, she'd be satisfied. After all, the original aim of the interview had been to protect Laryea, and that mission had already been accomplished.

By midafternoon she was ready to go after Leviathan. Unfortunately, she wasn't sure where to look first. Tilda had a substantial database of people to consult when it came to finding old TV actors, movie stars, and even one-hit-wonder musicians, but comic book artists were something new.

The first step was to Google Leviathan. Admittedly, Joni or her secretary or whoever had probably tried that first, but Tilda knew that using a search engine could take finesse, and not everybody was as good at it as she was. She used "Leviathan," "Pharos," and "Dylan O'Taine" as search terms to see what she came up with. The answer? A whole lot of hits. There was nothing to do but start going through them.

After an hour of sorting through websites and bulletin boards, she was ready to admit that Leviathan did not have a website for selling old sketches and reliving his glory days. Nor did he have a presence on Facebook, MySpace, or LinkedIn. That was hardly a surprise, because Joni would have found him herself that way, but Tilda would have felt like a complete idiot if she hadn't looked and Leviathan was on one of those places.

With the easy sources exhausted, she took a break to grab a glass of Dr Pepper before hitting the specialized comic book sites. Though Tilda had read comics on and off for years, she knew she was no expert.

She learned that *Pharos* was originally published by Regal Comics, but the company had long since gone out of business and she had zero luck tracking it down.

The next step would have to be talking to a real, live comic book fan. Which, in her case, meant Cooper. She called him at work.

"Cooper, I need to pick your brains about comic books. Do you know—"

"Oh, now you've got time to talk. When I needed your help, you were busy busy busy. Maybe I'm busy busy busy, now."

"What if I were to tell you what John Laryea is like in person? And how pissed off he got when a former costar showed up? And about the former boyfriend of mine who showed up with his head in my lap? Or would you like to hear about an interesting bit of detective work I've been hired for?"

There was a pause. "Okay, you've got me. What do you need?"

"Two things. First off, do you have any copies of *Pharos* I can borrow? The original comics, not the graphic novel."

She had read them, but she'd borrowed then from an old boyfriend and didn't have her own set.

"Nope, I'm not big into supernatural stuff. Other than Neil Gaiman's *Sandman*, of course, because it's brilliant."

"Then I guess I'll hit the Million Year Picnic. Now who can I talk to about the business end of comics?"

"There's a dude named Tony Davis—he's got connections and he knows comics like you know old TV shows."

"Great. Where can I find him?"

"When you get to the Million Year Picnic, look at the cash register. Tony will probably be standing behind it. He owns the place."

"Boffo! Then I'm off to Cambridge."

"What about all the gossip you owe me?"

She launched into a swift but detailed description of all the topics she'd promised, finishing with, "Tomorrow I'm heading back to the Cape to hang around the filming."

"But Tilda! Everybody knows how boring movie-making is. You'll be spending hours and hours sitting while the light gets just right, or for somebody to get their makeup fixed for the umpteenth time."

"I know."

"It totally destroys the magic of the movie when you see how unromantic those love scenes really are, and how those daring leaps from cliffs that are really only from two or three feet off the ground."

"True that."

"And the actors can be such bitches to everybody!"

"You're right again."

There was a pause. Then Cooper said, "God! I am so jealous I can hardly stand it."

"I know. But if you take me to dinner when I get back, I will share all the gossip with you."

"Bring pictures, too, and you've got a deal!"

# Chapter 10

No geek's visit to Harvard Square can be considered complete without a trip to the Million Year Picnic. Named for a Ray Bradbury story, the store is stuffed with comics and staffed by knowledgeable comic book fans.
—"EVERY GEEK'S GUIDE TO HARVARD SQUARE"
BY TILDA HARPER, GEEK TRAVEL

TILDA knew that the Million Year Picnic had been in the same downstairs shop front in Cambridge's Harvard Square for eons, other than a brief period of relocation when recovering from a fire. It was tiny and crowded with shelves filled with comic books and graphic novels, plus T-shirts, action figures, and other related miscellany. It was, in short, geek heaven, and Tilda had always loved the place.

Figuring that spending money was always a good way to get a store owner to talk to her, she first went to the boxes of back issues to see if there were any copies of *Pharos*. Clearly somebody had been keeping up with Hollywood news because there were several sets of the full run of *Pharos* bundled together in Mylar bags, and Tilda could see where the prices had been crossed out and higher ones marked. She picked out the cheapest set of the ten issues and took it up to the counter.

The guy at the register, a curly-haired man with mocha skin, a Green Lantern T-shirt, and wire-rimmed glasses said, "I should warn you that some of the comics in that bundle are second or third printing."

"Is there any difference between them and the first printing?"

"Only the word *first* in *first printing*, but some collectors insist on first printings."

"I just want to read them."

"In that case, we've got it in a graphic novel format, too, and it would be a little cheaper and hold up to reading better."

"Is there anything in the comic book that didn't make it into the graphic novel? Or vice versa?"

"The actual books have the letter columns, and ads for other Regal Comics titles. The graphic novel has an interview with the guy who edited *Pharos*. It's right there on the shelf on your right."

Tilda picked it up, flipped through it, decided it was worth the extra expense to buy both versions, and put it onto the counter with the package of actual comic books. Considering how quickly the guy had known what was in the comics and the graphic novel, she hazarded a guess. "Are you Tony Davis?"

"That's me."

"My name's Tilda Harper. I'm a friend of Cooper Christianson's, and he recommended I talk to you for a story I'm working on."

"About *Pharos*, I'm guessing."

"You guess correctly. I'm trying to track down the guy who wrote it."

"Oh yes, the mysterious Leviathan."

"I don't suppose you know who he is."

"No, not me. Of course there's been a lot of speculation about Leviathan in comics circles, thanks to the movie, but that's about it. You want to hear the theories?"

"Let me guess. Leviathan is somebody famous who doesn't want anybody to know he did comic books—maybe Andy Warhol. Or he was murdered. Or he was kidnapped to draw for some rich guy's personal pleasure. White slavery. Something to do with the Kennedys, Elvis, or Marilyn Monroe. Anything else?"

"You forgot the idea that he's actually a current comic book artist who changed his name. Nobody has a style that comes close, but I think Frank Miller is the leading contender."

"What about the idea that he was just this guy who drew a comic that didn't do all that well and when it was cancelled, he went on with his life?"

"You know, that's never come up. What fun would that be?"

She had to laugh. "What about you? Do you have any favorites?"

"Your explanation is really the most likely, even if it is hopelessly boring. The only question is why he hasn't come forward now, but he could be dead—from natural causes, I mean—or living in another country or just not somebody who pays attention to forthcoming movies."

"What about the comic book company? Regal Comics? I don't suppose you know anything about that end."

"Actually, I do," Tony said. "It was back when I was just working here part-time, during college. The manager gave us a lot of latitude in ordering new titles, and I'm the one who found *Pharos* first. Regal was a small-time operation, which meant that they weren't with any of the usual distributors, so I had to order directly from them. The woman in charge of orders was something else."

"Oh?"

"I never actually met her, but she had this amazing voice. I kept the store carrying Regal titles longer than I should have, just so I could call and talk to her." In a dreamy tone, he said, "Her name was Alicia."

Tilda lifted one eyebrow.

"Hey," he said with a shrug, "it's not like a whole lot of hot girls were coming into the shop back then."

"What about the guy in charge of Regal? The editor or publisher or whatever he was."

"I didn't talk to him as much, but he seemed pretty cool." He scratched his chin. "What was his name? Marc something?" He picked up the copy of the *Pharos* graphic novel and turned to the front matter. "Here it is. Marc Fitzwilliam. The company address will be in the old issues, but I might have something more recent." He turned to the computer that apparently did double duty as a cash register and tapped away for a few minutes. "This is a few years old, too, but he might still be there." He scribbled down the address on a piece of paper, complete with phone number and e-mail, and handed it to her. "Maybe this will help."

"Thanks, I really appreciate it."

"No sweat. And if you talk to Alicia, tell her I said hello."

"Will do."

"Do you still want to buy the comics?"

"Absolutely." And since he'd been both helpful and nice, she let him talk her into buying a graphic novel of *Nazrat*, another cult favorite from the 1980s boom in black-and-white independent comics. She wouldn't be able to claim it as an expense, but maybe they'd make a *Nazrat* movie someday.

# Chapter 11

The success of *Teenage Mutant Ninja Turtles* showed the industry that the smallest comic book company, even if run out of a garage or back bedroom, could provide a hot product. The downside was that so many people living in garages and back bedrooms produced such bad products.

—*TEENAGE MUTANT NINJA ARTISTS: THE BEST OF INDIE COMICS* BY JERRY FRAZEE

IT was after five by the time Tilda drove back to Malden, but since the number Davis had given her was for the Chicago area, she figured there was a reasonable chance she'd get the office while it was still open. So after letting the dogs out to do what they needed to do, and cleaning up same, she made the call. Somebody answered on the first ring.

"A-1 Printing."

"May I speak to Marc Fitzwilliam please?"

"Speaking."

"Is this the same Marc Fitzwilliam who edited *Pharos*?"

"Man! Did Shelton put you up to this?"

"Excuse me?"

"When is he going to quit ragging me over this? If he doesn't believe I published *Pharos*, tell him to just say so."

"Mr. Fitzwilliam, my name is Tilda Harper. I'm a reporter, and I'm trying to find Leviathan, the creator of *Pharos*."

There was a pause. "Seriously?"

"Seriously."

"Wow. How did you track me down?"

"It's what I do," Tilda said, which sounded more impressive than going to a comic book store. "I'm doing some work with the director of the movie *Pharos*, and we'd love to be able to talk to Leviathan to get his take on the film's casting and script. Do you know how I can get in touch with him?"

"Sorry, no. The truth is I never met the guy. Never even talked to him on the phone. We did all our stuff by mail."

"Then you must have his address."

"It was a PO box but the last few things I sent him bounced back marked 'Return to sender—address unknown.' And that was years ago, not long after the last issue came out. I guess he didn't need the PO box anymore. He never published anything else."

"I knew he didn't bring out anything with that name— I thought he might have used a different name for other work."

"Maybe, but I never saw anything that looked like his style. And I don't know what his real name is."

"How did you address stuff to him? And write checks?"

"Mr. L. E. Viathan."

"You're kidding me. What about tax records?"

"Now you're kidding me. I was a twenty-something-year-old kid running a comic book company out of my parents' basement. I paid an advance and royalties, and he took care of his own taxes. I figured he had some reason for living off the grid and I thought it was kind of cool. Like maybe he was on the run or something."

Or worried about being fired from his real job, Tilda thought. Or embarrassed about writing comic books. Or dodging alimony, or hiding from the mob, or any of the other speculations from the comic book community.

She asked, "If you never met him, how did you acquire *Pharos*?"

"It was an over the transom submission. I went to the Heroes Convention in Charlotte right after I decided to start up Regal, and I gave out a stack of business cards to wannabes. A couple of months later, I got photocopies of the first issue of *Pharos* in the mail. Leviathan said in his cover letter that we'd spoken at the con, but honestly, I didn't remember it then, let alone now. The stuff was so good that I really didn't care how he'd found me. It was the best thing I'd had come across my desk." He laughed. "Hell, it was the best thing Regal ever published, and that includes the books I wrote myself. A couple of titles sold better, but that was just chance. *Pharos* was head and shoulders above anything else."

From the other Regal titles Tilda has seen, she agreed with him, but didn't think it would be particularly diplomatic to say so. "And everything was by mail? How did that work? The editing process, I mean."

"Well, it wasn't very formal," Fitzwilliam said with a laugh. "I was still new to the business—*Pharos* was only the third title I brought out. Basically Leviathan would send me the script and the thumbnails for the pages, plus cover sketches. I'd take a look, and then send my comments and corrections. I didn't have many—he was way more professional than I was."

"Wait, if you don't know who it was, how do you know it was a guy?"

"I just assumed. It was pretty much a boys' club. There still aren't that many female comic book artists."

"I suppose not," Tilda said. When she herself went to buy comics, she was often the only woman in the place. "Sorry for the interruption. Please go on."

"So I'd mail back my comments, and a few weeks later, he'd send me the finished pages."

"He did it all by himself? I thought pencils and inking and lettering were done by separate people."

"They are usually, but like I said, I was new at it and didn't know any better. Besides, he wanted to do it all. He even did the coloring for the covers."

"What happened after you got the pages?"

"I'd make another pass, but I don't think I changed anything at that point more than three or four times. Honestly, he was like a dream for me, especially compared with the other guys I was working with. The only sticking point was having to do everything by mail, but he worked the extra time into his schedule and still made all his deadlines with days to spare."

"Why did you cancel the book if it was so good?"

"I just ran out of money. When I first started up, people were so excited about indie comics that any lousy book could sell out a print run of 20K. Naturally most of them were pretty bad, and a lot never even put out a second issue. People were buying comics for investments, as if every title was going to be another *Teenage Mutant Ninja Turtles*. It was all about the money."

"I'm sure all you publishers were in it purely for art," Tilda said dryly.

He sniggered. "Yeah, yeah. I was hoping to make a fortune, just like everybody else. But when the investment buyers realized that most of their comics had zero resale value, and the publishers realized they weren't going to get rich, titles started dropping like flies. By the time we got to the eighth issue of *Pharos*, the print run was down to 5K. I was leaking money, and something had to give. So I told Leviathan he had two issues to wrap up any plot threads, and he did such a great job I hated to see it end. I kept Regal going for maybe a year after that, but the craze was over and I had to get on with my life. I was lucky to find somebody to buy the whole shebang, and I still lost money."

Tilda checked her notes. "You sold your back titles to MasterWork Comics, and MasterWork sold their assets to Allman Ink, and then Joni Langevoort bought the movie rights for *Pharos* from them, right?"

"That's what I hear. I didn't really keep track after I sold to MasterWork."

"How did that work? Did Leviathan get any money out of the deal?"

"He got paid for the first printing, and then a little bit in royalties. The character and the right to reprint those issues belonged to me."

"But Leviathan created *Pharos*."

"I told you I didn't know what I was doing. I got a

look at a Marvel or a DC contract, and those guys kept all rights, so I thought that was what I was supposed to do. I swear, I wasn't trying to pull anything."

"It seems to me that creators' rights were an issue even then."

"Hey, I didn't force Leviathan to sign the contract. He could have tried someplace else."

"Yeah, sure," Tilda said in disgust. She'd met an awful lot of hungry writers, artists, and musicians who'd worked so hard and dreamed so long that they'd sign the first contract somebody put in front of them. She didn't know if Fitzwilliam had really been that ignorant, or just sleazy, but it didn't sound fair to her.

Fitzwilliam said, "If it makes you any happier, I didn't make any money out of the movie deal, either, because I signed away all those rights way back when, long before Hollywood came calling. Nobody has even bothered to talk to me about it until now." He sighed. "I sure wish I had a piece of that."

Tilda was tempted to say that nobody had made him sign his contract either, but since she might need more information from him, she resisted the impulse.

"I'm really dying to see the movie," Fitzwilliam said. "Hey, you think you could maybe get me into a movie preview or a premiere or something?"

"I could try. I bet they'd love the publicity if they could bring Leviathan and his original editor together." Okay, she knew no such thing, but she'd write up the story herself if nobody else was interested.

"But I told you. I don't know who Leviathan is."

"You've got to have some clue. Didn't he ever mention anything about where he was from, for instance?"

"Hell, it was over twenty years ago."

"What about Alicia? Would she remember anything?"

"Alicia?"

"Tony Davis from the Million Year Picnic in Cambridge said he used to order from a woman named Alicia—he sends his regards."

"Hang on." Fitzwilliam must have moved his mouth from the receiver, but Tilda could still hear him yell, "Ma! I thought I told you not to flirt with my comic book customers." There was a muffled response. "You remember some guy in Cambridge? Tony Davis?" Tilda heard giggles, and more answers. Then Fitzwilliam came back to the phone. "Alicia is my mother. She used to handle phone orders for me. I may have been working out of my basement, but I didn't want anybody to know about it. Ma says to tell Davis that she remembers him, too, but she doesn't know any more about Leviathan than I do."

"Do you still have any files or anything you can look at, see if there is something you've forgotten?"

"I should still have some copies of our letters. I could look through them to see if there's anything there, then let you know."

"That would be great." She gave him her contact info, and was about to end the call when he said, "I really hope you find him. I'd like him to get the credit he deserves. I mean, he really deserved a better publisher than me."

Tilda said, "At least you had enough sense to bring

out something good, and not another teenage mutant ninja creature. Though I kind of liked the hamsters."

"Yeah, but the kangaroos were better."

After a discussion that fortunately did not deteriorate to who was stronger—the Thing or the Hulk—they parted friends.

# Chapter 12

**Episode 16**
When the Blastoffs land on a planet covered mostly by water, Sid wants to cancel their concert and blast off immediately. Marty realizes his big brother is afraid of water, and tries to help him through it. But it's not until Marty falls in rough seas that Sid overcomes his fear to rescue him.
— *SATURDAY MORNING SPREE* BY CHARLES M. LUCE

TILDA wasn't overly thrilled with her progress, but she wasn't overly discouraged, either. It was just going to take a little more digging. She wasn't ready to pull out the shovel that minute because both the clock and her appetite told her it was time for dinner.

Since she was going to leave for Cape Cod the next day, she took the opportunity to empty out a combination of doggie bags, starting with half a Caesar salad from Boston Market, followed by part of a quesadilla from the Border Café, and ending with a third of a bowl of fettuccine Alfredo from Polcari's. As meals go, it was both economical and tasty. The only downside was the intense scrutiny she was under from both Honeypaw and Calvin. Dianne swore she never fed the dogs from the table, but since the dogs clearly knew what a doggie bag represented, Tilda wasn't sure she believed her.

By the time Dianne got home from work, Tilda had disappointed the dogs by actually finishing her own meal, and was on her way back to her room to fire up her computer and see what she could find out about Leviathan on the Web. As Tony Davis had told her, the comic book boards were buzzing about the upcoming Leviathan movie. In between posts speculating about who was going to play Dylan O'Taine's mermaid love interest and those trashing the script as antithetical to *Pharos* and perhaps the Constitution of the United States as well, there were quite a few filled with rumors about Leviathan's identity and whereabouts. Sadly, most of the theories were ludicrous.

Still, not all the posts were from loony tunes, so she composed one herself, explaining that she was a reporter looking for Leviathan and asking people to send her any substantiated information they had. She knew, of course, that most of the "substantiated information" would be complete gibberish, but that was why she first created a brand-new e-mail account for the responses. She preferred to put all her Internet nuts in one virtual basket.

She went on to a number of comics sites and bulletin boards, and on each, asked for information. When she felt she'd spread enough virtual bread crumbs, she started for the living room to watch shows she'd saved on TiVo. But when she met a heavily laden Dianne on the stairs, she grabbed one of the two PetSmart shopping bags her roomie was carrying to help her bring it upstairs.

"All done with work?" Dianne asked.

"Just finished," Tilda said, but could have slugged herself when she heard what came next.

"Could you give me a hand cleaning out the guinea pig cage?"

Tilda's options were limited. She could agree, but she really disliked handling guinea pig poop. Or she could refuse, with or without a lecture about how the pets were Dianne's responsibility, but that would probably get her the silent treatment for several days.

With some of her past roommates, the silent treatment would have been a blessing, but Dianne had the world's noisiest version. Though she wouldn't talk to Tilda, she would hold one-sided conversations with the animals to make sure Tilda knew how thoroughly she was being snubbed.

Thinking quickly, Tilda came up with a third choice. "Tell you what. I'll hold Tama and Hershey for you, and keep you company."

Dianne actually liked that idea, and Tilda wondered if she'd made a misstep. What if Dianne was trying to get Tilda to bond with the creatures, making her more vulnerable to future entreaties? The problem was, Tilda realized as she sat cross-legged on the floor stroking one pig with each hand while the piggies made chut-chut sounds at each other, that method just might work. They were pretty cute as long as they didn't pee on her, and a couple of times, they even purred, which made Dianne look on approvingly. Oh yeah, it was a trap.

To distract herself, Tilda said, "Did you find a pet-sitter?"

"My mother is going to look in twice a day to take care of everybody. I just have to make sure that Ka is fed before I go. Mom says she can't handle mealtime for him."

They discussed work—Dianne was a physician's assistant—and boyfriends—Dianne had a long-term one and was starting to become impatient about him proposing. Having met him and seen his hair recede month by month, Tilda didn't think he was much of a catch, but he was as rabid an animal fancier as Dianne, which made him a rarity.

"Except he doesn't like guinea pigs," Dianne said sadly. "He says they look like rats."

"They do not," Tilda said indignantly. Then she felt a warm, wet feeling on her jeans. "Shit! Tama just peed on me."

Dianne was nearly done, so she took the pigs and put them back into their cage. "I'll go fill the water bottle if you put some pellets in their bowl."

"Fine," Tilda said, no longer enthused by the creatures. She suspected that their cute little noises were laughter at her damp pants. So she dutifully filled the food dish, and then, not knowing where Dianne stored the bag of pellets, put it on top of the cage.

She was halfway back to her room to change when the pigs started squealing loudly, sounding like nothing so much as a car alarm.

"What did I do? What did I do?" Tilda asked as Dianne rushed in.

"Did you put that up there?" Dianne said, grabbing the bag from the top of the cage.

"Yeah."

"You frightened them. Guinea pigs are a prey species, and many of their natural predators fly. They thought something was trying to get them."

"Really?" With the bag gone, the piggies had ceased their squawks and were happily eating. "I didn't realize they were so stupid."

"They're not stupid!"

"They were afraid of pellets."

"Evolution taught them to avoid things flying over-head. To you it was a bag of pellets, but to them it was a predator."

"Good thing it wasn't a pack of their honey treats. That would have been really scary."

Dianne gave her a look, and Tilda thought that maybe she'd managed to avoid bonding with the piggies after all. As soon as she changed her pants, she went down-stairs to watch *The Daily Show*.

# Chapter 13

A good director's not sure when he gets on the set what he's going to do.

—ELIA KAZAN

THE next morning started out well enough. Tilda got e-mail from *Entertain Me!* approving the article about *Power Pets* and accepting the John Laryea interview. Three of the places she'd queried about the Wilder interview were interested, and the deadlines were loose enough that she could wait awhile to actually write up the pieces.

But then she checked her Leviathan-specific e-mail account, and found nothing but spam.

She spent the next couple of hours washing clothes and packing for her stay at the Cape. It was tricky. The weather was notoriously changeable during the fall. That meant her coat and what salesclerks called layering pieces. And there was always the chance that she'd get invited somewhere nice, and she'd want something appropriate to wear. In the end, she stopped just short of packing her entire wardrobe.

Work-related stuff was more straightforward: laptop, camera, tape recorder, phone, and all the thumb drives and memory cards and cords and chargers to keep it all up and running. Plus actual pads and pens—they were traditional, after all.

Once all that was loaded into her car, she slipped her latest mix disc into the CD player and took off for the Cape. Even with a stop for gas, she was only an hour later than planned getting out of Malden, which was an hour earlier than she'd actually expected.

The two hours plus of the drive weren't too bad, though admittedly not as nice as when she was riding in the limo with Pete at the wheel. It was early afternoon, so the rush hour hadn't started and there weren't many people heading to the Cape in October. Had it been spring or summer, it would have been a vastly different story on a Friday afternoon, but in the fall, weekend travelers were more interested in heading north for leaf peeping.

Tilda pulled in at the Glenham Bars Inn just before five, and went in to check with the front desk and see what arrangements had been made for her accommodations. With so many film people around, she was half afraid she'd be stuck in a broom closet in the basement, so she was pleasantly surprised to find out she had been assigned to one of the cottages. It wouldn't be as convenient for the restaurant and bar as the inn would have been, but, on the plus side, she'd get lots of privacy and it would be a whole lot quieter.

She got back into the car for the short drive down Shoreline Drive to Atlantic Breeze, as the inn's clerk had insisted on calling her cottage. It was on the ocean side of the road, giving her a view and fresh air along with everything else. "Do not get used to this, do not get used to this," she kept repeating to herself as she unloaded her car and started marking her territory by arranging her belongings.

There were two bedrooms, and naturally Tilda picked the larger one, which was attached to the Jacuzzi-equipped master bathroom. There was a desk in the room, too, so she set up her work equipment, and then jumped on the king-sized bed a few times just for the fun of it.

When she went into the eat-in kitchen to get a drink, she found that not only was the kitchen fully equipped with dishes and pots and pans, but that somebody had stocked the refrigerator with Dr Pepper and her preferred sandwich fixings. Only after she'd gloated over the food did she notice the manila envelope on the counter.

Her name was on the outside, and inside was a note from Joni, a shooting schedule, a parking pass, and a security badge with lanyard. While she was looking it over, and of course continuing to gloat, her cell phone rang.

"Tilda? Nick. Did you make it back down here okay?"

"I did, and I'm standing in my sumptuous cottage. Do I have you to thank for the refreshments?"

"Only in the sense of my telling Joni's minion what you like."

"Said minion must not have realized that I'm just a freelancer."

"It may be that I mentioned your byline has been seen frequently in national magazines of the highest caliber."

"That explains the deli ham instead of the cheap stuff. I could easily get spoiled by this. And there's not a four-legged, two-legged, or slithering creature in sight!"

"Excuse me?"

"New roommate, new set of problems. Let's leave it at that."

"Consider it left. Do you have dinner plans? The off-duty half of our security team is getting together for dinner at a Mexican place in town. Would you like to come with? It'll be me and Dad and some of the other guys you've met."

"Me and a tableful of guys? How could I refuse?"

Of course she should have stayed in and gone to work sifting through any e-mails that might have helped her track down Leviathan, but the aforementioned table of buff security men was too good to pass up.

The guy-packed limo picked her up a few minutes later, though she was surprised to see that Pete wasn't driving. Nick told her he had a date, and the speculations about said date would have become risqué if Dom hadn't cleared his throat significantly.

It was Pete's loss. The food was great, the margaritas were tasty, and the guys had some hilarious stories about celebrity misdeeds. Naturally all were either told anonymously or off the record, since Tolomeo Personal Protection had a reputation to protect.

Tilda reciprocated with stories of interviews gone wrong, or just wacky, including the time a TV executive wouldn't answer any of her questions in any depth until a parrot—which Tilda had thought was only a decoration—suddenly squawked loudly and came to sit on Tilda's shoulder. That turned out to be a sign that she could be trusted, and she got one of her most candid interviews ever. It was worth a little parrot poop on her shirt.

As far as Tilda was concerned, they could have continued swapping stories and sipping margaritas all night,
but Dom kept a pretty tight ship. Before it got too late, he
herded them all back to the inn, and when they dropped
her off, he himself made a sweep of her cottage to make
sure it was secure.

Since it was still fairly early, and since the shoot
wasn't going to get rolling until late the next day, Tilda
figured it was time to start earning her keep. She booted
up her laptop, and grinned in happy anticipation at the
number of e-mails waiting, especially since she saw
more than one with the subject line, "Leviathan identified." But as she started going through the notes, her
happy mood started to fade, and before she was done,
she was ready for another pitcher of margaritas.

It wasn't that she hadn't found Leviathan. It was the
fact that she'd found too many Leviathans. Even when
she weeded out the obvious crazies, there were twelve
different notes from people either claiming to be Leviathan or to know who Leviathan was.

There'd been rare occasions when she couldn't find
an actor she was looking for, but this was the first time
she'd found an even dozen.

# Chapter 14

In the past decade, imposters (midgets, dwarfs, and average-sized people) have continued to poke their heads out and claim involvement in *The Wizard of Oz*. Why do they do it? If only for some recognition, some profit perhaps, or a bit of adulation, that's why these imposters make these wild claims.
—*THE MUNCHKINS OF OZ* BY STEPHEN COX

"BUT why?" Joni wanted to know when Tilda called her the next day, by which time the list of contestants for Who Wants to Be an Obscure Comic Book Writer had swelled to fifteen. "What's the point?"

"You've seen reality television—some people will do almost anything to get that fifteen minutes of fame. Pretending to be Leviathan is a lot less drastic than pretending that one's child has gone up in a balloon."

"I suppose. But wouldn't an imposter want to pretend to be somebody more famous?"

"Not necessarily. You're bound to get caught if you fake being somebody obscenely famous. Obscure people are easier. A few years back a dance instructor in Texas claimed to be Tommy Rall, who was a not terribly well-known hoofer in movie musicals. The real Rall had long since retired while the phony one was using his name to sell foxtrot lessons. Before that, there were all kinds of midgets pretending to have been munchkins in *The Wizard of Oz* to earn appearance fees. Some had even been in the movie, but pretended to have had bigger roles—a bunch pretended to have played the mayor of Munchkinland instead of anonymous soldiers and such."

"But money was involved in those cases, right? We own the rights to *Pharos*, free and clear. There's no money in it."

"Not directly, but the real creator could get some nice TV interviews and print coverage, maybe hit collector's shows and comic book shows to sell his autograph. If the movie does well enough, he could use that as a hook to sell a new project or trunk book."

Joni sighed. "Okay, I'm convinced. It's an actual phenomenon."

Tilda was relieved. She'd run out of case studies pulled from the Web and used up the fifteen minutes' worth of secondhand analysis from her sister June the research psychologist.

"The question is," Joni said, "what do we do now?"

"Well, if you still want me to find Leviathan . . ."

"I definitely do."

"Then I'll start weeding out phonies."

"How?"

"There are a few tricks I can try," Tilda said, hoping she sounded mysterious, yet capable.

She must have nailed it, because Joni agreed, and Tilda promised to keep her up to date on progress. Once they hung up, Tilda let loose the sigh of relief she'd been holding in to maintain her air of competence, and threw herself down on the couch.

When she'd realized what she was up against the night before, she'd had to scramble to come up with enough background information to sound as if she hadn't been totally blindsided. She really wanted this story and the chance to hang around the *Pharos* film shoot, which meant that she had to sell Joni on the idea that it was still feasible. Now that she had, all she had to do was figure out how she was going to work it.

Since sprawling on the couch was probably not her best option, she went back to the Web to find out how the phonies she'd mentioned to Joni had been found out.

With the ersatz Tommy Rall, a woman named Carole Shmurak was a fan and had posted some biographical information about Rall on IMDb, including the fact that the dancer was retired. A woman from Texas had e-mailed Shmurak and said she knew a dance teacher who said he was Rall, but she wouldn't give his name. Anybody else might have left it at that, but Shmurak was a mystery writer, and decided to track the guy down— Tilda had to respect that. It turned out there were all kinds of inconsistencies in the guy's story, and he was quickly exposed.

As for the munchkins, some were found out because they were way too young to have possibly been in the movie. Others were revealed by the real munchkins, who knew their fellow actors, and others because movie buffs knew far more about *The Wizard of Oz* than they did. When you know who the real mayor of Munchkinland was, it's easy to identify imposters.

Tilda would've loved to have used the last method— finding the real Leviathan—but for the present she could focus on figuring out which of the wannabe Leviathans knew enough to put together a credible story.

First things first. She made a list of all the candidates and their e-mail addresses so she could keep them straight. Yet another wannabe popped up as she was setting up the file, but since he couldn't even spell Leviathan or Pharos correctly, Tilda ignored his existence. For the time being, she'd stick with her fifteen.

She sent an e-mail asking each of the wannabes how he or she had come to be published by Regal, and what his or her meetings with Fitzwilliam had been like. Since she already had Fitzwilliam's version, she thought that would help her eliminate a few. She carefully avoided any mention of the other claimants.

While waiting for replies, she turned her attention to the actual comic books. It had been a long time since she'd read *Pharos*, and it was even better than she'd remembered. The comics of that era had been a bit heavier on exposition than current readers preferred, and in that respect, *Pharos* had been ahead of its time. The art held up well, too. Being in black and white gave the drawings a sense of drama and dignity.

The story was not overly complex. Dylan O'Taine was the keeper of the lighthouse Pharos, which was a mystic citadel that protected the walking world from the powers of the sea, and sometimes vice versa. The main villains were the Asrai, who were translucent creatures Leviathan hinted might be the ghosts of drowned sailors, and their femme fatale leader Ceto, who used illusions to conceal her ugly form and nature.

O'Taine also fought the Blue Men of the Minch, who

were blue-skinned mermen who gathered treasure by using a magic wand to conjure whirlpools to crash ships. Their Chieftain had a code of honor, and would let ships go free if the captains could best him in a battle of wits.

When O'Taine wins such a battle by calling forth a storm of his own to overcome the whirlpool, the mermaid Melusine is washed up onto the shore near Pharos in the wake of that storm. They quickly realize they are soul mates, but since she's the daughter of the Chieftain, of course their love is doomed. But instead of moping about it the way comic book heroes often did—Tilda remembered getting really tired of the Silver Surfer whining about his lost love—they kept their romance going as best they could. It was surprisingly adult.

The Jengu seemed to be enemies at first, but were actually underwater shamans who taught O'Taine some of their magic. The Fosse Grim was a kind of aquatic pied piper, not wholly good or evil, and Flotsam and Jetsam were a pair of friendly seals who acted as pets for the lonely lighthouse keeper.

Tilda was enjoying the stories so much that she was disappointed to reach the last page of the final issue, which made her annoyed with Fitzwilliam for not continuing to publish the book, even if he wasn't making money.

She'd been too anxious about her forthcoming conversation with Joni to eat much breakfast that morning, so she took a break to take advantage of the sliced ham and cheese that had been left for her and made a couple of generous sandwiches.

Once they were gone and the crumbs wiped up, she

went back to the comics and made notes of things that she might ask the Leviathan Legion about. Something about the name Pharos rang a bell, and she hit Google to see if Leviathan had pulled that name from somewhere specific.

As it turned out, he had indeed—Pharos had been an ancient lighthouse in Egypt. That led to further investigation, and the realization that most of the characters and races in *Pharos* were borrowed from mythology, including Dylan O'Taine himself, who was a Welsh sea god. She jotted down notes about the origins of names and such, planning to use the info to eliminate candidates. Admittedly any of them could find this information the same way she had, but only if they thought to look. She was hoping some of them were boneheads. That would make her life a lot easier.

Tilda checked her e-mail, and found three replies: one Leviathan wannabe claimed to have met Fitzwilliam at Comic-Con while the other two described the many phone calls they'd had with him. Those last two were out immediately—Fitzwilliam had said he only dealt with Leviathan by mail. A quick phone call to Fitzwilliam established that he'd never been to Comic-Con, so that one was out, too.

That took the list down to twelve until another reasonable-sounding note arrived, bringing it back to thirteen. Still, she was making progress, and just in time for her to take a trip down to the beach where they were going to begin filming for *Pharos* the movie.

# Chapter 15

It bears repeating: by the first day of the movie, *the fate of the movie is sealed*. The point, once again, is that if you have prepared the script right, if you have cast it right, both actors and crew, you have a shot. If you have made a grievous error in either script or casting, you are dead in the water.

—WILLIAM GOLDMAN, *WHICH LIE DID I TELL?: MORE ADVENTURES IN THE SCREEN TRADE*

ACCORDING to Tilda's info packet, the film crew was set up at a private beach half a mile or so down the coast. When she arrived, one of the security guys she'd met at dinner the night before waved her toward a mostly filled gravel lot across the street from the beach, where another guy helped her find a space big enough to squeeze her car into. Even though the schedule said it was to be a sunset shoot, clearly the gang was mostly already there.

By the time Tilda crossed the street, Nick was waiting to help her over a bright yellow rope marking the restricted area.

"I don't want to be a pain," he said, "but you said you'd never been on a film shoot before, and I thought you could use a few pointers."

"Point away."

"One, do not approach Joni. Off set, she is as nice as

she can be. Once she's on-site, she is hyperfocused, and interruptions make her extremely irate."

"Fair enough." Tilda had only a vague idea of how much money was being spent for every moment of location time, but she knew it was a ridiculous amount. The last thing she wanted to do was cause delays.

"Two, turn off your phone and keep it off. Don't even leave it on vibrate mode."

"But—"

"I know, I know. Apparently both Joni and Laryea have had tricky shots ruined by phones going off, and Joni nearly went insane when a phone was left in a drawer and kept vibrating at random intervals. So if you have to make a call, go back over the rope—keep it off while you're on this side of the rope."

Tilda obediently pulled her cell phone from her pocket and powered off.

"Three," Nick went on, "do not get in front of the camera, or anywhere the camera might be moving toward. And do not get into the sight line of any actor. Which in this case is Laryea, since he's the only one on-site."

"Got it. What else?"

He pointed. "The craft table is over there—you're welcome to nosh unless it's a covered tray with somebody's name on it." He pointed again. "The facilities are over there, but unless you're desperate, I'd advise you to hold it. I think they cheaped out on them."

"Thanks for the warning. Anything else?"

"I don't think so, but if you need help, you can ask any of us security guys." Tolomeo's guys were all wearing royal blue polo shirts. "Or you can ask one of the production assistants, if you know which ones are PAs."

"That's easy," Tilda said. "PAs are the ones with the darkest bags under their eyes, the thickest clipboards, and the biggest coffee cups."

"Then you're ready to dive in. I'd offer to serve as escort, but my guys have caught sight of that damned stalker trying to sneak past the barricades twice today."

"The bathroom photo bug?"

He nodded grimly. "I'm going to find that guy, and when I do, I'm going to lift him by his carrottopped head and drop him off the Sagamore Bridge."

"Not taking it personally, are you?"

"Then I will fish him out and head for the Bourne Bridge and throw him into the canal from there."

"I wouldn't dream of standing in your way. Good luck!"

"Thank you. Enjoy your little slice of Hollywood." He waved her into the thick of it with a flourish that reminded her of Willy Wonka welcoming kids to his chocolate factory. Not a bad comparison, Tilda decided, since movie sets were also supposed to be places where dreams came true. But when she stopped to pull out a pad to write down that profound bit of analysis for her article, two guys carrying a crate of what looked like parts from a disassembled robot nearly ran her down. Nick hadn't warned her to keep moving, but Tilda was pretty sure that he should have.

Tilda knew that most of *Pharos* was going to be shot on a soundstage in Los Angeles. The Cape Cod shoot was mostly for establishing shots and background

footage which would be merged into the rest of the
film with CGI and other editing tricks. Therefore she'd
assumed the actual shoot would be fairly quiet, small,
and controlled. By the fifth time she'd ducked out of the
way of heavily laden people, she'd decided that if this
was quiet, small, and controlled, she would never sur-
vive a shoot that was noisy, loud, and chaotic.

The location where they were filming was a nice bit of
beach in a tiny inlet with a sea view devoid of buildings—
presumably an important point. The sand was liberally
dotted with stones, as were most New England beaches,
and as Tilda watched, techs of some sort were actually
sweeping the beach to get rid of debris and give it that
natural touch. Tilda didn't need a warning from Nick to
know that it would be a serious mistake for her to walk
on that sand.

All of the equipment was to one side, where it wouldn't
be seen by any of the cameras. It was on that side that
Tilda found a spot where it seemed relatively safe to settle down—a graffiti-spattered wooden bench at the end
of the path between the road and the beach, where she
could still see most of the action.

After an hour or so of watching, she admitted to herself that it really was as boring as she'd always been told,
and considerably more confusing. At any given moment,
three quarters of the people she saw were standing
around and drinking coffee and eating and none of the
work the other quarter was doing seemed particularly
germane to filming.

Then suddenly the mood shifted dramatically. The food
disappeared, the noise abated, and even posture improved.

A moment later, Tilda saw the reason. Joni and Laryea had arrived, and they strode down the path right past her, with Dom, Foster, and a trio of PAs close at their heels.

Tilda sat up straighter herself, sure something was about to happen. Then the director and the star—and of course their entourage—disappeared into a trailer on the beach. There was still a lot of activity, and it somehow seemed more purposeful, but since Tilda couldn't tell what the purpose was, it wasn't exactly invigorating.

She was itching to check her e-mail, and was about to retreat from the restricted area when Edwina strolled by. "How's it going?" the woman asked Tilda.

"Good," Tilda said. "This is fascinating to watch, and I'm getting lots of background information."

Edwina looked at the pad on Tilda's lap, which was blank other than a doodled mermaid. "I can see that. Mind if I join you?"

"Please do. I need somebody to wake me up in case I doze off."

"I'll wake you if you wake me."

The producer looked almost relaxed, which Tilda hadn't expected. "I'm surprised you're not in the middle of the frenzy," she said.

"My frenzy comes before, when we're trying to get the funding, set the budget, and cast the picture. Or after, when I have to figure out where we're bleeding money. I'm mostly superfluous at an actual shoot—this is Joni's department. I just like to show up and watch other people going crazy."

"There is something soothing about being the only person not working," Tilda agreed.

They watched for a while, and Tilda soon realized the advantage of hanging with a producer. When a PA started to zip by, Edwina stopped her with a single lifted finger. "Hold on a minute. Tilda, would you care for something to drink?"

"A Coke would be great."

"Katrina, could you bring us two Cokes? And if they've got any fresh nachos, some of those, too."

The PA nodded and, in less time than it would have taken Tilda to find the craft services table, was back with a tray neatly arranged with ice-filled glasses, cans of Coke, and two heaping plates of nachos. The PA showed every willingness to stand and act as a table while they ate at their leisure, but Tilda and Edwina scooted to the sides of the bench so they could put the tray down between them.

Edwina said, "Thank you, Katrina!" and before Tilda could add her appreciation, the PA was gone.

"Wow," Tilda said.

"Yeah, I live for that," Edwina said with a mischievous grin. "And I'm not just being a putz. I've found that if I eat from the craft table myself, they don't dare serve substandard food. As much as we pay the caterers, they owe us the good stuff."

"Very dedicated of you," Tilda said, and after a few bites, added, "I think you're getting your money's worth this time. Great nachos."

They were about halfway through their plates when Edwina said, "I hear you had a setback in your Leviathan hunt."

"You might say that," Tilda said, "but it wouldn't have been much fun if I'd found him right away anyway."

Edwina looked skeptical, but didn't argue the point.

She knew she was taking a chance, but what with the nacho-induced camaraderie, Tilda couldn't resist asking, "Can I ask you a question? Why are you against my looking for Leviathan?"

When the producer took her time before answering, Tilda had to wonder if Edwina was stalling. She finally said, "I don't like borrowing trouble. We own the rights and we're doing right by the material. That should be enough. The last thing we need is the creator showing up and making a fuss because we switched a character's name to something easier to pronounce or changed the time of year for a battle to make sure we don't give Laryea pneumonia. Not to mention bad press if he starts complaining that he's not getting any money out of the deal. You remember how the guys who created Superman got all the sympathy press when the first movie came out?"

"I tend to think Siegel and Schuster deserved some of the money." As a writer herself, Tilda was more than a little concerned with creators' rights.

"They had a contract—they gave up the rights. Same as Leviathan. And speaking off the record now, our budget is tight enough that we can't afford any kind of court battle if Leviathan were to try to sue."

"Do you think that's a possibility?"

She shrugged. "Who knows? It's like I said before, I don't want to borrow trouble."

Tilda thought about it, but had to say, "The thing is, I promised Joni I'd find the guy."

"I know you did, but nobody is going to hold it against you if you try your best and don't succeed. We won't chase you off the set or out of that cottage, and you'll still get your pass to Comic-Con. So don't knock yourself out if you hit a dead end."

"I'll keep that in mind."

"Well, I need to go make a few calls," Edwina said, scooping up cheese and chili onto a final tortilla chip. "Enjoy the show!"

Tilda couldn't help speculating as Edwina headed back toward the road. If she didn't know better, she'd think that maybe there was something fishy about the *Pharos* deal, and she didn't mean Dylan O'Taine's girlfriend the mermaid. The fact that Edwina was sending a different message than Joni was more than a little interesting, too.

# *Chapter 16*

I'd had makeup put on before and was familiar with the feel of the wet sponge and the smell of the typical film makeup, usually served up in a flat blue container labeled Max Factor Natural Tan. I always thought it was hilarious that they called this stuff natural. It was without a doubt the most unnatural color you could possibly paint a person.

—ALISON ARNGRIM, *CONFESSIONS OF A PRAIRIE BITCH: HOW I SURVIVED NELLIE OLESON AND LEARNED TO LOVE BEING HATED*

WITH those unsettling thoughts in her mind, the last thing Tilda wanted to do was to continue sitting by herself, so she decided it was time to explore some more. First she pulled her camera out of her backpack to check the battery and memory card. Some behind-the-scenes photos would definitely help out her article. She'd already seen a studio photographer taking official candid shots, but Tilda was hoping to actually take some that weren't staged. Her photography skills were basic at best, but with the wonders of digital photography she could use quantity to make up for her lack of quality.

Edwina had left the food tray behind, and Tilda was trying to decide if she should take it back to craft services or not when Katrina the PA suddenly appeared to whisk it away and, like the Lone Ranger, didn't even stay long enough to be thanked.

"I am going to be so spoiled," Tilda muttered to herself.

She headed toward the backstage part of the beach, being careful not to disturb the carefully groomed sand. Tension seemed to be rising, particularly for the crew setting up the massive banks of lights. There was something ironic about needing so many lights for a sunset shoot, and Tilda decided that it was worth a couple of photos. Then she caught a pair of assistant somethings consulting a laptop to see if any airplanes were scheduled to fly over while they were filming. Her cousin's wedding was the only occasion when Tilda had seen so much time and artifice expended on making something look natural.

Speaking of time and artifice, Tilda spotted Laryea himself sitting in a director's chair outside the makeup trailer and went closer to get her first look at the actor in costume. Since the actual comic was still fresh in her mind, she was able to admire the attention to detail: the blue gray flowing shirt ready to be ripped off at a moment's notice so O'Taine could slip into the water, the snug breeches, the ornate torc that gave him the various mystic defenses the plot demanded, and the mismatched bracers—one with runes to protect creatures of the land and the other to protect the ocean.

Tilda had attended enough comic book show costume pageants to know that it wasn't always easy to translate an illustration to actual clothing, but the costume designer for the movie had done a terrific job with

O'Taine's garb. And every bit of it suited Laryea right down to the ground.

Well, almost to the ground. While she was admiring, Laryea stood up to talk to a starstruck PA, and Tilda noticed that he was wearing ornate leather boots. In the comic books, O'Taine had gone barefoot. She'd have asked the actor about them, but mindful of Nick's warnings earlier, she decided to settle for taking pictures of the star preparing for his role.

But as she raised the camera to aim it, Foster jumped in front of her to block the shot.

"Stop!" Foster commanded. "Don't you dare use that pose." He bustled in and pushed Laryea back into the chair, prodded the makeup artist to do something useless, and the PA was now leaning over so that her face didn't even show in the picture. In other words, Tilda's candid photo now looked as informal as a Noh play. She took a few shots anyway, and thanked them.

"Let me see," Foster said, reaching for her camera.

"Excuse me?" Tilda said, holding it just a bit higher than the shorter man could reach without strain.

"I have to approve all photos of Mr. Laryea. It's policy."

"That may be your policy, but it's not mine."

Foster actually snatched for the camera, and would have followed when Tilda took several steps back had Nick not suddenly been between them.

"It's about time," Foster said. "Tolomeo, get that camera."

"I don't think so," Nick said evenly.

"Excuse me? You work for us."

"Actually, I work for the movie company, and I was hired to protect Mr. Laryea, not to manhandle the press."

"Protection includes protection from shoddy journalism."

"Shoddy journalism?" Tilda said, drawing out each syllable. "You little—"

"Hey now," Laryea said, coming up to put one hand on Foster's shoulder. "What's the problem?"

"Your watchdog here seems to have some funny ideas," Tilda said.

"She won't let me see the pictures she took," Foster said indignantly. "How do I know what she's made you look like?

"Foster, Foster, Foster," Laryea said. "I know you have my best interests at heart, but you don't really think Tilda is trying to make me look bad, do you?"

"I should hope not."

"Of course she isn't."

"I'd be happy to show you the photos before I send them to *Entertain Me!*," Tilda said, though she carefully did not say she would give Laryea—or Foster—veto power.

"That would be great, wouldn't it Foster?"

Foster just glared at her before ostentatiously taking out his Blackberry to make himself look far too busy to deal with a shoddy journalist. Tilda thought about reminding him that it was a cell-phone-free zone, but decided it wouldn't be wise.

Laryea put his arm chummily around Tilda, which she had to admit was aesthetically quite pleasing, though she didn't usually date men wearing so much makeup.

"Are you enjoying seeing the magic come to life?" he asked.

"Definitely," she said. "Your costume is terrific. One question, though. Why the boots? Dylan O'Taine is always shown barefoot in the comics."

"Insurance regulations," he said with a laugh. "Crazy, isn't it? I can see why they wouldn't want me performing stunts, but here they are worried about my stubbing my toe on a rock. I guess it's just part of the price I pay when the production depends on me."

Even though that statement was probably completely accurate, given the nature of moviemaking, it still made Tilda's skin crawl to hear Laryea say it.

"Well, I better get out of your way," she said, moving out of range of his arm. "I know you need to concentrate."

"Don't go too far! You're going to want to see this scene come together."

She smiled and nodded but didn't stop.

Nick came with her and said, "No offense, but you might want to be careful with Laryea."

Tilda raised one eyebrow. "That's a bit dog-in-the-manger-ish."

"No, no, I'd be perfectly happy to see you with a good guy—some of the fellows from last night wanted to know if you were available, as a matter of fact. It's just that Laryea has a tendency to date women in order to make professional connections."

"Oh, and he really needs a freelance reporter in his corner?"

"He has a good eye for potential. He spotted Joni

when she was directing commercials, and Edwina when she didn't know squat about the business."

"You mean Laryea and . . . Both of them?"

"I believe he introduced them, actually."

"Wow."

"Have you met the scriptwriter?"

"Dolores? Her, too?"

He nodded.

"He must be something special. Maybe I should go back over there."

Tilda could tell Nick wanted to argue, but he manfully controlled himself and only said, "If that's what you want to do."

She socked him in the arm. "As if! Seriously, he's not my type."

"Glad to hear it," he said with a sigh of relief.

"So tell me about the guys from last night. Which ones are helplessly in love with me?"

Before he could answer, a claxon horn went off and an amplified voice said, "Sunset in thirty minutes. Be ready and in position in ten." A moment later, the voice added, "Everybody knows how much it cost to build that platform and that it has to come down tonight. If anybody does anything to make us miss this sunset, you will be thrown into the water and you will then be walking back to the hotel."

There were a few nervous chuckles, but all extraneous sound stopped.

"What platform?" Tilda whispered.

"The one out there," Nick said, pointing to what looked like a square, wooden pier, except it was planted in splendid isolation a few yards from the shore. "Joni wants to film from the water to get the sunset behind Laryea, and that means they had to build that thing. They're not sure how sturdy it is, so they need to get the shot today, before the tide comes in."

"It is even legal?"

"Mine is not to wonder why, mine is just to keep the set secure." He headed off, presumably to keep things secure, and Tilda got as close as she dared to the cameras so she could see what was happening. And since she knew how cold the water could be off the coast of the Cape, she checked again to make sure her phone was turned off.

In no more than five minutes, Joni was up in a contraption where she could survey the entire area, a flotilla of rowboats had delivered the camera and cameraman out to the platform, more cameras were in place on the beach, and Laryea was standing just out of range, relaxed with a half smile on his face. Then they waited, and to Tilda it seemed much longer than half an hour, probably because she was afraid to move.

Just as she started to notice the shadows deepening, Joni gave a signal and the traditional clapperboard was snapped shut. Laryea immediately tensed and strode through the sand, heading straight for the ocean but stopping just short of the water's edge to stare out into the distance. His expression was one of such longing that Tilda knew that O'Taine must be thinking of his love Melusine, the mermaid with whom he could never completely share his life. He slowly knelt, picked up a perfectly shaped shell, and brought it to his lips for an instant. Then he flung it into the surf just as the sun dipped down below the horizon.

For an instant, nobody seemed to breathe. Then the man with the claxon yelled, "CUT! Print!" Laryea turned and bowed with a flourish. Tilda didn't know if it was planned or not, but the applause that broke out sure seemed spontaneous to her. She was clapping and cheering, too.

Maybe all of the equipment and people and money and time and effort had been worth it. Even if the rest of the movie turned out to be absolute crap, they'd created one moment of pure magic.

# Chapter 17

Though Wilder's cartoon-hosting days are long over, he says he still misses it. "I know I had a good run, first on *The Blast-offs* and then on *Quasit's Cartoon Corner*, but it feels as if it went by in an instant. Life changes very quickly."
—"HEY KIDS! IT'S CARTOON TIME!"
BY TILDA HARPER, *ENTERTAIN ME!*

WITH that one glorious moment in the can, the shoot was finished. So began the incredible task of packing everything up and lugging it back to wherever it belonged. Tilda took a few pictures of the tumult but, as interesting as it was from a logistical viewpoint, she didn't think readers or editors would be so interested that she needed to hang around to chronicle the entire process. Instead she dodged and weaved her way back to her car, and drove back to her cottage.

It was dinnertime, but after all the nachos, she wasn't ready to eat, whereas the time she'd spent disconnected from both phone and e-mail had made her antsy. So she logged onto her computer to see what had happened with her baker's dozen of Leviathans.

Five more had responded, and three of those gave such inaccurate tales of hooking up with Fitzwilliam at Regal that she could cross them off the list immediately.

One of the other's answers were vague enough that they could be true, and the other one said he'd never met Fitzwilliam, so he was still in the running, too. That got it down to ten.

Tilda took care of some other e-mails that had come in, including a few minor editing requests from *Entertain Me!*, then did a quick and dirty description of the film shoot she'd just seen while it was still fresh in her mind. She downloaded her photos to her computer, too, hoping that she'd got a shot of Foster with his mouth hanging open or picking his nose or something to laugh at, but no such luck. She'd have to try harder.

Once all that was done, the nachos were a fond memory, so she was ready to head up to the inn and get something to eat on the film crew tab. It was a warm night, and rather than drive such a short distance, Tilda decided to walk. The streetlights were few and far between, but there was a flashlight in the kitchen junk drawer, complete with fresh batteries.

Plenty of cars passed her on the way, and she guessed that the film crew was returning from the shoot, and when she got to the lobby she wondered if she should have eaten sooner. The hostess at the restaurant said it would be at least an hour before she could be seated, which made a burger from the inn's bar sound wonderful. There were a few places left there, so she grabbed a stool and shamelessly eavesdropped as crew members chattered about the day's shoot and what was coming next. They seemed equally divided about whether a successful first shoot was a good omen or a warning of disaster to come.

About the time her order arrived, Laryea showed up, dressed in running clothes. He made a circuit of the lobby to briefly work the crowd, then headed out. Foster was trotting along behind him, and Tilda briefly wondered if his job included fighting off dogs and removing sticks from the great man's path.

Since people continued to come in and seating space was tight, Tilda didn't linger after she ate. It had been a long day, and she was more than ready to head back to her cottage, take a quick e-mail check, and hit the sack.

Her cell phone rang just as she stepped out into the moonlight. It was Cooper, and she filled the first part of the walk with telling him about the shoot and Leviathan, ending with complaints about Dianne. It was just after hanging up from talking to him that Tilda saw two people on the other side of the road, coming toward the inn. And a minute after that, the limo came roaring down the street, swerved across the oncoming lane, and, as Tilda watched, slammed into them.

# Chapter 18

A lot of life is dealing with your curse, dealing with the cards you were given that aren't so nice. Does it make you into a monster, or can you temper it in some way, or accept it and go in some other direction?

—WES CRAVEN

LATER on, Tilda thought it likely that she'd screamed, but at the time, she didn't notice. She was running toward the other people, not even looking for traffic as she crossed the road. The flashlight was still in her hand, and it showed the blood on one man's face. It was Foster, and he wasn't moving.

Tilda hadn't much liked Foster—in fact she'd loathed the little worm—but it didn't make her any happier to see the man's crumpled body lying in the sandy weeds on the side of the road. His eyes were open, staring, and she didn't think he'd ever insult anybody again.

Just a few feet away, Laryea was moaning and cradling his arm. "Foster, get some help! That bastard hit us!"

Tilda said, "I'm sorry, I think he's dead."

"What? What!?" He started to scramble up, but Tilda went to kneel by him.

"Don't move. I'll call for help."

She pulled out her cell phone, dialed 911, and told the

woman who answered what had happened, where they were, and that they needed an ambulance right away. In a lower voice, she added that she thought one man was already dead.

As soon as she hung up, she dialed Nick's number and thanked God when he answered right away. "Nick, it's Tilda. There's been an accident. Mr. Laryea is hurt, and Foster is . . . I've called an ambulance, but you better let people there know, too."

"Where are you?"

Her mind went blank when she tried to think of the street name. "We're on the road that goes right by the front of the inn. Come out the front door, and go left. You'll see my flashlight."

"Hang on!" He barked orders at whomever he was with, and said, "I'm coming."

"Okay." She hung up, and then said, "Help is on the way."

"Please don't leave me."

"I won't."

"Are you sure Foster is . . . ?"

"Yeah, pretty sure." Tilda put her hand on Laryea's shoulder, afraid to hurt the man but wanting to comfort him. He didn't speak, but he clasped her hand to his chest and she thought he was crying.

Maybe five minutes later, Nick showed up at a dead run, and threw himself down next to her. "Are you all right? Where are you hurt?"

"Not me—I'm okay. It's Mr. Laryea who's hurt. And Foster." Nick took a quick look at Foster, then looked back at Tilda. He'd come to the same conclusion she had.

"How are you doing, Mr. Laryea?" he said. "You hang in there. Help is on the way."

As if in response to a cue, a police car and ambulance pulled up, and their headlights illuminated the area in lurid detail. For an insane second, Tilda started to suggest that somebody bring the lights from the film company so they'd be able to see better, but stopped herself just in time.

The EMTs looked at Foster only briefly. Then, after checking to see that Tilda was uninjured, they politely but firmly pushed her out of the way to tend to Laryea.

Nick tentatively put his arms around her. New girlfriend or not, Tilda hugged him back fiercely, telling herself she would have done the same thing if it had been Dom who were there. A second later, Dom was there, and he did indeed give her a hug before asking what was happening.

Events moved too quickly for Tilda to keep track of. At various points, Joni, Edwina, and Dolores showed up. The ambulance took Laryea away, but from what Tilda could hear, his injuries weren't severe. His three ex-girlfriends argued over which one would accompany him, and when Joni won, the other two dashed off to get a car to follow them to the hospital. Meanwhile, Foster's body was covered up, which helped.

The cop car had multiplied when Tilda wasn't looking, so there seemed to be a dozen cops around when an officer finally came to where Nick was still holding her. "I'm Lieutenant Sidell. I understand you witnessed the incident."

Tilda nodded.

"Your name?"

"Tilda Harper." In response to his other questions, she told him her home address, phone number, where she was staying, and why she was on the Cape.

"I know this is upsetting, but if you could just answer a few questions, it would be a big help."

"Of course."

Nick backed up a step, but was still close enough to hold her hand.

Sidell said, "Can you tell me what you saw?"

"I was walking away from the inn, heading to my cottage, and I saw Laryea and Foster walking toward the inn. Only I didn't know it was them. It was too dark."

"Okay," he said, taking notes.

"I heard a car coming."

"From which direction?"

"That way," she said, pointing. The next part was embarrassing, but she didn't want to leave anything out. "I kind of stepped farther off the road when I heard it."

"Why is that?"

"It's kind of a phobia. I was nearly hit by a car once, so . . . I wasn't expecting this to happen, or anything like that. I just don't like to get too close to moving cars."

"Fine. And that's when the vehicle lost control?"

"I don't think it lost control. I think he drove off the road right at Mr. Laryea and Foster."

"Deliberately?" he asked, sounding skeptical.

"That's how it looked to me."

He made a note. "You say the vehicle didn't stop?"

"No. It kept on going."

"Did you get a good look at it?"

This was the part she should have been dreading, but she'd been so caught up she hadn't realized what was coming next. Maybe she was in shock. Why in hell hadn't she warned Nick or Dom what was coming? Now there was no way she could dodge it. "Yes."

"What kind of car was it?"

"It was a black stretch limo." She felt Nick stiffen beside her.

"Did you see the plate?"

"It was TOLO4."

"You're sure."

"I'm sure."

Sidell called out, "Rico, I need you to run a plate for me. It's—"

"Don't bother," Nick said in a flat voice. "That's one of our limos."

"Your limos? And you are?"

"Nick Tolomeo, Tolomeo Personal Protection. We're handling security for the film shoot."

"And it was one of your limos that did this?"

Tilda wouldn't have blamed Nick for saying that she must have been mistaken, or even accusing her of lying. But what he said was, "If that's what Tilda saw, then I guess it was. I need to talk to my father. Dom Tolomeo. He's the boss."

Lieutenant Sidell sent another cop to fetch Dom from where he was talking to a group of people from the inn.

"Nick, I'm so sorry," Tilda said. "I should have told you. I wasn't thinking—this is all so unreal."

"It's okay. If that's what you saw."

She thought about it, even closed her eyes to replay those awful seconds. "It was your limo, Nick."

"Did you see the driver?" Sidell asked.

"No," she said. "Maybe it was stolen."

"We'll check it out," was all the lieutenant would say.

Dom came up then, and Tilda had to stand there and watch his face as Sidell repeated what she'd said. Again, she would have expected denial or argument, but all he said was, "I don't know anything about the limo being out tonight, but I can tell you where it's supposed to be."

"Why don't we go see?"

"Yes, sir."

Sidell said, "Miss Harper, is there anything else you can tell me about the incident?"

"I don't think so."

"Then you're free to go."

"Nick," Dom said, "take Tilda back to her cottage."

"But Pop—"

"The police and I are going to get to the bottom of this. Make sure she's okay, then give me a call."

"Sure, Pop." But he kept watching as his father walked off, surrounded by cops. Only when they'd driven off did he say, "Let's get you back to your cottage. Are you okay to walk?"

Tilda said, "Look, go with Dom. I'll be fine."

He flashed a shaky grin. "Hey, I'm not going against what the boss says, especially not tonight." He took her elbow and started her in the right direction, but neither of them spoke until Tilda was on the porch of her cottage, with the door open.

"Nick, I don't know what to say."

"You did the right thing, Tilda. If our limo was stolen, we need to know. If it was one of our guys driving . . . Then we need to know that, too."

"I should have told you before the cops asked."

"I won't say I wouldn't have liked a little warning, but—" He shrugged it off. "It wouldn't have made any difference. You saw what you saw."

"Then we're good?"

"We're good," he said firmly. "Are you okay now? Do you want me to come in with you?"

"No, I'm fine. Okay, not fine, but I'll be okay. You go take care of your father."

"Call me if you need me."

"I will," she lied, knowing that she'd suffer a thousand nightmares alone before calling him again that night.

As it turned out, she only had the one nightmare, a doozey about a rampaging limo destroying the film shoot. There might have been more if she hadn't given up on sleep after that. Instead she played computer games until dawn, when she finally drifted off to dreamless sleep.

# Chapter 19

Rather than focus on a cliffhanger to lead into the final issue, the penultimate issue of *Pharos* follows Dylan O'Taine as he goes through a normal day: trading messages with the Jengu, studying his spell books, crafting a gift for Melusine, and even playing with Flotsam and Jetsam. It is only on the last page that Leviathan gives a hint of the climax coming in the next issue.

—*Teenage Mutant Ninja Artists:*
*The Best of Indie Comics* by Jerry Frazee

WHEN Tilda finally woke, close to noon, she went straight to the computer to see if she could find out anything about Laryea. According to a breaking-news entry on the *Cape Cod Times'* site, Laryea had been taken to the hospital to be treated for bruises and scrapes. Though he'd been kept overnight for observation, he was expected to be released in the morning.

She checked the clock and saw that he was probably already back at the inn, which must have been a huge relief to Joni and Edwina.

Foster's name was being withheld until his family could be notified, and Tilda was glad to see she was identified only as a member of the film crew who witnessed the collision. Unfortunately, Dom's name was all too prominent. An unnamed member of his team had been found drunk, and was presumed to have been driving the limo.

"Shit!" Tilda said. She knew that she'd had to tell the cops what she'd seen, and she knew that Dom and Nick wouldn't blame her, but she couldn't help feeling as though she'd betrayed them. Part of her really wanted to pack up her car and head back to Malden, but the larger part of her—the part that made her a reporter—needed to know what was happening. Which meant that she was going to have to go to the inn and see people.

After she grabbed a sandwich and took a quick shower, Tilda headed out. She thought about walking again, but instead got into her car. Though she told herself it was because it looked like rain and that she might need to go elsewhere that day, the fact was she just didn't feel like walking down that road again, even in broad daylight.

There was a TV news truck in the inn's parking lot, but only for a local station. Tilda was surprised. She'd have expected more of a fuss, but maybe the vultures had come and gone, or were controlling themselves for once. Of course, she knew it was the height of hypocrisy to insult the press when she was a reporter herself, but she'd long since learned to live with the contradiction.

The lobby was as filled with people as it had been the night before, but the mood was considerably more subdued. Dom was talking to a pair of his security guards, and when he saw Tilda looking around, he waved her over.

"How are you doing?" he asked.

"I'm all right. How's Laryea?"

"Some bruises, but nothing broken, thank God. We just brought him back to the hotel."

"That's good," she said.

"I guess you know what happened with the police."

"Not all the details, but I saw on the news that it really was your limo last night."

"Oh yeah. When the cops and I went to find it last night, the evidence was right there on the bumper. Pete hadn't even tried to wipe off the blood and tissue."

"Pete? Pete Ellis?"

He nodded. "He'd been keeping the limo at his cottage in case we needed him in a hurry—which we do sometimes, with our clients. Anyway, after we looked at the limo, we found Pete inside the cottage, passed out drunk. Must have gone on a bender."

"Shit," was all Tilda could think to say. Driving drunk in a stretch limo? They'd been lucky he hadn't taken out the whole inn. "And they're sure he was driving?"

"Who else would it be?"

"What does he say?"

"That it wasn't him." Dom shook his head sadly. "I knew Pete was in recovery—he was up front about it when I hired him. Even offered to submit to random sobriety tests, but him offering was enough for me. I swear to God, I thought I could trust him.

"Even after we found him that way, too drunk to even talk to us until this morning, I was ready to do what I could for him. I know alcoholism is a disease, and I could have understood it if he'd owned up to having driven when he shouldn't have. It would have been stupid, criminally stupid, but understandable. But to just say it wasn't him? To look me right in the eye and lie? It was all I could do to keep from slapping him." Dom ran his fingers through the hair that looked two shades grayer than it had the day before. "Hell, it was myself I was mad at as much as it was him. I took a drunk and gave him keys to a limo. That poor bastard, Foster, is dead because of me."

"Screw that!" Tilda snapped. "You weren't the one driving drunk!"

"I know, I know. Nick told me, his mother told me when I called her. Everybody told me. But . . . Tilda, you remember when we first met? How I told you the secret to running a security operation was knowing people?"

"I remember."

"I won't say that I'm never wrong, but I've never been wrong about somebody I've spent as much time with as I have with Pete Ellis. I'd have sworn he was a good guy. If I can't hire good people, then I can't do my job—maybe it's time to give it up. Maybe I'm getting too old for this business."

"Bullshit! You're great at your job."

"Thanks, sweetie, but Joni and Edwina may not agree with you. I've got to go talk to them and see if they want to replace us."

"Don't you have a contract?"

"You think I'd make them honor a contract under these circumstances?"

"I suppose not. But they're idiots if they don't still want you." Tilda wasn't big into casual touching, but she had to pat him on the shoulder, even if it was awkward. After a second, Dom suddenly drew her into a hug, and

Tilda tried to give as strongly as she got. Then he headed toward the elevator.

Tilda looked around for Nick, wanting to see how he was handling it, but her phone buzzed before she could find him, and she stepped out onto the veranda to take the call.

"Hey, Cooper."

"Tell me you weren't anywhere near that hit-and-run last night," he commanded.

"I wish I could." She told him what she'd seen.

"Shit, Tilda. Are you okay?"

"Yeah, I'm fine."

"Liar."

"Okay, I'm still shaky." Then she thought of something. "Hell, does Jillian know I'm the witness?"

"I don't think so."

"Hallelujah!"

"Why?"

"I don't want her fussing about my not calling in with the story. It didn't occur to me until just this minute. I know that's nutty for a reporter, but I'm not used to *new* news—I'm a features gal, and my features are usually well aged. Besides, I'm not sure about the ethics anyway, what with my being embedded into the production. I don't think I should be talking to anybody without checking with Joni and Edwina. I can try to ask them—"

"Tilda, relax. Jillian isn't going to care about this story."

"Why not?"

"Our sources say Laryea is fine. He doesn't even have any broken bones."

"What about Foster? He's dead!"

"I know, but he's not exactly newsworthy."

"Excuse me?"

"Come on, Tilda, you know how the game is played. The man's death is a tragedy, nobody is saying anything different, but it was a drunk driver, right? That's just not an *Entertain Me!* story."

Now Tilda realized why there hadn't been any major media players at the inn. It was because nobody gave a shit about Foster. If it had been Laryea who'd been killed, the place would have been filled with representatives from all the networks, but since it was just his assistant, it wasn't worth the trouble. Everybody else could get live feeds from the local guys, if they had time to fill.

"You know what?" she said. "This business sucks sometimes."

"Yeah, I know," he said.

"Sorry. I shouldn't be snapping at you about it."

"Text me some good gossip when you're feeling better, and we'll call it even."

"You got it."

"I have to run. Call if you need to talk."

"Will do. Give my love to Jean-Paul."

Tilda put her phone away, but instead of going back inside, found a chair to sit in and stared at the ocean. Foster dead, and Pete Ellis the cause. It just didn't feel real. If the press didn't care, how real could it be? That sense of unreality was only enhanced when one of the most bizarre vehicles she'd ever seen pulled up in front of the inn.

It was a van painted the same eye-blinking green as

Hugh Wilder's Quasit suit, and it had "Blastoff for fun with Quasit!" emblazoned on the side. The license plate number was *Quasit*, just in case anybody hadn't caught the subtle hints. Wilder himself got out, and Tilda was tempted to ask him to tap his horn, just to see if it played a snippet from *The Blastoffs* theme song or their one song that had climbed to the bottom of the *Billboard* charts.

Wilder went to the back of the van to pull out a bouquet of Mylar *Get Well* balloons that looked large enough to lift a small child.

"Hi, Mr. Wilder," Tilda said.

"Oh, Tilda, isn't it terrible?" he said in a hoarse voice, his eyes red-rimmed from crying. "Is Johnny okay? I went to take these to the hospital and they said they'd already sent him back here. That's not right—they should be calling in specialists to make sure there aren't any internal injuries."

"I think he's fine."

"I couldn't stand it if anything had happened to him. And that other young man—what a terrible thing for Johnny to see."

"It was pretty bad," Tilda said. At the question in his expression, she said, "I was there, too. Not with them, but close enough to see it happen."

"You poor thing." He made as if to hug her, but couldn't figure out a way to do so and still hang onto the balloons, and settled for repeating, "You poor thing."

"Do you need help getting those up to the front desk?" Tilda asked.

"No, no, I'll take them up to Johnny myself. He's going to need his friends with him at a time like this."

Tilda thought about trying to talk him out of it, but decided it wasn't her job to run interference for Laryea. Maybe he would find his old costar's presence comforting as long as Wilder wasn't dressed in his fur suit. So she just held the door open and let events take their own course.

In fact, she concluded, there wasn't anything she could do for anybody in the inn, and she really wanted to be somewhere else. Deciding it was time to get back to work on the Leviathan hunt, she got in her car to drive to her cottage.

She'd finally received responses from all of the candidates describing their interactions with Fitzwilliam at Regal, and two of them had given such patently false stories that she was able to knock them off her list. That left her with eight.

Unfortunately, she also had a handful of increasingly annoyed e-mails from the first guy she'd eliminated, wanting to know why she hadn't replied. Given the lousy day she was having, she told him exactly why—because he was a phony. The minute she sent the e-mail, she knew it was a mistake, and ten minutes later, she really knew it. That's when the guy's venomous screed arrived, accusing her of stealing his work, pretending to be a reporter, and various other unspecified perfidies. Tilda was torn between deleting it and posting it to Facebook to share with the world, but settled for blocking more mail from the guy and saving the note in case of further reactions.

She was trying to come up with the next step for eliminating some of the legion of Leviathans when her cell phone rang.

"Hey, Nick," she said. "What's the word?"

"Well, we've still got a job."

"Good. I don't see how anybody could blame you guys for what happened anyway."

"Pop does."

"Yeah, I talked to him earlier."

"Anyway, I thought you'd want to know the film schedule is changing. Laryea is too sore to do anything for a couple of days, and then he wants to fly back to California for Foster's funeral."

"Do you know where it's going to be? I want to send flowers." She didn't think there was a preprinted card that said, "With sympathies from one of the people who saw your loved one die," but she would find something appropriate.

"I'll get you the info, and if you want an updated schedule, I can drop it by."

"That would be good."

"What are you up to?"

"Hunting the Great White Leviathan."

"Going well?"

"I've narrowed down the field a bit, but now I'm starting to get some collateral damage." She told him about the flames from the eliminated candidate. "Apparently people don't like being caught lying."

"Are you surprised?"

"I shouldn't be, but I was thinking of them more like cockroaches. You know—you turn on the lights and they skitter away."

"This guy may be more the cornered rat type, so be careful."

"If you feel the impulse to come guard my body, I wouldn't say no."

There was a long silence, and Tilda wanted nothing so much as a rock to hit herself in the head. "Just kidding," she finally said, as lightly as she could. "I know your heart belongs to another. Your other parts, too."

"Um . . . Right. I'll get that revised schedule to you soon."

"That would be very nice."

They hung up, and Tilda considered going outside to look for a rock. Okay, Nick was a great guy and she wasn't exactly happy that he'd broken up with her. Even though they hadn't had time to get superserious about each other because of his travel, she'd hoped it would happen, and seeing him had reminded her of why she'd had those hopes. He was good-looking, smart, kind, and had a great sense of humor.

But he'd been nothing but honest about the state of his affairs. Even though he'd provided an awfully nice shoulder to lean on the night before, that only meant he was a good friend. It wasn't his fault that his holding her had reminded her of just how good he was in bed.

"Take a cold shower!" she told herself firmly. Nick was dating somebody else, and it was apparently serious, so she had no business thinking of ways to seduce him away from the hated Cynthia. She wasn't a poacher. The one time she and her sister June had seriously fought was when Tilda had expressed interest in one of June's dates, and after that, she'd sworn to never, ever poach.

When there was a knock on the door a little while later, she was ready to avoid any suggestive banter, but she needn't have bothered. It wasn't Nick—it was Hoover, one of the other guys she'd hung with at the Mexican restaurant. And he'd come with an invitation to dinner.

Before answering, Tilda took time out for two thoughts. One, nothing would convince Nick that she'd moved on like her going out with somebody else. Two, Hoover wasn't a bad-looking guy. So she agreed, and after a moment to brush her hair and decide against makeup, they took off for a nice Italian place in Glenham.

Dinner was fine, but it became clear to Tilda even before they finished their entrées that she wasn't interested in seeing Hoover again. Though he was perfectly nice, he missed most of her jokes and clearly knew nothing about classic TV or movies. When they got back to her cottage, he hinted at his willingness to come inside for the night, but Tilda decided to test the waters with a kiss first. It was also only nice, without the first hint of a spark, so she nicely thanked him for dinner and nicely turned him down.

Then she grabbed the graphic novel of *Pharos* so she could at least take Dylan O'Taine to bed with her.

# Chapter 20

**Episode 3**
Sid and Marty hire a young boy to help set up their show.
When some of their equipment goes missing, the club's manager blames the boy, but it's not that simple. It turns out he's
the heir to the planet's throne, and moreover, he's a girl in
disguise. And she's being framed.
— *SATURDAY MORNING SPREE* BY CHARLES M. LUCE

WITH Laryea out of the picture for the next couple of
days, the film crew was going to be filming establishing shots and background stuff that didn't much interest Tilda. She spent most of the next day in her cottage
weeding out Leviathans. Asking them which city the
Leviathan PO box was in got rid of a couple. Then asking for them to send scanned character studies of any of
the denizens of *Pharos* knocked out one more. That left
her with five.

On the negative side, two more of the candidates
she'd eliminated were becoming irate that she wasn't
bowing down in their virtual presence, including the
guy who'd sent the worst excuse for a sketch of Dylan
O'Taine that she could imagine. As far as she could tell,
he'd traced a picture of Prince Namor the Sub-Mariner,

including the Atlantean's pointed ears. Dylan O'Taine did not have pointed ears.

Dinnertime approached, and as Tilda was trying to decide between eating out or making yet another ham sandwich, there was a knock on the door. She was hoping that it wasn't Hoover there to try his luck again, and she got her wish in an unexpected way. It was Pete Ellis.

"Hi," she said, which she later added to her Top Ten List of Lame Greetings.

"Hi. I was wondering if I could talk to you for a minute."

She'd thought he was still in jail, and she really wasn't sure if she should let him in or not. On one hand, she was the main witness to identify the limo he'd been driving. But on the other hand, the physical evidence had trumped her testimony, so Pete had no reason to blame his arrest on her. Then again, on a hypothetical third hand, if he'd been drinking, all bets were off.

Pete must have seen the complete lack of decision on her face, because he said, "I'll understand if you'd rather not."

Tilda didn't know if he was painfully sincere or really good at reverse psychology, but she said, "Come on in."

Though Pete couldn't have been in custody very long, the time had weighed heavily on him. His face was drawn, and the shadows under his eyes hadn't been there the day Tilda met him.

He sat down in one of the armchairs in the living room while Tilda took the couch and waited for him to talk. She really didn't know what to say.

"I was wondering if I could ask you a couple of questions about the night Foster was killed," he said.

"Sure."

"The cops said you saw the limo."

"That's right."

"Are you certain it was me driving?"

She raised an eyebrow. "Don't you know?"

He shook his head. "Sometimes I black out when I'm drinking. It hasn't happened in a long time, but it has happened. I remember sitting in my cottage drinking, and then I remember Dom and the cops waking me up. In between is just a blank."

She must have looked skeptical, because he said, "You think I'm lying, too, don't you?"

"I'm not sure yet. Tell me what you do remember."

She knew he must have gone through it many times already, so she wasn't surprised when he spoke in the monotone that usually meant an interview subject had been asked the same questions one time too many.

He said, "After I went off duty that day, I drove the limo into town to get dinner."

"Why didn't you eat at the hotel?"

"It was too crowded, too noisy, too fancy. I found a takeout place and got an order of fish and chips, and ate at an outside table so I could watch the ocean. When I was done, I walked over to a convenience store and picked up some things. Then I drove back to my cottage."

"And you were alone the whole time?"

He nodded.

"What did you do at your cottage?"

"I turned on the TV."

"And?"

He looked away. "And I started drinking. That's what I went to the convenience store for. I wanted beer."

"Dom said you're in recovery."

"I was. I'd been clean and sober for three years this past August."

"Why did you start drinking all of a sudden?"

"Are you a drunk?"

"No."

"Then you wouldn't understand."

"You could explain it to me."

He took a deep breath. "I know it was a dumbass thing to do. I should never have bought that beer, and once I did, I should never have taken it back to my cottage, and I should never have opened it."

"And you should never have gone out driving?"

"I didn't!" He wiped his face with his hands. "Do you know any other drunks?"

"A few."

"Then you know we've all got our justifications. 'Maybe I drink too much, but only on weekends.' Or, 'I never drink before five o'clock.' Or, 'I only drink beer, never hard liquor.' Something we cling to so we can pretend that we're not completely out of control. My excuse was always, 'I never drive drunk.' And I never did. Ever."

"Until the other night."

"Did you see me driving?"

"No, the limo was going too fast."

"Then that's all I need to know."

"You really don't think you were driving drunk?"

"I was drunk—I know that. I just don't believe I was

so drunk that I'd go out in the limo and forget about it. They can't make me say any different, and they can't prove that I was driving. Hell, why would I have gone anywhere?"

"Maybe you ran out of beer."

"No, I had two more six-packs in the refrigerator. I was set for the night."

"Then what do you think happened?"

"All I can figure is that somebody took the limo and went joyriding."

"How? Did somebody come by your cottage and get the keys?"

"It's possible. My door wasn't locked."

"You didn't lock the door?"

"I guess I was in a hurry to get that first beer open," he admitted. "Anyway, Dom said it was unlocked when the cops came by."

"Okay, somebody came in, saw you passed out, and took the keys. Then he went out joyriding and accidentally hit Foster and Laryea. Realizing what he'd done, he then drove the limo back to your cottage and left it there. And took the keys back inside?"

"The keys were left in the ignition. Which I never do."

"Yeah, and you never get drunk either."

"Of course I get drunk. I'm an alcoholic. But even alcoholics have behavior patterns. I have a routine for drinking—at least, I used to have one. I came in, put the keys up, and stuck the beer in the refrigerator. Then I went to the bedroom and changed into a pair of gym shorts and a T-shirt so I wouldn't fall asleep in my clothes.

I left my shoes by the bed, put my socks and shirt in with the dirty clothes, and folded my pants and left them on the chair. Then I got the first six-pack and carried it into the living room, turned on the TV, and started drinking. I kept drinking until I passed out. That's what I do."

"Every time?"

"Yes!" He threw his hands up in the air. "What's the use? You don't believe me. Nobody believes me."

"I'm trying to believe you, Pete, but look at it from my perspective. The one time in over three years that you're passed out, somebody just happens to decide to take the limo."

"I wasn't the only one drinking that night, not by a long shot. You've seen those film crew guys."

Tilda thought about all the people she'd seen in the bar celebrating the successful shoot. "They do like to party."

"And limos are sexy. Dom can tell you how many clients we've had who've wanted to drive it. So a guy or maybe a couple of guys came by wanting to borrow it. Except they find me passed out, and they see the keys on a hook by the front door. Just like that one." There was an iron whale by the front door to Tilda's cottage, with a hook for the tail. "They take off in the limo, ride up and down the road a bit, and then lose control of the thing. A vehicle that long is a bitch to drive when you're not used to it, and you know how narrow and curvy that road is. You saw the limo lose control, right?"

She hesitated. "Sort of."

"What do you mean?"

"It didn't look to me like the driver lost control. It was more like he hit Laryea and Foster on purpose."

"What the hell?"

"I told that to the cops, but they didn't believe me."

"Yeah, join the club."

"It was dark, and when they found you were drunk, I figured I'd seen it wrong. But . . . Okay, if you really weren't driving, then maybe it wasn't an accident at all."

"Meaning what?"

"Meaning that whoever was driving that car intentionally hit Foster and Laryea, and now that person is framing you."

"Are you sure you don't drink?"

"Oh, I'm supposed to believe you, but you won't believe me? I'll admit it sounds a lot crazier than a known alcoholic falling off the wagon and driving drunk, but if you're sure that didn't happen . . ."

"It didn't. I swear it didn't. But I'm having a hard time getting my head around the idea of murder. Why would anybody want to kill Foster?"

"Because he was a pain in the ass?" She shrugged. "I didn't really know the guy—he could have had a dozen people gunning for him. I can't be the only one around that he annoyed."

"Killing somebody is way beyond being annoyed."

"True." She considered it. "Okay, what about this? Maybe Foster wasn't the target. Maybe whoever it was meant to kill Laryea."

"Why would anybody want to kill John Laryea?" Pete asked.

"I don't know. He's a big star. Maybe he stepped on

a few toes on his way up, or stabbed a few people in the back. Maybe one of his ex-girlfriends has a grudge—I know that three of them are right here on the Cape, and he could have a dozen more lurking. Maybe somebody else really wants to play Dylan O'Taine, or doesn't want *Pharos* made. What about that stalker Nick has been watching for, the guy from the airport bathroom?"

"I don't know, Tilda. Sure, Laryea has probably pissed off plenty of people. But murder?"

She looked at him directly, deciding it was time to talk about the elephant in the room. "How about this then? What about a former costar angry at Laryea's success, maybe even angrier because Laryea didn't even recognize him."

He looked down at his hands. "No, that wasn't it."

"The police might consider that a really good motive, especially if such a person were here on the Cape. They might think the former costar got drunk enough to go after Laryea. Or they might even think the guy went after Laryea when he was sober, then got drunk afterward to cover his tracks."

"I guess they might, if they knew. Do you think they're going to find out?"

She thought about it, and it occurred to her that she'd as good as told Pete that she was the only one around who could provide the police with a motive for him to commit murder. It also occurred to her that she was alone in a fairly isolated cottage with him, and that nobody knew he was there. Dom, she told herself, you better be right about this man.

"Pete, how long have you been working for Dom?"

"Six months," he said, surprised. "Why?"

That settled it. She just couldn't accept that Dom could be fooled for that length of time. "I don't think the cops are going to find out anything else because they aren't looking. They think you're the guy. But you're not."

"Then you believe me?"

"Yeah, I do. I trust Dom, and Dom trusts you."

"He used to."

"He still wants to. So I'm going to trust you for him." She paused. "Did that make any sense?"

"If you'll believe that I didn't go out driving drunk, then I don't care if you make sense or not."

"Dude, I think this is the beginning of a beautiful friendship."

That seemed like a good opportunity to serve drinks—the nonalcoholic kind—so Tilda poured them both glasses of Dr Pepper.

"So the question is," Tilda said, "what do you do next?"

"Talk to the police, tell them I think it was attempted murder, not just a drunk driver?"

"Why do you think they'll believe you?"

"I don't, but maybe my lawyer can at least get them to investigate the possibility. He thinks I'm guilty, but still—"

"Your own lawyer doesn't believe you? Why did you hire him?"

"Dom found him for me and vouched for him. I don't think it matters if the guy actually believes I'm innocent."

"I guess not. Then you should talk to him right away and see if he can get the police to do their thing."

"I could talk to other people, too. Ask around to see if anybody else saw someone in the limo, or if anybody has heard rumors of somebody with a grudge against Laryea. I have to stay in the jurisdiction anyway, and Dom has suspended me until this is settled, so I've got nothing better to do."

"No offense, Pete, but do you really think people will want to talk to you? The film crew is convinced that you killed Foster and nearly got Laryea, too, which would not make you their favorite person."

"Yeah, you're right," he said, chagrined. "And the lawyer did say I should lay low."

"Do you have a place to stay?" Tilda asked, really not wanting to invite him into her cottage.

Fortunately he said, "Yeah, Dom said I can stay where I was. He's really doing right by me."

"Then you better head back there and call your lawyer."

"What about you? People will talk to you. I mean, I know I shouldn't ask anything more of you, but . . . You're the only one who believes me."

Tilda regarded him with no particular enthusiasm. She had encountered murderers before, but it wasn't by choice, and she really couldn't see herself interrogating suspects and looking for clues. But then she thought about Foster, who'd nearly been forgotten. If he'd been murdered, even by somebody going after Laryea, he deserved to have his murderer caught, whether or not Tilda liked him.

Then there was Dom. He'd been so disturbed by the idea of no longer being able to trust his own judgment that he'd talked about quitting the business he loved. If

Pete really was innocent, then Dom would get his confidence back. Unless, a nasty inner voice said, the real killer was one of Dom's other employees. Tilda told the nasty inner voice to take a hike.

Out loud, she said, "I'll keep my ears open, and if I hear anything useful, I'll let you know. Okay?"

"Thanks Tilda."

"No guarantees," she said, "but what the hell. Being nosy is my job."

# Chapter 21

I only sound intelligent when there's a good scriptwriter around.

—CHRISTIAN BALE

ONCE she'd shooed Pete out, Tilda went back to her computer, hoping for some sort of inspiration for eliminating more of the last five Leviathans. When nothing sprang to mind, she opened up the file where she'd transcribed her notes from talking to Marc Fitzwilliam. He'd said something about looking for any letters from Leviathan, and since he hadn't called back, she figured it wouldn't hurt to check in again.

Apparently the guy lived at his business, because once again, he was the one to answer the phone.

"Marc? This is Tilda Harper."

"Any luck finding Leviathan?"

"I've got more luck than I need." She explained the problem. "What I'm trying to do now is weed out the phonies, and I wondered if there were any clues in your correspondence with Leviathan that might help. Did you have a chance to go through your files?"

"I did, and I've been looking over the letters, but I don't see anything. Leviathan never put in much personal stuff. All we ever wrote about was the comic—how it was selling, what the deadlines were, the edits I needed. He was all business."

She knew she was grasping at straws, but still said, "Would you mind letting me take a look at the letters myself?"

"I suppose not, if you think it will help."

"It couldn't hurt." If the process kept on much longer, Tilda was seriously considering seeing whether or not she could get the letters from Leviathan dusted for fingerprints. She found the fax number for the inn and read it to him, and he promised to send the letters right away.

Tilda spent a good five minutes trying to decide if she wanted to drive to the inn or walk, and finally decided to drive—her excuse was that she might want to go somewhere else after picking up the faxes.

The faxes hadn't shown up when she got to the inn, so she peeked into the bar to see if anybody was around. Dolores the screenwriter was sitting alone at the bar. According to Nick, Dolores was one of Laryea's ex-gal-pals, which meant that she might know if he had any particularly nasty enemies. And if not, she might have some juicy gossip. Either way, it was a good way to kill a few minutes.

"Hey, Dolores," Tilda said casually. "Mind if I join you?"

"Sure, have a seat."

Tilda climbed onto a bar stool, and when the bartender looked her way, asked for a cosmo.

"How's it going?" she asked the screenwriter.

"Other than being exhausted and frustrated, it's great. How's your quest?"

"Exhausting and frustrating. I guess you've heard how many Leviathans have shown up."

"Joni told me. Of course you can't blame them. Why wouldn't somebody want to pretend to be an almost unknown comic book writer? I mean, the life of a professional writer is so glamorous. Of course, Leviathan's life isn't as glam as a screenwriter's."

"Or a reporter's," Tilda said.

The two women looked at each other and started laughing. That led to comparing notes of their encounters with people who really did think their lives were like something from the movies.

When that subject ran dry, Tilda said, "I meant to ask how Mr. Laryea is doing."

"He's fine. He left this morning for LA to arrange Foster's funeral. Joni and Edwina went with him, but I figured they didn't need me. It's tacky to speak ill of the dead, but as far as I'm concerned, Foster put the 'ass' in 'assistant.' "

"Did anybody like him? Other than Mr. Laryea, that is?"

"Nope, not a soul. I knew him back from when John and I were an item, and I think he'd already managed to alienate everybody else in the world. But he was good at his job—I'll give him that. So I'll drink to him." She and Tilda clinked glasses and did so.

"Mr. Laryea must be doing better if he was able to travel."

"He was never that badly hurt in the first place," Dolores said dismissively. "The man gets a bruise, acts like it's a broken bone, then makes a big deal of overcoming the pain."

"I had a boyfriend like that," Tilda lied. "That must have been tough to live with."

"I never lived with John, thank God. He took one look at the mess in my office and I took one look at the clothes in his bedroom, and we knew we were never meant to share a roof."

"Did you two date a long time?"

Dolores gave her a look. "Are you working?"

"Nope, just curious." Then, knowing that the majority of Hollywood denizens loved publicity, she added, "Unless you want me to use it."

" 'Screenwriter tells of dating a big star.' " Dolores shook her head. "Nah, I don't think it would do me any good in the business. Screenwriters aren't supposed to make news unless they look like Diablo Cody. Which I do not."

"Then it's off the record."

"Good—I will commence to dish. You wouldn't be considering taking a ride on the Laryea express yourself, would you?"

"He's kind of old for me, no offense."

"That never stopped John. He has only two requirements in his choice of women. One, he likes them goodlooking, and you're okay there. But two—and more important—he likes women with talent. He doesn't want a hanger-on or arm candy. He honestly likes a woman he can talk to."

"Really? He gives the impression of just wanting to flirt."

"Well sure he flirts. It's good for business. But for anything more than a one-night stand, he demands brains. Look at the three of us working on *Pharos*. Joni is a damned good director, and Edwina could convince a conservative to back a biography of Obama. And me . . . Well, modesty forbids me from pointing out my own gifts."

"I really don't think I'm his type."

"Don't sell yourself short. I've read some of your pieces. You've got a good voice, you know the old stuff backward and forward, and you respect the material. Yeah, John could go for you in a big way, and I happen to know that he's currently unattached. But I should warn you. You can't get too attached to John Laryea. He is the personification of serial monogamy. He won't fool around on you, but it won't last forever, either. Six months, nine months, a year at best, and he's gone. He and I made it seven months to the day."

"Did that bother you?"

"Hell, no. I knew what he was like. He's honest about it."

"Still, there's a difference between theoretical knowledge and actually getting dumped."

But Dolores was shaking her head. "Did you ever have a summer romance? At camp or whatever? You knew that when summer ended, the romance would end, too. I didn't have that strict a timeline, but I knew the end was coming. We were done."

"It sounds so civilized."

"Crazy, huh? If it weren't so civilized, do you think I'd be working with him now? Let alone working with Joni and Edwina."

"No hard feelings there either?"

"Not that I ever heard of. Don't you ever stay friends with your exes?"

"Sometimes," Tilda admitted, thinking of Nick.

"There you go then." Dolores downed the rest of her beer. "Well, I need to get my nose back to the grindstone. The glamour awaits."

# Chapter 22

I don't believe in the no-win scenario.
  —CAPTAIN JAMES T. KIRK IN *STAR TREK II: THE WRATH OF KHAN*

WITH Dolores gone, there was nobody else around Tilda knew, so she went to check on the faxes from Fitzwilliam and found a fat stack waiting for her. The inn's restaurant looked pretty full, so she retraced her steps and found a table at the bar big enough for her papers and the chicken Caesar salad she ordered.

Her dinner was long gone, and she was nearly through the stack of letters when she noticed somebody standing next to her.

"Hey, Nick. What's up?"

"Just keeping an eye out."

She wasn't sure if she should ask him to join her or not, considering their last phone call, but then decided that if John Laryea could manage to work with three ex-girlfriends, she could certainly maintain a platonic friendship with Nick. "Have a seat and catch me up on the news."

"Sure, okay." He caught the waitress's eye, and ordered a beer for himself and a refill on Tilda's Coke. "I hear you and Hoover went out."

"Yeah, but . . . Did you know he's never seen a single

episode of *Glee* or *True Blood*? I don't think I can take a man seriously when he's so far out of the cultural zeitgeist."

"Hey, *Glee* is just in its second season. He can catch up on Netflix."

"Maybe, but I don't think he's my type. Thanks for the fix-up, anyway. Keep me in mind if somebody more aware of post-Boomer culture comes around."

"Will do."

Tilda felt they were back on an even keel again, which was a relief. She, like Dolores, wanted to be civilized.

"What's with all the paperwork?" Nick asked.

"I'm reading correspondence between the guy who published *Pharos* and Leviathan, trying to get a clue about him I can use to cross off a wannabe or two."

"Anything there?"

"Not so much. No characteristic misspellings, no verbal tics, and no regional word choices. And definitely no references to anything personal. The guy was focused on the book. They talked numbers, and they talked edits. That's it."

"Sorry to hear that."

"It was worth a shot."

"Any more threats, veiled or otherwise, from the non-Leviathans?"

"Yes, but nothing very creative."

"You do need to be careful, you know. Take this seriously."

"Seriously, I am. None of them have my address or my unlisted phone number and even if they went online hunting for my address, I've moved so many times they wouldn't know where to find me even if they found the right T. Harper."

"Still, I don't like it."

"I'm not crazy about it, either, but I'm saving all the nastygrams in case it escalates." It was past time to change the subject, so she said, "So how's your father doing?"

"He's okay. Still on the job, but you know, Pete Ellis killing that guy has really shaken him."

"Do you really think Pete did it?"

"Is it even in question?"

"It is to me. He came by my cottage today, and I'm just not sure."

"According to the police, it looks pretty cut-and-dried."

"What about your father's sixth sense about people?"

"He's the best at sniffing out bad guys, but I'm not saying Pete is a bad guy. He made a mistake."

"And lied about it?"

Nick shrugged.

"What is with you?" Tilda asked, suddenly angry. "Has your father ever been wrong about a person before? Even once?"

"No, but—"

"Whereas the cops have been known to be wrong before, right?"

"I don't know these cops," Nick objected.

"You don't know them, but you trust them more than you trust your father?"

"But Pop himself said—"

"Do you trust your father?"

"Of course, but—"

"If somebody had asked you a week ago if you could

trust Pete, going purely on Dom's say-so, what would you have said?"

He thought about it for a minute. "I'd have said that Pop is never wrong."

She just looked at him, waiting.

"Let me get this straight. You're saying that since Pop is never wrong about a person, and he trusted Pete, I should trust him, too."

"That's what I'm saying."

"Huh." He took a swallow of his beer. "So if Pete wasn't driving the limo, who was?"

"Hell if I know. And it gets worse." She explained the conclusion that she and Pete had come to, that somebody had gone after either Laryea or Foster on purpose, though she avoided mentioning Pete's secret past. "Does that sound completely insane?"

"Not completely, but— Any thoughts about which one was the target?"

"It's hard to say. Foster was a pain in the ass, but Laryea is the famous one, and famous people often have enemies. Including, maybe, that stalker you've been chasing after."

"Son of a bitch! I saw him again today. When I drove Laryea and the ladies to the airport in Hyannis, I spotted him in the parking lot. I almost had him, too."

"Then maybe he is the killer. A crazed fan running down the idol who ignored him. Or the idol's assistant, because he blocked him from his idol."

"How could he have gotten to the limo?"

"The guy seems to be everywhere. He could have

skulked around to figure out where the limo was left—
he saw it at the airport so he knew it was the one Laryea had taken before. Then he saw Pete show up with
his booze and watched him through the window until
he passed out and snuck in to get the keys and . . ."
Tilda saw the expression on Nick's face. "Yeah, it's
kind of thin. Tell you what. Catch the guy, and we'll
ask him."

"That's a plan I can get behind. If you see a beanpole
with red hair and a camera, ping me."

"Will do."

"You know, I'm thinking I should talk to Pop about this.
If somebody is after Laryea—the stalker or whoever—
we need to tighten security." He pulled his cell phone out
of the holster at his belt. "You mind if I ask him to join
us? He's watching TV in our room."

"Of course not."

A few minutes later, Dom came in and sat in the chair
Nick pulled out for him. He looked better than he had
the last time Tilda had seen him, but only a little.

"What are you two up to?" he asked.

Taking turns, Tilda and Nick explained their theories,
though Tilda really wished it sounded a bit more solid.

When they were done, Dom didn't say anything for
a long time, just rubbed his chin slowly. Finally he said,
"You two are killing me here."

"I don't understand," Tilda said. "I thought you'd
want me to help."

"Help with what? Pete got drunk, and he got in my
limo, and he killed some poor guy. What he needs is a

good lawyer—which I got him. If we can keep him out of jail, he needs to go to rehab."

"But Pop, you've never been wrong about anybody before," Nick said.

"I'm not perfect, Nick. I'm just a guy who's managed to hit it lucky in the past. We don't need luck to run our business—we need smarts. Do you honestly think this theory you two have cooked up sounds smart?"

"What happened to all that stuff you told Joni and Edwina about me? That I was such hot shit?" Tilda said.

"When you stick to your job, you are hot shit. Now tell me, how is this your job?"

Tilda couldn't very well answer that—she knew as well as he did that it wasn't her job.

"As for you, Nick, you've got a job, too, and that's working for me. Right?"

Tilda could tell how hard it was for Nick to control himself, but he nodded.

"Good. Now I'm going up to bed. Mr. Laryea will be back the day after tomorrow, and I want to make sure everything goes smoothly. And we've got to get things arranged for the big shoot the day after that. Are you coming, Nick?"

"In a minute."

"Fine." He started to leave, then turned back. "Tilda, I know you mean well, but see it from my point of view. The press hasn't made a big deal out of this, which means that the business's reputation is still intact. You start stirring things up, and there's no telling what will happen."

"I know what will happen if I don't stir things up.

Pete Ellis will go to jail." When Dom started to say something else, "I'm not going to argue with you, Dom. You're not my boss."

"Then you do what you've got to do."

When he was gone, Tilda let out a breath she didn't even realize she'd been holding. "I guess it's a good thing we broke up after all. Pissing off a boyfriend's father is no way to keep a romance sizzling."

"Are you kidding? Ma gives him worse than that on a regular basis."

"Yeah? I've got to meet her one of these days. But in the meantime, I'm sorry for causing problems with you two. I won't ask you to go against his wishes and try to figure out what's going on."

"You don't have to ask. I think you're on to something, and it's like you said. Pop's never been wrong about anybody before. He may have lost faith in himself, but I haven't lost my faith in him." He leaned over and gave her a kiss on the cheek. "You call me if you need me."

"Deal," she said, but once he was gone, she went into full brood mode. Could she really be destroying Dom's business? Was Pete really in trouble if she didn't stick her nose in? Did she have a right to keep information from the police? "Screw it," she finally said to herself. If she was right and managed to find the real killer, then both Pete and Dom would be off the hook and the police wouldn't need to know anything she was hiding. She just had to be right.

# Chapter 23

There is a peculiar kind of satisfaction that comes from working for a powerful or famous person. Washing a car or serving
a meal may be considered menial, but when that car belongs
to a movie star or the meal is served to a world leader, the
work is somehow elevated. The car wash attendant is now
helping to create award-winning film while the waitress aids
world peace. Being a full-time assistant to a member of the
elite is even more intoxicating.
— "To Serve in Heaven" by Lorinda B. R. Goodwin, PhD

TILDA headed back to her cottage for some strategizing.
Though she didn't intend to abandon Pete, Dom was
right that she had a job to do, which meant she had a
comic book writer to find. Plus she was still supposedly producing a series of articles about the making of
*Pharos*. That meant she was going to have to work her
time out carefully.

The first step was to look over the latest version of
the filming schedule. Nothing big was planned for the
next day because Laryea, Joni, and Edwina wouldn't be
back from LA. The day after would mostly be dedicated
to prep work for a major sunrise scene at the local lighthouse that would be standing in for Dylan O'Taine's
Pharos, with the scene itself set for the following

morning, weather permitting. She definitely wanted to be there for that.

Then there was supposed to be a day of minor background stuff, only some of which would even include Laryea. A little of that would go a long way, so she'd have most of that time free for tending to other things.

The last scheduled day of filming was going to be a biggie, requiring two full days of prep. They were going to be filming a slice of the climactic battle between Dylan O'Taine and Ceto's army of Asrai, which was going to involve pyrotechnics on the beach. Tilda was counting on that shoot for some nice vivid descriptions for her article.

It added up to an uncomfortably short amount of time for all she wanted to accomplish. Admittedly, Joni hadn't given her a cast-in-stone deadline for finding Leviathan, but it would look a lot better if she could get the job done while the director was still around to appreciate it. As for figuring out what had happened to Foster, that would be nearly impossible once the film crew headed back to Los Angeles. And of course she couldn't very well observe the film shoot once it was over.

She was going to have to manage it all in a week.

Her examination of the letters from Leviathan hadn't given her any ideas, so she put them aside for the time being. As for finding a killer, she was going to need to talk to people for that, and she couldn't do that in the middle of the night. That left her series of articles, and she fired up the computer and got to work, which filled up the rest of the evening and left her tired enough to sleep like a log.

The next day was a wash as far as finding Leviathan or solving Foster's murder went, but it was promising in terms of story ideas. When Tilda woke unexpectedly early and went by the inn for breakfast, she ran into an ambitious second-unit film crew who'd decided to use the free time to wander around the Cape taking footage that might or might not end up in *Pharos*. If it did, they'd look good, and if not, it was at least good practice.

Since Tilda found up-and-comers nearly as interesting as the lost-and-forgotten, she asked to ride along and spent the day taking pictures of them at work. That night she hung around the inn, chatting with people at the bar and taking enough candid shots of the crew at rest to fill up the rest of her memory card. Hugh Wilder was there, too, talking about Laryea, and as more beer was consumed, people actually started to find his stories amusing.

When Tilda herself started to giggle, she decided she'd had too much to drink and walked back to her cottage.

The next morning, she hoped to kill two birds with one stone by talking to Edwina and Joni—they'd promised her interview time and surely there'd be a chance to slip in some questions about any enemies Laryea might have. Plus it wouldn't hurt to talk to Laryea himself. Though she was sorry about Foster, at least his absence might make it easier to get access to the star.

A quick text message exchange with Nick told her they were all due back on the Cape by noon, and she left messages for both women at the inn, asking if they'd be free for an hour or two that day or the next. Laryea would be trickier, since she'd already interviewed him.

Then she remembered the man was both bereaved and injured, and according to Dolores, liked being made much of at such times. That gave her an idea.

Next she needed to do some serious research. First she hit the Web to find out enough background about Joni and Edwina so that she could do decent interviews. There were times when Tilda had gone in cold, but it went a lot better if she knew enough to ask the interesting questions right away. She had no idea how freelancers had found out such things before the advent of the Internet, and was devoutly grateful that she didn't need to know. After a couple hours of intense Web surfing, she had enough to work with.

Next for a bit of background on Laryea. There was nothing online that helped with what she needed, so she called Dolores, figuring that in seven months, the woman would have learned Laryea's preferences. That led to a call to the inn's concierge, followed by a trip to the Choco House in Glenham.

With all that, Tilda still managed to be in the lobby at the inn when Nick and Dom escorted Laryea, Edwina, and Joni in. The trio looked moderately jet-lagged from flying in on the red-eye flight, and the women headed straight for the elevator. Fortunately Laryea paused to talk to one of the film crew, and Tilda took the opportunity to head his way, carrying a large white box.

But before she could get to him, she was stopped by a slight man with jet-black hair and a long nose designed for looking down at people, despite his being shorter than Tilda herself. "I'll take that," he said, reaching for the box.

"I don't think so," Tilda said.

"It is for Mr. Laryea, isn't it?"

"Yes."

"Then I'll take it." He reached again.

"And who are you?"

Nick came over. "Tilda, this is Sebastian Fontaine, Mr. Laryea's new assistant. Sebastian, this is Tilda Harper, a reporter for *Entertain Me!*"

Nick knew darned well that Tilda didn't work for *Entertain Me!* full-time, so presumably he had a good reason for pretending otherwise. The patently false smile that appeared on Sebastian's face confirmed it. He wouldn't have bothered speaking to a freelancer.

"I'm so happy to meet you," the new assistant said.

Laryea finished up his conversation, and came to join them. "Tilda, good to see you." Then he actually sniffed. "Is that what I think it is?"

"Look and see." She bypassed Sebastian to hand the box to him herself.

He opened it, then looked at her with a huge smile. Inside was a batch of chocolate chip cookies so fresh that the bottom of the box was still uncomfortably warm. According to Dolores, the actor was a slave to chocolate chip cookies, the gooier the better.

He inhaled deeply. "How did you know?"

"Information is my business."

"Do you have time to come to my suite and share them with me?"

"Absolutely."

"Great. Sebastian, see if you can round us up some milk to go with these. And get plenty of napkins. I can see that these babies are going to be messy." He looked delighted at the prospect.

Sebastian said, "Right away!" and bustled off while Nick, Laryea, and Tilda started upstairs. Nick got them to Laryea's suite, which was on the same floor as Joni's and Edwina's, opened the door, then left them standing in the foyer while he made a quick sweep of the place. Clearly he was taking her suspicions that Laryea had been the intended target seriously.

When Nick was done, he said, "Will you be needing me for anything further, Mr. Laryea?"

"I think we'll be fine. Would you like to take a cookie with you?"

"As your bodyguard, I suppose I should test one," he said, which was as transparent an excuse as Tilda had ever heard. But if Laryea didn't mind sharing, she wasn't going to complain.

Once Nick was gone, Laryea said, "I'm waiting for the milk. Cookies just aren't the same without milk."

She was going to have to thank Dolores for the tip. This was clearly a man who loved his cookies.

But after he put the box aside, he said, "I'm glad to have a chance to talk with you, Tilda. I wanted to tell you how much I appreciated your staying with me that night . . . The night Foster died."

"I couldn't have just left you there," she said awkwardly.

"Sure you could have. You could have gone the other way and pretended you hadn't seen it. But you came running to help. It meant a lot, having somebody with me."

"You'd have done the same thing," she said.

He smiled. "I'm glad you think so. And if there's any time I can do anything for you, you just ask." He reached out to pat her hand, and for once he wasn't flirting.

It was terribly sweet, and Tilda was terribly uncomfortable. As her sister the psychologist often reminded her, she didn't do well with emotions. So she was thoroughly relieved when the door to the suite opened, and Sebastian came in with the milk and napkins.

Not that he was carrying it himself, of course. Instead he'd dragooned somebody from the hotel staff to wheel in a cart with a pitcher of milk, stemware, china, a bundle of cloth napkins, and even a rose in a vase. As soon as the cart was where he wanted it, he sent the man away without even giving him a tip. Presumably the opportunity to serve John Laryea should be enough of a gratuity for anybody.

"I hope these cookies are as good as they smell," Laryea said, opening the box and taking another good whiff.

"I did some quality control earlier," Tilda said, "and I think you'll be satisfied."

"So you won't be staying for more?" Sebastian said, and Tilda was fairly sure he was hinting.

"I only had one, and that was a while ago," she said. "Besides, I didn't have any milk."

"Milk makes all the difference," Laryea said.

Sebastian poured three glasses of milk, then laid out cookies on each plate. Tilda noticed that he put three on Laryea's plate, two on his own, but only one on Tilda's. Oh, he was a subtle fellow.

Conversation for the next few minutes was confined

to happy noises as Laryea devoured his cookies. Tilda went a little more slowly, but still managed to put away the measly one on her plate plus one she got out of the box herself. Sebastian nibbled his.

When Laryea was finishing up his third cookie, Tilda said, "I hope your trip went as well as possible."

"It was rough," Laryea said, "but I wanted to be there to say good-bye to Foster. He'd worked with me for over three years, and I'm going to miss him. I was expecting to have to rough it for a while, but I ran into Sebastian at the funeral, and when I realized he was available, I offered him a job immediately."

"Did you know Foster, Sebastian?" Tilda asked.

"We'd met a few times," he said. "We worked through the same agency, and I'd stepped in for him when he went on vacation when Mr. Laryea needed him." It was obvious from his tone that Sebastian would never leave Mr. Laryea in the lurch. "So I've been able to hit the ground running, so to speak. Give me a week, and I'll have Mr. Laryea's correspondence caught up and his wardrobe sufficiently organized."

Charming, Tilda thought. He'd managed to build himself up and insult a dead man in just a few moments. It gave her an idea. She'd been assuming that Laryea was the target, just because he was the famous one, but couldn't Foster's death have been a means to an end? Sebastian being *available* was just a fancy way of saying he needed a job. Could he have needed one badly enough to kill for it?

"Have you ever been to the Cape before?" she asked him.

"No, why?" he said, eyes narrowed.

"I was just thinking that late fall isn't the best time to see it for the first time. It's wonderful during the summer, and winter is lovely here, too."

"I suppose so, but I'm not here for sightseeing."

So much for small talk with the new guy. Now to see if she could find out anything from Laryea. "John, I suppose you heard that Pete Ellis was arrested."

He looked blank.

"The limo driver?"

"Oh, right. I didn't know his name."

"The police think he was driving the limo that hit you."

"Only 'think'? I thought it was pretty well established."

"More or less," she hedged, "but you know how it is when a celebrity is involved. They want to make sure everything is done properly. And a man of your stature sometimes becomes a target."

Tilda hadn't known what response to expect, but she hadn't expected a big laugh. "You must have been talking to my publicist. He would love me to have a stalker— I told him about the guy in the bathroom at the airport, but what he really wants is a female stalker. He thinks it would make me sound more desirable if an attractive woman became fixated on me. He tried to talk me into hiring an out-of-work actress."

"Seriously?" Tilda asked.

"I love getting press—you know I do—but I don't think I need that kind of attention. Sure, I've got a few fans that take it a bit too far, but that goes with the territory."

"What about enemies? A knock-down drag-out with another star would be great publicity, too."

"You have been talking to him! No feuds, either, I'm sorry to say. I'm too self-centered to have enemies. I want everybody to like me. It's why I became an actor."

That was, without a doubt, the most quotable thing Laryea had ever said to her, and Tilda couldn't wait to put it into an article. Unfortunately, it didn't do a thing for her ulterior motive.

Sebastian picked that moment to take her plate and glass away, and started stacking up the remains of their cookie feast. "This has been lovely," he said in a voice that implied otherwise, "but Mr. Laryea has a very tough schedule tomorrow and he needs to get some rest."

Laryea threw up his hands in mock despair. "He's only been with me for a day, and he's already running my life."

"That is his job," Tilda said, earning a tiny nod from Sebastian.

Laryea walked her to the door, where he took her hand and said, "Thank you for the cookies, Tilda. It was just the treat I needed." He patted his stomach. "I just hope I can fit into my costume tomorrow."

"Dylan O'Taine never looked so good," Tilda said, and let him kiss her on the cheek again before leaving. Laryea had said he wanted everybody to like him, and damned if she didn't like him herself.

# Chapter 24

In Issue 2, Dylan O'Taine feels that he is being watched even though none of Pharos's mystic safeguards have been triggered. Then, during a nighttime swim, he is attacked by assailants he cannot see, the transparent Asrai. He splashes them with squid ink to make them visible so he can defeat them. When he still has that feeling of being watched, he sets a trap, and captures two seals—Flotsam and Jetsam—who just want to be friends.

—*TEENAGE MUTANT NINJA ARTISTS: THE BEST OF INDIE COMICS* BY JERRY FRAZEE

NICK was waiting for her in the lobby.

"If you're hoping for more cookies," she said, "I left the box upstairs with Laryea."

"What about that box in your car?"

"You peeked!"

He grinned. "Any luck with Laryea?"

"Other than milk and cookies, not so much. Oh, and I did get a chance to bond with Sebastian. What a sweetheart! We're Facebook friends and everything now."

"I can only imagine."

"Honestly, where does Laryea find these guys? First Foster, and now Sebastian, who may be even nastier."

"He's definitely shorter."

"Not that size matters," Tilda said dryly.

"I take notice of these things. If he were to suddenly attack Laryea, I would need to be aware of his weaknesses and strengths."

"So how would you judge him as a driver?"

"Excuse me?"

Tilda explained her thought that Sebastian could have killed Foster to get his job.

"So he snuck into the inn, despite our security arrangements, hung around until he figured out where the limo would be, figured out Pete was going to be drinking, knew where Laryea was going to be—"

"Okay, stop there. It makes no sense. He might have had the motive, but nothing else. Unless he hired somebody . . ."

"Who then snuck into the inn, despite our security arrangements, hung around until he figured out where the limo would be, figured out Pete was going to be drinking, knew where Laryea was going to be—"

"Point taken. I'll continue to assume that Laryea was the target, which means I want to talk to the other two-thirds of his trio of ex-lady friends." She pulled out her phone to check e-mail. Unfortunately, both Edwina and Joni had begged off for the day. Between jet lag and the next day's shoot, they didn't have time for an interview. "So much for that idea. I suppose there's nothing left for me to do but take my box of cookies back to my cottage and enjoy them in solitude."

"Let me walk you out to your car."

"You're not getting my cookies."

"Just one? I'll—"

But Tilda never got to hear what he was going to

offer, because as they stepped out the door and onto the veranda, there was a rerun of the night they'd arrived at the inn. Nick stopped, swore, and started running.

Hugh Wilder's van, unmistakable in its coloration, was stopped on the driveway, and a tall guy with an orange-red mop of hair was taking a photo of Wilder waving and smiling from the driver's seat.

Tilda knew it had to be the stalker Nick had been chasing all week, but this was the first time she'd gotten a good look at him.

"Shit!" she said. "Nick, stop!"

Realizing he couldn't hear her, she saved her breath and started toward them. By the time she got to Wilder's car, Nick had already wrestled the guy to the ground and was talking into his ever-present earpiece. People had heard the commotion and were coming out of the inn to watch, and she saw more than one cell phone camera at work.

"Nick!" she said. "NICK! Let him go!"

Nick and his captive both turned to look at her, but Nick didn't let go.

"Is this your bathroom stalker?" Tilda asked.

"Damned right he is. And he's not getting away this time!"

Had she and Nick still been dating, Tilda would have tried to hold it in, but given their current status, she felt no compunction about starting to snicker.

"What's so damned funny?" Nick asked.

"If you'd spent a little more time in Boston this past year, you'd know who this guy is. He's no stalker. Well,

I guess technically he is, but he's harmless. He's the Photo-Operative."

"Come again?"

"She's right. I'm on the Web," the Photo-Operative said. "Photo-operative.com."

"He's a college student or something," Tilda said.

"Boston University," the guy put in.

"He finds out who's coming to Boston, where they're staying, and where they're going to be. Then he stakes them out until he can meet them so he can takes pictures of himself with them. He puts the pictures up on his website."

"He puts pictures of people pissing on the Web?" Nick asked.

"No!" the guy squeaked indignantly. "I just wanted to get a picture of me and Laryea. The bathroom at the airport was just the first chance I had to talk to him. I've been trying to get to him ever since, but you guys have been stopping me. All I want is a picture!"

Nick looked doubtful. "Are you sure about this guy, Tilda?"

"Fairly sure."

Nick finally turned him loose, and helped him up from the ground. "Sorry about that, buddy. You okay?"

The Photo-Operative seemed to be torn between wanting to complain and a guy's natural instinct to claim that it would take a lot more than *that* to hurt him. He settled for, "Yeah, I'm good. But jeez, guy, get a grip!" He turned as if to go toward the inn.

"Oh no, you don't," Nick said, blocking him.

"But you heard her! I've got a website."

"You and half the country. That doesn't give you the right to bother Mr. Laryea."

"I'm not going to bother him! I just want to get a picture of him and me together."

"Not today," Nick said firmly. "Only guests are allowed inside the inn."

Before the guy could argue, Dom and one of the inn's own security guards came running up, and Nick turned to talk to them.

"Thanks for keeping him from giving me the bum's rush," the Photo-Operative said to Tilda. "Are you with the movie crew?"

"Nope, I'm a reporter. Tilda Harper." She fished a business card out of her satchel and handed it to him. "I've seen you around town, but I don't remember your name." He'd been at the Boston Film Festival, the Music awards, and at several of the Oldies 103 concerts at the Hatch Shell.

"Greg Dickson," he said, handing her a card of his own, complete with a photo of him looming over Tom Cruise, probably from when the actor had filmed *Knight and Day* in Massachusetts. "Do you think you can get me in to see Laryea? You know, as a professional courtesy?"

Since when was a college student with a camera and a website a professional? "Sorry, it's not going to happen," she said. Still she felt sorry enough for him being manhandled to add, "Laryea's probably not leaving his room for the rest of the day. He's got an early shoot tomorrow."

"Where?"

"Oh, you're not showing up there, but I think he'll be

back here in the early afternoon. If you wait here—outside the inn—you might be able to get that picture."

"Awesome!"

By then, Wilder had parked the Quasit-mobile, and was coming toward them.

Seeing a way to make Wilder and Dickson happy, she said, "Greg, did you know that Mr. Wilder here used to be on TV with Mr. Laryea?"

"That's right," Wilder said, beaming. "We were on *The Blastoffs* together."

"What's that?" Greg said.

Some professional. Had the guy not even bothered to read up on Laryea's background? "It was Laryea's first acting job. Mr. Wilder played Posit the wisecracking Twizzle."

"Sorry, I never heard of it."

"Then why were you taking pictures of Mr. Wilder's van?"

"I just thought it would make a cool picture, you know."

Dom and Nick came over, and Dom said, "I hear there's been a misunderstanding."

"Yeah, there sure has," Dickson said.

"So let's make a deal. You agree not to make a fuss about Nick apprehending you, and we agree not to turn you over to the police for trespassing."

"Trespassing? I just want to get a picture."

But Dom wasn't having any of it, and the hotel security guy got involved, too. While they bickered, Wilder asked Tilda, "What's going on?"

"The redheaded guy has been sneaking around

trying to get a picture with Laryea, so they thought he was stalking him."

"Shame on him!" Wilder said indignantly. "That youngster has no right to bother a man like John Laryea. Even public figures have a right to privacy. The press these days—it's totally out of control." Then, realizing who he was talking to, he said, "Not you, of course. You've shown John and me nothing but respect."

"Thank you," she said, hoping it sounded sincere.

She wasn't sure if Nick wanted to talk further or not, but didn't want to interrupt, so she said, "Were you going up to the inn?"

"I was, actually. I thought I'd go see John and see how he's feeling. I missed him the other day. He was already napping when I brought his balloons."

Tilda didn't think Wilder would get any closer than the Photo-Operative had, but she walked back inside with him, and as he headed to the front desk to call up to Laryea's room, casually mentioned that she was going to get something to drink at the bar. Sure enough, he came to join her a few minutes later.

"John's sleeping," he told her. "His new assistant seemed very nice, though. Very conscientious."

"Sebastian certainly gives that impression."

They ordered sodas and Tilda thought she might as well pick the older man's brain while she waited for Nick.

"Hugh, can I ask you something kind of odd?"

"Certainly, you can ask me anything."

"You've known Mr. Laryea a long time, probably longer than anybody else around here."

He puffed his chest out in pride.

"Do you know of anybody who might have a grudge against him?"

"Against John? No, of course not. Everybody loves John! Why would you even ask such a thing?"

"Just something I heard somebody saying," she said, which wasn't even a lie. She'd heard herself say it, hadn't she? "Somebody was speculating that maybe the accident with the limo wasn't strictly an accident."

"That's crazy talk! Didn't the police arrest the limo driver? I heard he was as drunk as a skunk."

"He says he wasn't driving the limo that night."

"Of course he says that. And, to give the man his due, he might not even remember what he's done. Too much alcohol does things to a man's memory, you know."

"Still, just for argument's sake, is there anybody you know of who might wish Laryea harm? Maybe even from as far back as *The Blastoffs*?"

"Absolutely not! Didn't I tell you how we were like a family?"

"People kill their own relatives all the time," she pointed out.

But he was shaking his head. "I just don't believe it. Everybody loves John Laryea."

Tilda gave up on digging up any dirt, and said, "He is amazingly talented." That was enough to get Wilder going on about various scenes in *The Blastoffs* that showed just how brilliant an actor Laryea was, and Tilda did some brilliant acting of her own to make him believe she was interested. She was relieved when she saw Nick come in, and she excused herself to go talk to him.

"Everybody happy now?" she asked.

"Nobody's particularly happy," he said, "but that guy isn't going to sue me for tackling him or for throwing his camera into the toilet, and we aren't going to have him arrested. That'll do." He shook his head ruefully. "I can't believe I wasted all that time chasing that loser."

"How could you have known he was an über-fan? It's not like stalkers wear uniforms or something."

"Yeah, well, I'm not Pop, but I'm supposed to have some instincts for things like that. Anyway, I've got to go on duty, so I guess I'll see you at the shoot tomorrow."

"Location shots at the lighthouse, right?"

He nodded. "Which is good news and bad news for us. On the good side, there's nobody who lives anywhere around there, so we won't have to worry much about rubberneckers."

"Are you kidding? I've toured that lighthouse. It's right in the middle of town."

"You didn't read your schedule carefully enough— you're thinking about the Glenham Lighthouse. They aren't using that one because it's not atmospheric enough. They're using the Monomoy Point Lighthouse instead."

"Where's that? And do not say 'Monomoy Point.'"

"It used to be Monomoy Point," he admitted, "but ever since the Blizzard of '78, it's been South Monomoy Island, which is off the coast of Chatham. There's nothing there other than the lighthouse and the lighthouse keeper's quarters, and the wildlife."

"So you'll be protecting Laryea from what? Bears? Mountain lions?"

"Deer, gray seals, and enough different birds to make a bird-watcher drool."

"Seals aren't so tough. You can take 'em."

"Yeah, but those deer are mean mothers. Seriously, though, it's mostly about protecting the animals from the ravages of Hollywood. The island is a wildlife refuge, and many papers were signed and promises made to ensure that the island will look the same when we leave as before we arrived."

"Trusting souls," Tilda said, having seen the condition of houses after they'd been rented for location shots.

"They probably wouldn't be letting them film there at all if they weren't looking to raise money to overhaul and preserve the lighthouse."

"Wouldn't it be easier to use the Glenham Lighthouse?"

"Probably, but wait until you see Monomoy."

"How do I get there?"

"Easy. Just show up at the dock and they'll get you on the first available boat."

"Sounds like fun."

"Did I mention you need to be there at 4 AM?"

"You're kidding me."

"Nope. Four in the morning."

Tilda groaned. She wasn't a morning person, a fact Nick knew full well. "For God's sake, why?"

"Joni wants to capture the sunrise."

"She's making John Laryea get up at that hour?"

"Actually, he won't have to come until later. They're just doing exterior shots of the lighthouse at first. He doesn't have to be there until five thirty."

"Lucky him."

"What are you complaining about?" he said. "I've got

to spend the night on that island watching the equipment they already took over."

"Whereas I'm going to go back to my cottage and go straight to sleep. Thanks—that does make me feel better."

"Sure, rub it in."

"Tell you what. Walk me out to my car for real this time, and I'll split the cookies with you. I think you need them."

"That's the best offer I've had all day."

When she got back to her cottage with the remainder of the cookies, she wondered if she should have kept them all to comfort herself. That was when it occurred to her that if the mysterious stalker was the Photo-Operative, then she'd lost her most promising murder suspect.

# Chapter 25

Melusine once asks Dylan O'Taine about his lighthouse home. He replies, "To those at sea, Pharos is a beacon, a guide to safety. To those on land, it's a bulwark against the power of the ocean. And to me, it is both my haven and the source of my strength." Fans speculate that had Pharos ever been destroyed, O'Taine would have died, too, but Leviathan never established the link with any certainty.

—*TEENAGE MUTANT NINJA ARTISTS:
THE BEST OF INDIE COMICS* BY JERRY FRAZEE

AT 3:55 the next day, a time of the morning she usually only saw by staying up extra late, Tilda was on a dock with a satchel of supplies and a freshly charged laptop, ready to board the next boat with an empty seat. It was still dark when she arrived at South Monomoy Island, but she had a flashlight and managed to find her way across the tiny island to where the shoot was taking place. By the time the sun rose, she was on the beach.

She found a spot safely out of the way of the frantic moviemakers, and picked a semiflat rock to sit on to wait for sunrise. The sky was clear, the water had only the gentlest of ripples, and when the sun started out as a tiny disk at the edge of the horizon, it was as though the world was winking at her.

Nick showed up next to her as the light grew. "Sleep well?" he asked.

"Like a baby. You?"

"I'll tell you when I actually get to sleep. But I think seeing this sunrise may be worth it."

"If not, it comes pretty close."

"Aren't you going to take a picture?" he asked, nodding at the camera in her lap.

"Nope. I'm feeling selfish—I want to keep the view all to myself."

"What about me? Should I close my eyes?"

She wondered if he would have, but she said, "I suppose there's enough to share with you."

The sounds they heard were not quite so idyllic. The cinematographer cussed his way through framing shots, sighting angles, and getting as much footage into the can as possible. From what Nick told Tilda, the man knew he might not get another opportunity to film on the island, so he was making the most of his chance.

"Have you seen the lighthouse yet?" Nick asked once the sun was mostly up.

Tilda shook her head, and took the hand he offered to pull her up from the rock. He had remarkably strong hands, and under her breath, she whispered, "No poaching, no poaching."

"Beg pardon?"

"I was just thinking that poaching must be a problem around here," she lied.

Though the sunrise the film crew was so busy capturing was supposed to be visible from Dylan O'Taine's lighthouse, the real lighthouse was actually fifteen minutes' walk away. And when Tilda got there, she realized why it was that Joni had insisted on filming at Monomoy. Not for the sunrise, as glorious as it had been. It was the lighthouse. Monomoy Point Lighthouse *was* Pharos!

The cast-iron tower, with outer braces to hold it steady; the balcony circling the lantern room; the shingled keeper's house next it—everything was exactly the same as the one Leviathan had drawn in the comic book. The only difference was the color.

"Why is it red?" Tilda asked. "I thought lighthouses were usually white." Dylan O'Taine's had been black, which had been part of what made it so cool.

"They painted it so that sea captains would be able to spot it in the daylight."

"That makes sense." But she could see why Leviathan had gone for black instead. "Can we go inside?"

"I'm afraid not. They can't film in there, either, which made Joni crazy. It's historically significant and I suspect they'd never get the camera angles they'd want without destroying the place. They're going to set up some sort of tower near Glenham to put Laryea on, so they can film him looking out on the ocean and then stage his half of the climactic battle. Then with the magic of CGI, they'll combine footage of the lighthouse, the sunrise they just filmed, and the stuff of him on the phony lighthouse to show us O'Taine looking out over his domain."

"Sometimes I think it would be easier if they just built their own lighthouse."

Tilda heard a whisper that meant somebody was calling Nick on his headset.

"Sorry," he said. "Duty calls. Are you going to stick around here?"

"For a while, anyway," she said. Maybe she couldn't go inside the lighthouse, but she definitely wanted to get some photographs of it. Not only was it incredibly cool in its own right, but it was so clearly the inspiration for Dylan O'Taine's mystic fortress.

As she snapped photos, a happy thought came to her. She had a juicy new fact to use to figure out which of the wannabes was Leviathan. She didn't believe the resemblance between the real lighthouse and the fictional one could be a coincidence, so any wannabe who couldn't identify the inspiration for Pharos as the Monomoy Point Lighthouse was as phony as a three-dollar bill.

# Chapter 26

storyboard *n* A panel or panels on which a sequence of
sketches depict the significant changes of action and scene in a
planned film, as for a movie, television show, or advertisement.
—DICTIONARY.COM

THOUGH Tilda had packed a water bottle and a couple of
the previous day's chocolate chip cookies, as the morning progressed, caffeine began to sound like an excellent
idea. The shoot was more disorganized than the one at
the beach had been, but eventually she found the craft
services table. There were, sadly, no nachos, but a Coke
and a croissant made up for their absence.

Edwina was nearby, and in contrast to her ease during
the sunset shoot, she looked a bit frazzled as she talked
to one of the various technical experts whose roles Tilda
remained unsure of. She wandered closer, semicasually,
to eavesdrop.

"Just go with what's on the storyboard," Edwina was
saying.

"I can't!" the expert said. "Look at the angles." He
pointed to a stand of bushes. "Those things are in the
way, and you told me I can't trim them—"

"Don't even joke about trimming anything! You were

at the briefing—we're lucky they let us on this island at all."

"If we can't touch the bushes, then we can't get the shot."

"Don't tell me. Tell Joni!"

"Joni is in a boat chasing sea lions."

"They aren't sea lions. There are no sea lions on the Cape. They're seals."

"Whatever she's chasing, she's chasing them somewhere else. And we're going to lose the light if we don't do something now."

Edwina closed her eyes tightly and started muttering in some other language—Latin, Tilda thought. When she opened her eyes again she said, "Get me a piece of paper and a marker."

Since Tilda had both in her satchel, she said, "I've got it," and handed over a pad of lined paper and a black Sharpie.

Edwina nodded her thanks, took the clipboard with the offending storyboard pictures from the expert, and quickly sketched a series of shots that showed the lighthouse getting increasingly bigger, as if somebody was walking along the sandy path and suddenly saw it looming above the bushes.

"Do that!" Edwina said, handing it to him.

"Done!" he said and trotted away.

"Seals!" Edwina said, throwing her hands into the air. "Were seals in the storyboard?" She glared at Tilda as if expecting an answer.

"I'm guessing not."

"No, it was a totally seal-free shot. We're supposed to film seals later, in San Diego, where we don't have to shoot in one day and one day only to make the care-takers of the island happy. But Joni saw seals, and off she went. I'm sure the footage will be great—she always gets great footage. But not only did she endanger this shoot, but now we're going to have to match today's seal footage with San Diego's seal footage. What if they aren't the same size or color or . . . ?" She put the cap back on the Sharpie and gave it back to Tilda. "I better go make sure nothing else goes wrong."

Tilda nodded, and stepped well back as the producer stomped away. In fact, after that she decided to go the other way entirely. She spent the rest of the morning snapping photos and doing her best to stay out of the way of the film crew and not disturb any flora or fauna. It required enough fast stepping that she became convinced that it would make a terrific video game.

Laryea showed up at some point, dressed in his Dylan O'Taine finery, and Tilda got to watch the filming of several quick bits: O'Taine looking up at the lighthouse, O'Taine at the door of the lighthouse, O'Taine walking toward the lighthouse, O'Taine walking away from the lighthouse, O'Taine running toward the lighthouse, O'Taine running away from the lighthouse. These shots were coverage, seconds of footage that might be needed to fill in longer sequences.

Tilda couldn't resist taking a few surreptitious shots of Laryea relaxing between shots, including a great one of him dancing an impromptu tango with an exasperated Edwina. That she managed to do so without being caught by Sebastian gave her perverse pleasure.

The film crew continued to buzz around like bees

having panic attacks until just before noon when, according to a PA Tilda spoke to, they lost the light. Then it was
time to start packing up. Laryea and Sebastian weren't
about to stay for that, of course, and immediately headed
for the boat. Tilda did the same, and earned a huge smile
from Laryea by giving him one last, somewhat crumbly,
chocolate chip cookie.

The boat ride was too noisy and windy for conversation, so Tilda was happy to keep an eye out for any seals
that might have escaped Joni's camera. They split up at
the dock on the mainland, with Tilda heading for her car
while Laryea and Sebastian got into a waiting limo—
not, Tilda noted, the same one that had killed Foster.

What with the limo being harder to maneuver on
Cape Cod's narrow roads, and perhaps a driver who
wasn't as good as Pete Ellis, Tilda beat the limo back
to the inn and saw Greg Dickson standing on the lawn
outside, careful to not even step onto the veranda.

"Is Laryea coming or what?" he asked. "I've been
here for hours."

"He should be right behind me," she said. If he'd
asked a little more nicely, she might have introduced
them, but as it was, she decided to let him handle it himself. When she saw the limo pulling in, she stopped to
see how the encounter worked out, trying to decide who
she'd bet on in a smackdown: the irrepressible Photo-
Operative or the supercilious Sebastian.

To her considerable surprise, neither took the belt. It
was Laryea himself.

After the limo pulled up, Hoover hopped out of the
driver's seat and stepped smartly to the passenger side

to open the door. Laryea climbed out first, followed by Sebastian, who was lugging a pair of bulging tote bags. Dickson approached with a big smile and his hand held out.

"Mr. Laryea, I'm a big fan of your work, and I was wondering if you could stand over here with me for a picture?" He gestured to where his camera was set out on a tripod, ready for them.

Laryea glanced at him, then swept right past, ignoring the hand, the camera, and the smile. Sebastian sniffed at Dickson as he passed and said, "Hoover, get rid of that."

Poor Dickson was left standing with his mouth open. "What the fuck? Tom Cruise let me take his picture. Adam Sandler let me take his picture. Clint effing Eastwood let me take his picture. And this guy won't let me take his picture?"

"Sorry, man," Hoover said, looking embarrassed. "You've got to get going."

"Cameron Diaz, Cher, Helen Mirren, Anna Paquin. I've got them all. But not John Laryea." He glared up at Tilda, as if it were her fault. "What's the matter with that guy?"

"I've got no clue. He's been very open with me."

"What'd you do? Blow him?"

"Hey, hey!" Hoover said. "You get your ass out of here!"

But as Dickson grabbed his camera, he said, "Seriously, did you tell him not to talk to me or what? I mean, are you that worried about the competition?"

"Dude, the day I worry about competition from a college boy with a blog is the day I find a new job." Then she did her best imitation of Sebastian and swept inside.

Despite the pleasure of getting the last word, she was still disturbed. Not just by Dickson's being an ass, but by Laryea's behavior. Hadn't he said he wanted everybody to like him? So why hadn't that applied to Dickson, now that he knew the guy wasn't a stalker, just a fan with a website?

Come to think of it, why had Laryea been so resistant to letting Hugh Wilder get pictures for the local paper? Okay, he didn't want to be linked too strongly with *The Blastoffs*, which she could understand. But still, blowing off a former costar seemed a bit harsh.

Those incidents just didn't fit in with what she'd seen of the man. Was he faking being nice to her, or was she missing something?

# Chapter 27

Here it is: stars are not *not* **not** what you think. They are not remotely what the world believes them to be, either. Most of them are smaller than you think, and all of them are more frightened than you think—and don't you *ever* forget that if you are lucky enough to work with them.
—WILLIAM GOLDMAN, *WHICH LIE DID I TELL?: MORE ADVENTURES IN THE SCREEN TRADE*

AFTER a much needed bathroom break, Tilda headed to the bar for a bowl of tomato soup and a club sandwich, and was still eating when Nick arrived.

"I thought you'd be getting some sleep," she said when he sat down at her table.

"I'm on the way, but Hoover just told me what happened with that Dickson guy. Are you okay?"

"Yeah, I'm fine. But what a wanker! As if it were my fault Laryea wasn't in the mood for a photo op."

"Of course not. It's ours."

"Come again?"

"Sebastian called Dad to chew him out on Laryea's behalf. Apparently it's our fault that Dickson is allowed in the vicinity of Mr. Laryea, when any right-thinking person would have him deported immediately. The concept of public space is not familiar to Sebastian."

"I don't believe it," Tilda said. "Laryea managed to find an assistant who is even nastier than Foster."

"And shorter," Nick reminded her. "Do they grow these guys in a vat or what?"

"Sebastian says he works with a service. I'm guessing it's Assholes-R-Us."

"Or WankerExpress, when you absolutely, positively have to annoy somebody the same day."

"McPITAs?"

"You lost me."

"PITA equals 'pain in the ass.' "

"Not bad, but a little opaque. Anyway, going back to Dickson, Dad told Sebastian that we'll do our best, but we can't throw him into the canal unless he actually does something threatening. After today's outburst, are you still sure he's harmless?"

"Not as sure as I was," she admitted, "but all today really proves is that he's got a mouth on him."

"Maybe, but if you see him around again, call me or one of the guys, okay?"

She didn't answer for a minute.

"What?" he asked.

"I'm trying to decide if I should gratefully accept your manly protection or be offended by the implication that a modern woman like me can't defend herself."

"Would it help if I pointed out that many of our clients are men, or that some of our people are women and therefore supply womanly protection?"

"It would. Thank you for respecting my sensitivities."

"I am a modern guy, secure in my masculinity. Now,

if you will excuse me, I need to go find my blankie and take my afternoon nap."

Tilda laughed, and after he left, continued to enjoy her sandwich, but something Nick had said about Sebastian was niggling at her. He was short, wasn't he? Definitely shorter than she was. Shorter than Foster had been, too, and Foster hadn't been tall. Meaning that both men were considerably shorter than Laryea. She didn't know what the average height was for personal assistants to the stars, but it was an interesting coincidence.

It wasn't a thought she wanted to examine further in public, so after she finished eating, she headed back to her cottage and settled down for some Web investigation.

First she found Laryea's biography on IMDb. His height was listed as six feet. Then she found a selection of publicity photos of him in various movies with various costars. He invariably looked taller than the women and most of the men, even actors whose IMDb bios said they were over six foot tall.

Okay, that wasn't exactly lying. Maybe Laryea was playing men who were taller than he was himself. Elijah Wood wasn't really hobbit-sized, after all. It was no more dishonest than Keira Knightley enhancing her bosom when the role called for it, or William Shatner and his Starfleet approved wig.

But what about off camera? Tilda went trolling for semicandid shots of Laryea on red carpets and at award shows. In each, he managed to appear taller than most of his costars—no matter what their listed height was—even though the women were often wearing ludicrously high heels.

Finally she went to Celebheights.com, one of the more bizarre celebrity websites. The guy who ran it had spent vast amounts of time and effort trying to determine the actual heights of movie and TV stars, as opposed to what they claimed to be. He even explained how it was possible to fool the camera with shoe lifts, perspectives, and elevator shoes, and listed techniques for figuring out a star's real height. After a bit of playing around, Tilda still couldn't say for sure how tall Laryea was, but she was convinced that he was considerably less than six feet.

Suddenly some apparent anomalies made sense. Of course Laryea chose short assistants. Having them around made him look taller. The time Foster had gotten snotty about her taking pictures, Laryea had been standing— Foster had posed him sitting down. Then there were the boots he wore with his Dylan O'Taine costume instead of going barefoot. She'd bet her favorite *Banana Splits* T-shirt that they had lifts in them.

Laryea's real height even explained why he'd been so curt with the Photo-Operative. Tilda went to Dickson's website and confirmed her memory of him being fairly tall. He was a head above Tom Cruise, and taller than all the women he was pictured with. He'd have towered over Laryea, even if the star was wearing lifts or elevator shoes.

Tilda noted that in his newest photo Dickson was standing next to Hugh Wilder, and was only a tiny bit taller than the older man. But that was enough to show that Wilder was taller than Laryea, which would have been even more obvious if Wilder was wearing his Quasit costume. No wonder Laryea had dodged photos with either of them.

John Laryea, action hero supreme, was short.

# Chapter 28

Why did Demara do it? He stole no money and never hurt anyone. Asked his motives, he said, "Rascality, pure rascality." But other remarks he made suggest he wanted to lead an exciting life without going through a lot of tiresome training—and that he liked to prove himself superior to the people he duped.

—"'PURE RASCALITY' HAS LOST ITS SHINE SINCE LAST TUESDAY"
BY ROBERT FULFORD, *NATIONAL POST* (TORONTO)


TILDA couldn't help snickering, and wondered who she could share this snippet with without ruining her career—she had no doubt that publishing it would bring Laryea's vengeance down upon her. Briefly she considered the idea that he'd arranged for Foster's death because he was afraid he was about to break the height story to the press, but before her mind could go too far down that path, her cell phone rang.

She checked caller ID before answering. "June! Just the person I wanted to talk to."

"I thought I might be," her sister said.

"You're not going to believe this, but . . ." Tilda launched into the investigation of Laryea's height, complete with her brilliant deductions, ending with, "As far as I can tell, he's no more than five-foot-eight, no matter what he says in his biography. He's been dodging Hugh Wilder all week just because he's shorter than the guy, and today he wouldn't let this Photo-Operative guy get a picture for his website."

"Does being short make him less of an actor?"

"Of course not. It's not his height that's important. It's the fact that he lies about it. As famous as he is, as rich as he is, he fakes his height. It must weigh on his mind, too. Listen to how he describes his characters: 'rises to the occasion,' 'larger than life,' 'learning to stand tall.' Talk about your Freudian slips!" There was silence from the other end of the phone. "You're not chortling. I expected a chortle."

"There's a website devoted to figuring out how tall actors really are?"

"Sure. People like to see big shots taken down a peg. Pun intentional."

"So it seems to me that Laryea has every reason to be sensitive about his height—people are waiting to pounce on him. You know what they say. Even paranoids have enemies."

"Well, yeah, but . . ."

"Should I bring up the story of a young lady who seemed to think it was necessary to stuff her bra?"

"That was you, June, not me."

"Which is why I'm sympathetic to Laryea's feelings. And it's worse for him. I only had to fake the bustline for a year or so."

"Two years, wasn't it?"

"That falls under the heading of 'or so,'" she retorted. "Laryea is stuck wearing lifts and elevator shoes constantly.

Plus he lives his life in the spotlight, never knowing when he'll be caught flat-footed. So to speak."

"Who's making fun of him now?"

"At least I'm not going to publish an article outing the man's height."

"I'm not going to write about it, either," Tilda said. "For one, it would be mean and for another, it would be professional suicide unless I were planning to become the next Perez Hilton."

"And I'm sure you weren't planning to joke about it with your friends either."

Tilda was suddenly glad that she hadn't had time to call Cooper. "Okay, you're right. I should cut the guy a break." She paused, making sure that she hadn't made any more Freudian slips. "You know, it wouldn't hurt you to be wrong once in a while. Always being right is way annoying."

"I'm not always right," June said. "Remember how I thought my bridesmaids would be able to get more use out of their gowns."

"Ouch. Don't remind me." For some reason, the usually style conscious June had picked lime green dresses. With matching shoes. And as Kermit had always said, it isn't easy being green. "I used mine for a Halloween costume two years ago. I went as a Cyalume light stick and won third prize in the costume contest. People thought it was a scream."

"After I spent weeks picking out that dress, you wore it as a Halloween costume?"

"Um . . . Sort of." Tilda held her breath, waiting for the explosion.

"Then you did get more use out of it. Maybe I am always right."

"Did you call to remind me of that?"

"Actually, no. I called to see how you were dealing with witnessing a hit-and-run, considering your phobia about cars."

"I don't think it counts as a phobia. A phobia is an unreasonable fear. I have an excellent reason."

"Then I called to see how you were dealing with witnessing a hit-and-run, considering your reasonable fear of cars. Are you going to tell me, or are you going to stall some more?"

Stalling almost never worked with June—Tilda wasn't sure why she even tried. "I'm dealing with it okay, I think. I had bad dreams one night, but not since. And I'm not avoiding cars any more than I did before seeing it. Is that normal?"

"Define normal."

"Is it healthy? Am I in denial? Am I going to get post-traumatic stress syndrome and chase after my big sister while dressed as a Cyalume light stick?"

"Oh now I'm supposed to diagnose you when you didn't even bother to call me."

"I know, I'm an idiot. I should have called you. I did talk to Cooper, but he was the one who called me. And I assume that he's the one who called you."

"Never assume. I called him to get the name of a good caterer, and he asked how you were doing."

"Why do you need a caterer?"

"For a friend. Are you stalling again?"

"No. Maybe. Anyway, I talked to Cooper and I've talked to Nick."

"Nick Tolomeo? The one who dumped you via e-mail? I'm sure he was a big help."

"We've moved past that."

"I'd like to move past him with a stick." June had a tendency to blame Tilda's breakups on the men involved, which was comforting, though not always fair.

"The point is," Tilda said, "I've talked to friends and I think I'm okay. Mostly I've been distracted by trying to figure out who really killed the guy."

"The news I found on the Web said it was a chauffeur."

Tilda explained what she was trying to do for Pete Ellis. "I like the guy, and I think he's innocent, but I don't know that I'm really going to be able to help him."

"It's frustrating when somebody you know is in trouble, and you can't help."

Tilda suddenly realized that June knew far too much about that feeling—her sister had wanted to help *her* and instead she'd gone to Cooper and an ex-boyfriend. Tilda could have smacked herself, but settled for thinking furiously. She didn't know of any advice June could offer about Pete Ellis, but maybe she could help elsewhere.

"And if that weren't enough," she said, "I'm really stuck on this whole Leviathan search. Hey, maybe I can borrow some psychological insight from you."

"How much do you need? Half a cup? A whole cup?"

"Why do people pretend to be something they're not?"

"Okay, now we're talking a tanker truck. Can you narrow it down?"

Tilda had spoken to June briefly about the search when she was trying to find backup to make sure Joni didn't give up the search, but now she explained the story in more detail. "I've already eliminated a bunch, including the one who claims to be Leviathan reincarnated, but I've still got five Leviathan wannabes, and I'm running out of ways to figure out which one is the real deal. Maybe if I knew why somebody would fake it, I'd know who was faking."

"Would it help if I told you there are all kinds of reasons to fake an identity?"

"No."

"Too bad. Let's start with pathological liars. They lie to get their own way, as a way to avoid taking other peoples' needs into account. As in the mother at the kids' school who told everybody she had sciatica and couldn't walk very far, so she needed to use the handicapped spot during afternoon pickup even though she didn't have a handicapped tag. That worked until somebody saw her playing tennis."

Tilda pulled out a pad to take notes. "Okay, that could fit some of them."

"Then there's the compulsive liar. He lies out of habit, with no particular reason. The lies usually aren't very convincing, so he can be easy to catch."

"I think I already weeded those out," Tilda said, thinking of the guy who'd claimed to be the real talent behind Frank Miller.

"Some people lie to get attention and to look better than other people. Remember that friend of Lonnie's? She always claimed to have seen the hot kids' movies before we had, even when the movie hadn't opened yet. She's gotten over that, but some folks never do. Remember that Tony Curtis movie *The Great Pretender*?"

"That's a song. The movie is *The Great Imposter*. But I never saw it."

"How do you know a movie title when you haven't seen the movie?"

"How can you *not* know the title of a movie you *have* seen?"

Since this was a long-known difference between the two sisters, they put it aside.

June said, "Anyway, the movie is based on the real story of this guy who faked his way into jobs. He was apparently extremely smart and may have had a photographic memory. One time he posed as a doctor in the Canadian Navy, and actually performed surgery."

"Successfully?"

"More or less. None of the guys died, and some of them would have without the operations. But that's a very special case."

"What was his excuse?"

"He gave so many at various times that I don't know if he himself knew why he lied. The one I liked was 'pure rascality.'"

"I'm not sure pretending to be a comic book creator, even a cult figure, would be in his wheelhouse."

"Of course, almost anybody will lie if they've got a good reason. A con artist lies to cheat people out of money. Some people lie for sex—a doctor or a film producer is more likely to get laid than a guy who delivers pizza."

"That would depend on the pizza."

"Lots of people lie on their resumes. Maybe they promote themselves to manager when they were just office boy, or give themselves a degree they never completed. I've seen a lot about that in the paper lately."

"One of my wannabes is a commercial artist, and being a public comic book artist would have helped him get that first job. No, wait, he's already out. He told me an obviously phony story about meeting his editor in his last e-mail."

"You're doing this by e-mail? Are you insane?"

"What?"

"Tilda, you can't believe anything anybody says online. Even my kids know that. There are pedophiles pretending to be cute young guys, guys pretending to be girls in order to get virtual items on game sites, nobodies pretending to be celebrities, and all kinds of people pretending to be Nigerian royalty."

"I know that."

"Do you know why?"

"Because a lot of people are assholes?"

"Well, yeah, but they mainly do it because one, there's no accountability on the Web and two, it's so easy. When you talk to somebody, you get all kinds of unconscious cues to tell you whether or not to trust them. Tone of voice, whether they meet your eyes, do their clothes match their supposed identity, body language— all kinds of stuff. But online? All you've got to go on is a user name, spelling, and grammar. It's not enough. If you're going to figure out which one of these people is really Leviathan, you're going to have to meet them, or at least talk to them on the phone."

"I think you're right. Again. Of course, I don't know that for sure because we're only talking on the phone, but—"

"Anything else? Because I do have a life."

"Kiss kiss to you, too. Tell the kids not to take any virtual wooden nickels." Tilda hung up, satisfied that she'd allowed her sister to help. And in fact, June had helped a lot.

Of course, bringing five strangers to the Cape posed logistical problems. For one, she didn't know where they all lived. For another, considering how cranky the already eliminated wannabes were getting, she really didn't want to have to tell somebody to his face that he was full of plankton.

Before she started working out those details, she wanted to eliminate as many contenders as possible. So she sat down in front of her computer to send more e-mails to her remaining Leviathan wannabes, this time asking if there was any particular inspiration for the appearance of the lighthouse Pharos. If any of them didn't mention Monomoy Point, that would take him out of the running. The ones who were left standing after that would get an invitation to the Cape.

Once that was done, she started working her notes on the day's shoot into an article and got sucked in enough that she barely looked up for the next few hours. If she hadn't realized she was getting hungry, she might have kept at it for another hour or more.

June's brief mention of pizza deliverymen had given her a taste for something covered in cheese and Italian sausage, so she checked with the inn's concierge for a recommendation and then called the nearest delivery place to order a Greek salad and a small pizza.

The food arrived promptly. Not being in the mood to eat alone, Tilda put her laptop on the table and stuck a DVD in so Matthew Morrison and the rest of the *Glee* cast could sing to her. She knew it was pathetic, but it was also quite pleasant until her cell phone rang. It was Cooper.

"Heard from your sister lately?"

"Yes I have."

"Damn! I meant to warn you, but I got tied up at work and forgot. How many pints of Toscanini's ice cream do I owe you?"

"None. Well, maybe one. She wasn't angry—she was just very, very disappointed."

"That's the worst."

"Seriously, we're good. June was right—I should have called her. I've just been a bit overwhelmed by everything that's going on."

"Tell me all."

She did so, or at least most, since she decided to leave out the bit about Laryea's height, or lack thereof. She probably would tell Cooper later, but only when she was sure she could do so without making short jokes.

"I see what you mean. It sounds insane."

"A bit."

"Still, it's not all bad, right? I mean you, Nick, private moonlit beaches, a private pet-free cottage . . ."

"And me watching reruns of *Glee* on my laptop. Dude, I told you he's seeing somebody seriously now. I don't poach."

"You wouldn't have to keep him—just borrow him."

"No."

Cooper sighed. "You are spoiling my vicarious jollies. Can't you make something up?"

"Fine. There was a knock on my cottage door late last night and when I went to answer, I found a trail of wet footprints leading into the darkness. I was drawn to follow them, and I found him standing at the edge of the sea. At first I thought it was John Laryea in costume, but this was no actor. It was Dylan O'Taine himself, wearing nothing but a kilt of seaweed. He held his hand out to me, and gestured toward the softly lapping surf. Then he loosened his kilt and waited for me to untie the ribbons at the neck of my flowing gown so it could puddle at my feet."

"Yeah, you in a flowing gown."

"Okay, in my oversized T-shirt with the words 'And then Buffy staked Edward. The End.'"

"That I can picture. Keep going. This is good stuff."

"Yeah, it is, but the part about *Glee* reruns is the real story. At least it's a really good episode." They spent the next few minutes debating the charms of Will versus Finn versus Kurt before hanging up.

# Chapter 29

"I'd always avoided stuff like 'Where are they now?' or 'Whatever happened to?'" he explained in a telephone interview from his home. "Just 'No thanks, thanks for calling.' You tell me, have you ever seen a 'Whatever happened to' where they seemed anything but pathetic?," he continued.
—JACKIE EARLE HALEY, QUOTED IN "SOME GOOD NEWS ARRIVES AT LAST FOR A BAD NEWS BEAR" BY MARK OLSEN, *The New York Times*

AFTER hanging up the phone, Tilda knew she should keep working, but since there were no replies from the Leviathan brigade she was stymied there. She wasn't ready to do much more on the *Pharos* piece, and she didn't know what more to do on Pete Ellis's behalf. That left *Glee*, and she was too restless to watch the next episode.

She stepped out on the patio and was irritated to see that the night was just as alluring as the one she'd described to Cooper. There were no footprints leading into the darkness, of course, but she really did feel drawn to leave the cottage, which suddenly seemed unbearably stuffy. She grabbed the flashlight from the kitchen drawer, stuck her key and phone into her jacket pocket, and slipped into her sneakers. Leaving the outdoor lights on to make sure she could find her way back to the cottage, she headed for the ocean.

With the flashlight, the path down to the beach was pretty easy to navigate, and before long she was standing in the sand the inn's management must have had shipped in at exorbitant prices to cover the rocks that usually made up Cape Cod beaches. The sound and smell of the water had its usual effect on Tilda, which was to make her problems and concerns seem terribly small in comparison to the sheer size of the ocean. She turned off the flashlight and let her eyes adjust so she could soak it all in.

The solitude and peacefulness were slowly turning to boredom when she heard a noise. She looked down the beach to see somebody lighting a cigarette.

Tilda hesitated for a minute, but decided that anybody who'd meant her harm wouldn't have lit a cigarette to advertise his presence. "Hello?"

"Hey," a familiar voice said, and Tilda went close enough to recognize Pete Ellis. He was staring at the ocean much the same way she had been before.

"What's up?" she said, feeling guilty about not having called him.

"Not much," he said.

"Did you talk to your lawyer?"

"I did, but he didn't believe me, and the cops didn't believe him."

"I'm sorry," she said, which was wholly inadequate. "I've been asking around, but . . ." She shrugged, even though she wasn't sure he could see the gesture. She thought about her tenuous theories, but they all sounded so ridiculous she couldn't bring herself to tell him about them. "I'm not finding anything out. Nobody seemed to have a grudge against Foster or Laryea, or at least, nothing worth killing over."

"I appreciate your trying."

"I just wish I could help."

"It's okay. I'm kind of coming to terms with it. The Serenity Prayer, you know? 'God give me the serenity to accept the things I cannot change, courage to change the things I can, and wisdom to know the difference.' I'm thinking that maybe this is one of the things I can't change. Coming out here helps with that."

"If you want to be alone, I can go."

"No, it's cool. I've got a blanket if you want to sit down."

"Sure. I was wishing I'd brought one myself." It was a lie, but it sounded good.

Together they spread it out and sat facing the ocean. Tilda was once again struck by how comfortable Pete was to hang with, just as he had been when they first met. Was that the reason she didn't want to think he'd killed Foster? Would she have been more willing to accept it if he'd been annoying the way Foster had been?

"I'm trying to decide if I should tell my lawyer to plead guilty," Pete said. "Maybe it would be easier that way."

"Did you kill Foster?"

"No."

"Then don't do it. You know Nick believes you."

"Dom doesn't."

"He wants to. Give him time, and he'll come around."

"Maybe. But the cops are sure it was me. If I hadn't picked that night to fall off the damned wagon . . . Dom would have every right to write me off, just for that."

"It was really bad timing," Tilda admitted. "Why did you start drinking that night?"

He gave a half laugh, half snort. "You know why. Driving Laryea around, then listening to Hugh Wilder talking about the glory days on *The Blastoffs.* I thought I could handle it, but it brought back too many memories. You know what I mean. You must have figured it out that first day, in the limo. When I had to go make a fool of myself and say what I said. I saw the look on your face."

"Then you really are Spencer Marshall?"

Pete put the cigarette to his mouth again and inhaled, and the ember illuminated his face just for a second as he said, "Blasting off, bro."

Now that he'd finally admitted it, Tilda didn't know what to ask first. "Do you want to talk about it?"

"No, but it's time. You've been holding on to the secret for me—you deserve to know it all."

Tilda just waited for him to continue.

"Can I ask you something first? Was that moment in the limo when you figured it out? Or was it when you first met me? I should have begged off from driving Laryea, but I knew he'd never notice me, and I didn't realize until later how good you are at recognizing old actors."

"I'm not that good—just meeting you didn't do it. And even in the limo, it was as much the lighting as what you said that got my attention, and I was only half convinced. Then the questions you asked when you were driving me home combined with a picture I found on the Web got me up to eighty percent. I just couldn't get around the fact that Laryea didn't recognize you. Didn't that surprise you?"

"Not really. It's not the first time I've run into him. I had a bit part in one of his movies years ago, and when I tried to speak to him then, he blew me off."

"How could he not know who you were? You guys worked together day in and day out."

"It wasn't for that long. We filmed the show in about six months. Add in another few weeks laying down music tracks in the studio, and a few months of promo work. Then we did a lousy mall tour for about a month. That was it. Call it a year, all told. We didn't hang out together or anything—we just worked together. Would you remember somebody you'd worked with for a year, twenty years ago?"

"Probably not, but didn't you ever see each other? Hollywood isn't that big a place."

"Maybe we would have if I'd stuck around, but while John went from *The Blastoffs* to doing more TV work, I went to college. By the time I graduated, he was doing regular guest shots, making a name for himself. Me? *The Blastoffs* had been forgotten, and nobody knew who the hell I was. I did a few made-for-TV movies, but only as long as I was young enough to pass for a college student. Meanwhile John moved into films and started hitting it big while I could barely get speaking parts. That's when I started drinking."

"I can see why."

"No, it's no excuse. I could have kept at the acting, or tried something else. The drinking was just my way of giving up. It took me a long time in the program to learn that, but it's the truth."

Tilda had enough friends in various forms of addiction recovery to know what he meant by *the program*.

Pete went on. "Anyway, jobs are even harder to get and keep when you're drinking. By the time I sobered up, my reputation was wrecked. I was doing shit work until I got a job driving, and I realized I liked it. I stuck it out long enough to get my chauffeur license, but I knew I wasn't going to be able to keep driving people I used to know."

"Didn't they recognize you?"

"Some did. Some didn't. I never could decide which was worse. I knew I was going to start drinking again if I didn't get away from Los Angeles. But I liked the driving, so I talked to some of the other drivers, and that led to me getting the job in Dallas. That's went I went back to my real name. Spencer Marshall was a stage name, a combination of my father's middle name and my mother's maiden name. I only used it because there was already a Peter Ellis in the union.

"I stayed in Texas for just over ten years. Then I met Dom when he was in town handling security for a movie that was shooting down there. One of the actors he was watching got into a bit of trouble, and I helped him take care of it. Dom decided he liked the way I handled myself, and asked me to move to Boston to work with him full-time. I was tired of the heat in Texas, and figured it was time for a change. And I like Dom."

"But you never told him you'd been an actor?"

"Tilda, I don't even talk about it in program meetings—I tell them I messed up my career, but I don't say what the career was."

"Why keep it a secret?"

He hesitated long enough to finish his cigarette and stub it out in the sand. "Did you ever write one of those 'where are they now?' articles about Gary Coleman?"

"No, but I read them."

"Then you know that for a while he was a security guard for some studio. It wasn't for long, just when he was in a tight spot, but until he died, almost every article or TV story about him mentioned how he'd been a big star and ended up in a menial job. Just like I ended up driving a limo."

"There's nothing wrong with driving a limo."

"There's nothing wrong with being a security guard, either, but people laughed about it. If he'd been a drunk, too, it would have been even worse. I didn't want them laughing about me, Tilda."

She wished she could tell him that it wouldn't have been like that, but she knew it would have been. Maybe she wasn't as nasty as some of the reporters who'd covered Gary Coleman's fall from grace, but she'd written her share of stories about self-destructive stars. All she could say was, "I'm not laughing, Pete."

"I know you're not. That's why I don't mind telling you."

June or Cooper would have said something warm and comforting, but Tilda wasn't great with comfort. So she changed the subject. "I guess you never expected to run into any of your former colleagues around here. First Laryea, then Hugh Wilder. Wait! Did Wilder recognize you?"

"He didn't get a chance. After you interviewed him, I went and told him who I was. That night he came to my cottage so we could talk about old times. I told him that I was staying under the radar, and he said he'd go along, but I could tell he didn't get why I wanted him to."

"Really? A guy whose life work revolves around a part in a show all those years ago didn't understand a man who'd rather not talk about a role in that same show?"

"Something like that. Still, he said he wouldn't tell anybody, and he hasn't. You're the only other person around here who knows." He looked over at her. "So why didn't you tell the cops about me? Or anybody else?"

"Honestly? Because I wasn't completely sure until that day you came to my cottage. Before then, your past didn't matter—it's like I told you, I don't out people. Afterward, it only mattered if you were a real suspect for killing Foster, and I'd already decided you weren't. So again, I had no reason to tell anybody."

"Thank you."

She shrugged. "I probably would have if the cops had asked me, but they only asked if I'd seen who was driving the car. When I told them I hadn't, they really didn't have any more questions for me. They didn't even want to hear it when I told them about the car veering on purpose, but I was still pretty shaky. It all happened so quickly."

"It must have been a terrible thing to see."

"It was." Tilda took a deep breath, and realized she was tearing up. Accident or murder, she'd seen a man killed. "I didn't like Foster, but damn, he shouldn't have died like that. And it makes me crazy that the cops are never going to find who did it, at least not the way they're going. They've decided you're it, and that's enough for them."

"You can't really blame them. A hit-and-run by a drunk from Boston means that Glenham is still a safe place. But a murderer running wild? Who would want to bring their family here for vacation? What film crews would want to set up here? There's a lot on the line."

"I suppose."

"If I were them, I'd be looking at me, too. I'm a drunk, I'd been drinking, I had access to the limo, and the limo was outside my cottage. Case closed."

"Except for the part about you not being guilty."

"Yeah, except for that part."

They continued to sit quietly for a little while longer, but Tilda was both tired and talked out, so eventually she said, "Well, it's not getting any earlier. I think I'm going to head on back to my cottage."

"That sounds like a good idea."

They stood and shook the sand out of the blanket. Pete's cottage was in the other direction, but he politely asked, "Can you find your way back all right?"

"Sure, no problem."

"Sleep well."

She had a hunch he wasn't going to be sleeping much at all even with the Serenity Prayer to keep him company. She patted him awkwardly on the shoulder and started back the way she'd come.

# Chapter 30

The nighttime scenes were some of the best artwork in *Pharos*. It was there that Leviathan was able to take full advantage of the use of black and white.
—*TEENAGE MUTANT NINJA ARTISTS: THE BEST OF INDIE COMICS* BY JERRY FRAZEE

AT least she thought it was the way she'd come. At some point, Tilda realized how tired she must have become because of how much harder the trek back to her cottage was than the way down the beach had been. The moon had set, making it a lot darker even with the flashlight to guide her, which was probably why she took the wrong path, one that led her to a different cottage. Fortunately it was unoccupied or the people there might have wondered why she spent five minutes trying to get her key to open the door.

Eventually she figured it out, and backtracked to find the path to her own place. It would have been easier to spot if she'd left an outside light on, she told herself as she started toward the door. Then she stopped. She had left that light on, hadn't she? Of course, the bulb could have gone out, but it didn't seem very likely.

Normally the idea of somebody lurking at her cottage

wouldn't have seemed likely either, but it hadn't exactly been a normal few days. And it would certainly explain why there were no lights on.

The big question Tilda had to consider was this. If there was somebody lurking, was he inside or out? Should she stay where she was, hoping the guy was inside and hadn't noticed her approach, or try to get inside before the guy grabbed her?

Both of those ideas sucked. A lot.

The safest bet would have been to jump into her car and get the hell away—she'd have done just that had she not left the car keys in her satchel, which was in the cottage. She checked her pockets—all she had were the cottage key and her cell phone. Why hadn't she asked June for a Taser for Christmas?

She had to do something other than stand there. She decided to assume the hypothetical bad guy was expecting her, and therefore, sooner or later, would come looking for her. And since hypothetical bad guys tended to be huge, vicious, and armed to the teeth, Tilda decided she'd just as soon not be found.

As quietly as she could, she started away from the house. Should she go back toward the beach? No, Pete was probably long gone, and she didn't want to be caught out there by herself. Instead she went toward the road, not quite walking backward but angled, so she could watch behind her.

When she reached Shoreline Drive an eternity later, she was more than a little pissed that there wasn't the first sign of a car driving by. Though come to think of it, she'd have been leery about flagging down a car anyway,

after what had happened to Foster. She headed toward
the inn, still looking for any sign of pursuit.

Finally she found a couple of straggly trees that
offered a little shelter, and pulled out her phone. At first
she was going to call Dom, but after their last conversation, she was afraid he'd think she was making it up. So
she called 911. To her great relief, the operator didn't
sound even a little bit skeptical, just advised her to stay
where she was with the phone line open until the cops
could find her. Three minutes and thirty-eight seconds
later, a squad car pulled up beside her with siren blaring
and lights flashing.

Tilda felt a little ridiculous when explaining why she
was worried, but the cops took it in stride. One said,
"Better to be safe than sorry, right? Hop on in, and we'll
drive you back there to check it out."

There were still no lights on at the cottage, but no
sign of anything else, either. The officers instructed
Tilda to stay inside the squad car, then took her key to
go into the cottage. A moment later, Tilda saw the cottage lights come on, and she could see the cops moving
around. A minute or two after that, a security car for the
inn showed up, and that guard went to join the cops.

A full fifteen minutes later, one of the cops finally
came out. "The place is clear," he said, "but we want you
to look at something."

She followed him inside, blinking at the bright lights
after peering around in the dark for so long.

Something crunched underfoot as she walked into the
bedroom, and the cop said, "Watch your step. There's
glass on the floor."

"Does that mean there was somebody in here?"

"Unless you broke a window yourself. From the outside."

The big picture window that looked out onto the beach had a hole knocked through it, near the window lock, and the window itself was open.

"This is where he got in," the cop said.

Tilda nodded as if he'd said something clever.

"We want you to look at your things to see if anything is missing. Also, we think that knife is one of the set from the kitchen."

"Knife?" Tilda said stupidly. But once he pointed it out, it was all she could see. A carving knife had been thrust into the bed pillow.

# Chapter 31

The defenses of Dylan O'Taine's lighthouse are breached at the end of the ninth issue of *Pharos*. It is at that moment, when he is at his most vulnerable, that he finds a necklace left on his desk by an intruder. The expression on his face when he realizes that the necklace belongs to Melusine is worth the price of the issue.

—*TEENAGE MUTANT NINJA ARTISTS:*
*THE BEST OF INDIE COMICS* BY JERRY FRAZEE

WITH the cops' help, Tilda went through her belongings and confirmed that everything was intact, including her laptop and the money and credit cards in her wallet. That pretty much eliminated robbery as a motive for the break-in, not that Tilda had really thought it was a burglar anyway. A burglar would have been a lot less freaky—burglars didn't usually attack pillows.

Then the cops asked a bunch of questions about what she'd been doing in Glenham and why somebody might have wanted to attack her, but nothing she told them seemed to strike their interest until she mentioned her involvement in the hit-and-run incident. That caused silent communication between the two of them that she couldn't interpret.

The last question was whether or not she intended to

stay in the cottage, something she hadn't even had time to think about. Before she could answer, the inn security guard offered to move her to another cottage, or if she preferred, into the main building. Tilda decided that she'd had enough solitude, which meant she wanted to switch to the inn. He immediately got on the phone to arrange a room.

Once the cops gave her permission, she packed up her things and the security guard helped her load them into her car. The guard followed her on the short drive to the hotel, too, where the manager and a trio of bellmen were waiting. Without even stopping at the main desk, they whisked her up to a room where a fruit basket and selection of cookies and soft drinks were waiting. It wasn't until she thanked them all profusely and locked the door behind them that she realized that she wasn't in just a room—she was in a deluxe suite just as nice as Laryea's. More importantly to her, it was on the third floor, where nobody could break a window and climb inside.

She thought she was dealing with the night's events calmly and rationally right up until there was a knock on the door, and she nearly peed herself. After looking through the peephole, she opened the door. It was Nick.

"Are you all right?" he asked.

"I take it you heard about my little adventure," she said, trying to sound light and unworried as she shut the door. Either she failed miserably or Nick knew better, because he put his arms around her and just stood there holding her. Only then did she start crying.

"It's okay," Nick murmured. "You're safe."

"I know I'm safe," she said, her voice muffled by how

tightly he was holding her. "I did everything right and I outsmarted the guy and I'm fine. So why the hell am I crying?"

"It's a delayed reaction. Completely normal."

She nodded and let him hold her a few more minutes before pulling away. "I suppose you deal with this kind of thing with your clients all the time."

"Occasionally," he admitted. "Are you okay now?"

"You tell me. Am I likely to break down and cry any more?"

He took a long look at her. "No, I think you've moved past it. You're ready for the next stage."

"What's that?"

"Chocolate." He pulled a battered-looking Hershey bar from his pocket.

"There's nothing like having an expert around." And actually chocolate did sound like a good idea. "You want half? Or I've got cookies—they aren't from Choco House, but they look pretty yummy. The manager must be worried about me writing an article about his unsafe hotel or suing or something."

"Maybe he was just being nice."

"He brought fruit, too."

"Yeah, okay, he's covering his ass."

"Actually, an ass covered in chocolate chip cookies sounds pretty good. Depending on the ass in question, of course."

"You must be feeling better."

Since it was a suite and not the average hotel room, there was an actual dining room table with chairs for them to arrange themselves around as they munched.

"How did you find out what happened?" Tilda finally thought to ask.

"Hotel security," he said. "They called Pop, Pop pinged me, and here I am. Pop went to see what he can find out from the cops."

"What's to find out? Some guy broke a window, grabbed a knife from the kitchen, and waited for me. When I didn't come strolling in, he took off. Oh, and he took revenge on my poor helpless pillow."

"There might be fingerprints, or footprints, or tire prints."

"The cops were doing the CSI thing when I left."

"I suppose they already asked you about who might have it in for you."

"Standard operating procedure, I would imagine."

"What did you tell them?"

"I told them about the hit-and-run, but that couldn't be it. It's not like I identified the driver."

"You did ID the limo, which is what got Pete arrested. Didn't they speculate about revenge?"

"They didn't tell me what they were thinking, but revenge doesn't make sense. For one, the physical evidence would have led to Pete even if I hadn't been there. All I added was the fact that it looked deliberate, which the police don't believe anyway. For another, Pete knows I don't think he did it. And for a third, this time Pete has an alibi."

"He does?"

"Yeah. Me." She told Nick about finding Pete on the beach, though she didn't tell him everything he'd said. She didn't think Pete would want Nick to know he was

Spencer Marshall. "So even if Pete could have gotten to my cottage ahead of me and broken in, why would he have? He could have dragged me into the ocean and drowned me while we were alone on the beach."

"So what else did you tell the cops?"

"That the only enemies I've got handy are the wannabes, particularly the ones I've already eliminated. A couple of them had been pretending to be Leviathan in their little circles for a while now, and they aren't happy about having that taken from them. Or maybe a phony who's still in the running wants to make sure I don't find him out."

"That's kind of thin."

"That's what the cops thought, too, but I didn't have anything else. Nicole at *Entertain Me!* despises me, of course, but she'd rather destroy me professionally. I had to admit I've met real killers, but they've been put away. Of course, the big favorite was an ex-boyfriend, but you're the only one handy." Seeing the expression on Nick's face, she added, "I didn't even mention your name."

"I had an alibi anyway," he said, looking oddly uncomfortable.

"Talking to Cynthia on the phone?" Tilda guessed.

"On Skype, actually."

To tease, or not to tease. Tilda remembered the chocolate bar and the comforting shoulder he'd supplied. There would be no teasing.

"Anyway," she said, "that's all I could come up with."

"What about the Photo-Operative?"

"I didn't think of him," she admitted. "It would be great to get him put away for a few days, or even just

scare him back to Boston, but I don't think I could
sell it."

"So who does that leave?"

"There's always the chance of a random psycho, but
that doesn't strike me as likely. Which brings me back to
Foster's death. I've told a few people that I didn't think
Pete was driving, which means that word could be getting around. Maybe somebody doesn't like the idea of
my asking questions."

"You think? Why wouldn't a murderer like you stirring up trouble?"

"If I knew who the killer was, I could be more careful
about talking to him," she said, exasperated. "I wouldn't
have to 'stir up trouble' if the cops were doing their job, or
if somebody who was trained in security would take over."

She glared at him, he glared at her, and had there not
been a knock at the door they might have spent the rest
of the night glaring. Even with Nick there, Tilda checked
the peephole first. It was another Tolomeo: Dom.

He rushed in as soon as the door was open. "Tilda,
are you okay?"

"I'm good."

"I can't believe I got you mixed up in all this. First
that guy Foster, and now this. I only meant to do you a
favor, I swear."

"You did do me a favor, and I appreciate it."

"Nick and I went over the security system and proce-
dures ourselves. They've got good locks, plenty of lighting, security drive-bys—we thought it was safe."

"You couldn't have known anybody was going to
come after me."

"If anything had happened to you, I'd never have forgiven myself." He actually started to tear up.

"I'm fine," Tilda said firmly. "What could happen with you two looking out for me?"

"Sure, like I've been looking out for Pete," Dom said. "Here you've been trying to help him, and I yelled at you."

"Does that mean you believe Pete now?" Nick asked.

"Yeah, I believe him. I could swallow the idea of him getting drunk and lying about it, but I cannot swallow the idea of him trying to kill Tilda. My instincts may be getting a bit shaky, but not that shaky."

"God, that's a relief," Tilda said. "I was starting to think that I was the one whose instincts were off."

"Like hell!" Dom said. "Pete's damned lucky you were around to show me what a fool I've been."

There were a dozen things Tilda probably should have said, but all she could think of was, "Would you like a cookie?"

Dom was willing to keep apologizing all night long, but with Nick's help, Tilda eventually got him calmed down long enough to discuss Pete's situation. A little while later, when he caught Tilda yawning, he jumped up and started pushing Nick toward the door. The last thing the older man said was, "Don't you worry about Pete, Tilda. Nick and I are going to take care of him, and you, too."

After all that had happened, Tilda expected to toss and turn for the rest of the night, but she fell asleep as soon as her head hit the pillow.

# Chapter 32

When Dylan O'Taine first encounters the Jengu, he misconstrues their motives and treats them as enemies. It is only when Flotsam and Jetsam show their fondness for the strange-looking beings, that he realizes they may have things to teach him.

—*TEENAGE MUTANT NINJA ARTISTS:*
*THE BEST OF INDIE COMICS* BY JERRY FRAZEE

TILDA slept in the next morning, and considering the day and night she'd had, she didn't even feel guilty. When there was a knock on her door around eleven, she was expecting it to be either Nick or Dom-the-apologetic again, but when she looked through the peephole, she saw her sister June.

She opened the door and let her in. "Nick called you, didn't he?"

"Glad to see you, too. And actually it was his father." Then her eyes widened when she got a look at the room. "My gosh, I am in the wrong business!"

"It's a guilt suite," Tilda assured her. "The Glenham Bars Inn wants to make sure I don't make a stink about their security measures."

"Hey, if they were slack about security, you're damned well going to make a stink. And if you don't, I will."

"I don't think this was their fault," Tilda said. "Even Nick and Dom said they'd taken all the reasonable precautions."

"Nick!" June said in a tone of distaste. "Who cares what he says?"

"I told you that we're still friends."

"Why?"

"Because he's a nice guy."

"Nice guys don't dump my sister."

"Are you saying that I don't date nice guys?"

June wagged a finger at her. "Don't play word games with me. I reserve the right to bad-mouth any man who breaks up with you."

"Did you drive all the way from Beverly to bad-mouth my ex?"

"No, I drove down to find out why somebody is trying to kill you. Again."

"I think it must be my winning personality."

"Tell me, or I tell Mom."

Tilda knew her sister well enough to know that it was no bluff. "Okay, but can we get something to eat first? I'm starved."

"It's kind of early for lunch, but . . ."

"Lunch? I haven't had breakfast yet!"

After their usual sniping about whether it was better to be a night owl or a morning lark, they found the room service menu and ordered. Tilda didn't love the idea of explaining what had been going on where anybody else could hear them, and what was the fun of having a guilt suite if she didn't use room service?

While they waited for Tilda's breakfast and June's

lunch—the room service people saw nothing wrong in their ordering from different sides of the menu—Tilda told June what had happened the night before, including the gist of the conversations with Pete, Nick, and Dom. Though she hadn't told Nick and Dom about Pete's past, she did tell June. If she couldn't trust her big sister, then who could she trust?

The food arrived at an opportune pause, and Tilda dug into her omelet while June tackled her club sandwich. By mutual accord, they decided to forgo further discussion of murder during their meal. Instead they talked about June's kids and the latest challenges of parenting. Tilda didn't mind listening to it all—it was a great reminder of why she kept birth control handy.

"How about the *Pharos* article you're working on?" June asked after a lengthy description of the effort it took to produce a really first-class social studies project. "Does it feel strange to be working with a big-name star? Somebody who is still in the public eye, I mean."

"I guess."

"You guess?"

"It's just that the guys I usually interview are really open—they'll tell great stories about people they've known and worked with. Really funny stuff, and not just dirt, though there's plenty of that. Laryea is too intent on protecting his reputation. He'll only say nice things about people, but nothing too specific, and he'll only say how wonderful it is to be working on this movie, and how wonderful it is to be in Cape Cod."

"*In* Cape Cod?"

"He's not from around here, June. Anyway, it's not very satisfying."

"That's good to know, isn't it? Now you'll be able to go back to your usual kind of story knowing you're doing what you like."

Tilda ate a few more bites to avoid answering.

"Right?" June said pointedly.

"If I can," Tilda said. "I may have lost my touch."

"Excuse me?"

"There was this guy I was hunting for *Entertain Me!* I interviewed one of his costars, who swore up and down she didn't know where the guy was. Then as soon as I was off the phone, she called the guy and told him I was looking. The guy went directly to the magazine and left me in the cold."

"Ouch."

"Then there are all these wannabes I've been dealing with. It seems as if I should at least have a gut reaction about which one is Leviathan, but I've got nothing."

"What if it's none of them?"

"Then I'm in even worse shape. I networked my ass off to dig these guys up. And then there's Pete. If he hadn't told me, I still wouldn't know for sure that he used to be Spencer Marshall. Maybe I should stick with Laryea and people like him—they can be hard to get to, but they're easy to find."

"Let me get this straight," June said. "First, a professional actor—a professional liar, in other words—manages to fool you. Then you have problems finding a comic book artist from twenty years ago—bearing in mind that you're not a big comic book fan and had to make a whole new set of connections to even start searching. Then you recognize a man who was in a kids' TV show that you've probably only seen half a dozen times in your life, even though he was only a kid when the show was filmed, but you suck because you weren't willing to swear to it. Oh yeah, you're clearly losing your touch. It's time to find a new career, maybe something in fast-food preparation or domestic engineering."

"You have a peculiar way of expressing sympathy."

"If you needed my sympathy, you'd get it. When what you need is a swift kick in the pants, I'm ready, willing, and able to oblige."

Tilda finished the last of her omelet. "Okay, my pants have been sufficiently kicked. I can do this thing." Unlike TV or the movies, there was no musical crescendo, but she did feel as if she'd achieved at least a minor epiphany. "And with Dom and Nick taking over the murder stuff, I can concentrate on Leviathan."

June cocked her head. "You sound almost disappointed about that."

"Are you kidding? Do you think I like this kind of thing?"

"Are *you* kidding? Do you think you don't?"

Tilda wished she had more eggs to chew on along with the thought, but she'd have to navigate through this epiphany without a prop. "Here's the thing. Some reporters I know really enjoy being published, but sweat over the actual process of producing words. They like having written, but not the writing. I think I'm that way with the murders. I like having figured them out—the analog to being published. But the middle part of doing the work and being scared, not so much. Does that make sense?"

"Why are you asking me?"

"Why do you always answer my questions with another question?"

"Why shouldn't I ask questions?"

Tilda threw her napkin at June, June returned it with gusto, and the conversation went on hiatus for a few moments.

Afterward, Tilda said, "Anyway, I think what I said makes sense, and I hope that Dom and Nick getting involved won't take away from my smug satisfaction when they figure out who was really driving that limo. In the meantime, I have got to figure out who Leviathan is, and I've only got three more days."

"You are going to meet the candidates face-to-face, right?"

"I'm planning to, though I'm hoping that I'll have a smaller pool to draw from. Which reminds me—I should check e-mail." She set up her laptop and logged in. "Baby! Contestants Number One and Three didn't know that Pharos is based on the real Monomoy Point Lighthouse."

"I take it that this means something to you."

"It means that now I only have to meet with three people, instead of five. Since you're here, you can advise me on how to handle them."

She and June plotted the logistics of where and when, pulling Nick in by phone to arrange for a strong-arm presence in case anybody got unruly. When that was done, Tilda wanted to talk about the questions she'd pose to the wannabes to get them to prove their bona fides, but June said, "You still like Nick, don't you?"

"We're friends. I generally like my friends."

"You like him more than that."

"Maybe."

"Then what are you waiting for?"

"Make up your mind! I thought bad-mouthing him was your favorite hobby. Besides which, he's seeing somebody else."

"So?"

"So no poaching! Remember what you told me about girls who poach? Back in high school?"

"That was when you tried to flirt with my date! Besides if anybody poached, it was this other woman. You saw Nick first!"

"Nick chose her," Tilda said, which ended it as far as she was concerned. It took a little longer to convince June, but eventually she gave up and helped Tilda plan her attack on the Leviathans. She headed back home only after extracting a promise from Tilda to be careful.

# *Chapter 33*

Leviathan played with aquatic mythology and folklore from many cultures: Pharos was an ancient Egyptian lighthouse, Dylan O'Taine is from Welsh mythology, the Asrai and Blue Men of the Minch are Scottish, the Bunyip come from the Aboriginal Australians, and the Fosse Grim is Scandinavian.
—*TEENAGE MUTANT NINJA ARTISTS:*
*THE BEST OF INDIE COMICS* BY JERRY FRAZEE

WITH the arrangements in place, it was time to invite the final three contestants to come to the Cape. Tilda had thought it might be interesting to have all three show up at once, and then have a smackdown to see who got the Leviathan crown, but June convinced her that meeting them one at a time would probably work better.

Fortunately, all three lived within day-trip range, and had the weekend off. Though Tilda knew that Leviathan had used a Cambridge post office box back in the day, she also knew that he could have moved anywhere in the world. She was just glad she didn't have to try to play spot-the-phony via video conference.

There was a bit of back-and-forth with e-mail to get times scheduled, but eventually she had it all worked out. Contestant number one would come after lunch the next day, with the other two coming on Sunday. That was cutting it tight, since the last day of shooting would be the day after that, but she was hoping for the best.

While Tilda was hoping that just meeting the contenders would be enough to help her decide which one was really Leviathan, just in case her psychic powers were on the blink that day, she started putting together a list of questions to ask them.

She flipped through her *Pharos* comic books and came up with a couple of good questions, and then found another in the interview with Marc Fitzwilliam in the graphic novel, but she still wasn't satisfied. A good imposter might be able to bullshit his way past those hurdles. She needed something definitive, something that would leave no doubt in her mind.

She pulled out the stack of correspondence between Leviathan and Fitzwilliam and read the letters over again, and found something that might do the job. It all depended on the accuracy of Fitzwilliam's memory. She found his phone number and reached for the phone.

"Marc, this is Tilda Harper calling again."

"How's the Leviathan hunt?"

"Let me put it this way. Do you remember the time Dylan O'Taine had to fight the Asrai, and every time he defeated one, another one swam up? It's like that."

"Ouch."

"At least I've got it to the last three. I was looking at the letters that you faxed me, and I wondered about some of the edits that were made to the comic. Nobody ever did any editing on *Pharos* but you, right? You didn't have a copyeditor or anything?"

He laughed. "I didn't even have a dictionary. I had to check with Mom if there were words I didn't know."

"So you and he are the only ones who'd know what the original versions were, right?"

"Right." Before Tilda could get too excited, he added, "Only I never really changed his stories in a major way. There were just a few times I asked him to change wording, or redraw a panel."

"I see notations on your letters about 'a paragraph on page four' and 'misspelled word on page twenty-eight,' but it doesn't say what the corrections were."

"Yeah, I marked up the photocopied pages and sent them back to Leviathan—it was easier that way."

"I don't suppose you kept a photocopy of the markup."

"No, sorry. I didn't run a copy shop back then, which meant I'd have had to pay for every single page I copied. I was pinching pennies pretty tightly, so that was out. And I don't think I could remember what the original words were, if that's what you were going to ask next."

That had been exactly what she was going to ask. "What about the art? Do you remember any of those changes?"

"No, not really. Of course, if you had the pages themselves, you could see for yourself."

"Say that again."

"A few times when Leviathan sent me photocopies of completed pages, I found problems with the art on a particular panel. So I told him what I wanted done differently and he fixed it. Which means that he cut a piece of bristol board the same size and shape as the original panel and glued it onto the page. Then he made the correction."

"So I could peel off that corrected panel gently enough to see what was underneath?"

"It would depend on how he glued it down, but if they could figure out what was originally on the Sistine Chapel ceiling, there must be somebody who could do that for a comic book page."

"You're absolutely right," Tilda said.

"The thing is, I don't have any of the original pages. I sent them all back to Leviathan—it was part of our deal."

"That's all right. Thanks, Marc." Tilda hung up the phone, and then let herself get excited. Marc might not know where any of the original *Pharos* pages were, but she did. There were some just down the hall in Joni's suite.

Of course, she didn't know for sure that any of those pages had corrected panels, or if Joni would be willing to risk damaging them. So she tamped down on her glee long enough to consult her contact list, and hit the phone to do some research.

Several hours later, Tilda knocked on Joni's door. The producer was alone for once, and said, "I hope you've got good news about Leviathan."

"Not yet," Tilda admitted, "but I'm getting closer. I've got an idea for eliminating the rest of the pretenders, but I need to take a look at the pages you've got here."

"Sure thing," Joni said. The pages Dolores had fussed about carrying around were matted and shrink-wrapped in some kind of archival plastic for protection. Joni had ten different pages, and Tilda was momentarily distracted by the pleasure of seeing the original artwork in all its glory. Fortunately she wasn't so distracted that she didn't notice that a frame on a page from the final issue had been corrected. Now for the hard part.

"Joni," she said, "I need to ask a huge favor. You see how this page here has a panel that's been cut out and glued on top of the original piece of paper?"

Joni looked more closely. "You're right. I never noticed that."

"According to the man who edited *Pharos*, that panel is one where he asked Leviathan to change something, and the only way to do it was to cut out a new piece of paper, paste it down, and draw the corrected panel."

"Okay."

"I want to lift off the panel on top to see what's underneath."

"Why?"

"Because nobody has seen that original panel except the editor and Leviathan himself. So I'm going to ask the rest of the wannabes what's there." Of course, there was always the chance that Leviathan wouldn't remember, but she was betting that he would. Maybe Fitzwilliam hadn't, but he'd edited a lot of books. Leviathan had just drawn the one, and this particular panel was in a climatic section of the final issue. Surely he'd remember why he'd had to redraw it.

"Will it hurt the page?" Joni asked.

"Not if it's done properly, and I just happen to have just the right person for the job." It had taken Tilda some elaborate networking to find somebody both capable and willing, but thanks to the dozens of art museums around Boston, she'd tracked down an art conservator at Harvard's Fogg Museum who was a stone comic book fan and who'd be willing to drive to the Cape for no payment other than a chance to see some of the actual pages from *Pharos*. To sweeten the pot, Tilda was throwing in some swag from *True Blood* and some reading copies of old *Power Pets* comics. "She can be here first thing in the morning to take a look, and if she's not completely sure she can do it without damaging the page, she won't even try."

Joni still looked reluctant. "Is it really necessary?"

"Well, I'd like to say that I'll be able to identify the real Leviathan just from talking to the last three people, but I'd be a lot happier if I had something concrete to prove it. This would do the job. Besides, wouldn't you like to find out what's under there?"

"You know, now that you mention it, I would. Okay, bring on your expert."

Tilda spent the rest of the day making sure she had everything in place for the meetings, which included running into town to gather a few props. For dinner, she again indulged in room service and wondered how much money she'd have to make in order to be able to afford to live somewhere like the Glenham Bars Inn full-time.

# Chapter 34

> Though artists produce excellent work on the computer, I do miss being able to see the actual pages and know that Frank Miller and Bill Sienkiewicz make mistakes, too.
> —*TEENAGE MUTANT NINJA ARTISTS: THE BEST OF INDIE COMICS* BY JERRY FRAZEE

ART conservator Patricia Houchin, a sturdy woman with a firm handshake and thick glasses, arrived at Tilda's door a few minutes before eight the next day, which impressed Tilda all the more when she found out she had driven down from Cambridge that morning. Either she was really eager, or a very fast driver, or both. The first words out of her mouth were, "Good morning. Do you have the page?"

Tilda showed it to her, and that concluded the small talk portion of their day.

With Tilda carrying the page and Patricia toting a big red toolbox, they went across the street to one of the inn's boathouses. When they'd spoken on the phone, Patricia had told Tilda that the process could be messy and that she'd need someplace with good ventilation. Tilda had played the guilt card once more and the hotel manager had provided a work area, complete with the table and strong light Patricia required.

Once Patricia had her equipment in place, Tilda handed her the page and then disappeared from sight. At least, she supposed that she must have done so, because Patricia didn't look in her direction again for the next three hours.

Patricia did keep up a running monologue as she worked: "Okay, it's in good shape, no creases. Only used adhesive along the corners, which will help. India ink? Yeah, probably. Good-quality bristol board. Not so sharp with the trimming here. Wow, look at that."

Tilda found it entertaining for the first fifteen minutes or so, but after that she resorted to playing Bejeweled on her phone, wishing she'd brought her laptop along. She supposed she could have gone to retrieve it without Patricia even noticing she was gone, but she'd promised Joni that she wouldn't let the page out of her sight, so she was stuck as Patricia pulled out an impressive selection of solvents, knives even more exact than X-ACTO blades, and a digital camera to document every step of the procedure.

Finally, almost exactly four hours after Patricia had knocked at Tilda's door, the conservator triumphantly announced, "Got it. It's coming off now."

Tilda jumped up to watch as Patricia used a shiny pair of tweezers to lift the corrected panel off of the page.

They looked at the original panel, and Patricia started to say, "I don't see why—" just as Tilda started to snicker. When she explained what she was seeing, hilarity ensued.

Once they'd wiped their eyes, Patricia carefully packed up the page and the removed panel. Joni had said that she wanted to see the panel underneath before deciding if she wanted to paste the panel back on or not. So once Patricia cleaned up the work area and took her toolbox back to her car, Tilda showed her to Joni's suite. Edwina and Dolores were there with the director, so Tilda got to show all three of them the panel.

Hilarity ensued.

After everybody settled down, Joni let Patricia get a closer look at her other original pages, and the art conservator was almost incoherent with joy.

"I've loved *Pharos* since it was first published," she said, "and I've never stopped hoping that some of the pages would show up at a convention or on eBay or somewhere. This is the first time I've had a chance to see any of them."

Joni looked on proudly as Patricia oohed and ahhed, and even let her take photos. Then she thanked her for coming and gave her some *Pharos* swag, including a signed photo of Laryea dressed as Dylan O'Taine and a spiffy *Pharos* crew jacket.

After that, Tilda offered to buy her lunch, but Patricia said she needed to get back to Cambridge. Of course Tilda was fairly sure that what she really wanted was a chance to show off her new toys, but she could understand that. She wouldn't have minded getting one of those jackets herself.

It was just as well Patricia was in a hurry. The first Leviathan wannabe was due in a little over an hour, which didn't give Tilda much time to grab a bite and get prepped. And now she was sure that she had a question that only the real Leviathan could answer correctly.

# Chapter 35

The Fosse Grim wasn't so much evil as greedy. He used his Siren Pipe to play seductive songs that enticed sailors to throw their treasure overboard, but when the entranced men also threw over their food supplies, condemning themselves to starvation, Dylan O'Taine had to intervene.

—*TEENAGE MUTANT NINJA ARTISTS:*
*THE BEST OF INDIE COMICS* BY JERRY FRAZEE

FIVE minutes after shaking Roy Coombs's hand, Tilda knew that June had been absolutely right about meeting the remaining members of the Leviathan legion in person. Via e-mail, Coombs had come across as sincere and sensitive. In person, he sounded and acted like a used car salesman. It wasn't just the studied casualness of his sport coat and khakis, or the slight overuse of hair product. It was the plastic smile.

Still, it had been twenty years, and maybe those two decades had converted the creator of Dylan O'Taine to a fast-talker. So she went through the protocol she and June had devised.

Instead of inviting Coombs to her suite, Tilda had asked if the inn had a small function room she could borrow, and the hotel—still in make-Tilda-happy-so-she-won't-sue mode—had swiftly provided one. Tilda had also asked for and received chairs and a table. Dom had loaned her Hoover to act as security, and he was sitting to one side, out of the way but visibly and muscularly present.

Coombs was right on time.

"Mr. Coombs," Tilda said, offering him her hand. "I'm Tilda Harper. I really appreciate your coming down here today. I know it isn't easy to get away on short notice."

"It's my pleasure. Knowing that somebody still appreciates my work is so gratifying." He looked around the mostly empty room. "Will the movie people be joining us later?"

Tilda hadn't said anything about movie people being involved, or even implied it. "Maybe later. Right now, I'm just so excited to have a chance to meet the man behind Leviathan."

She started by asking about the sources of Dylan O'Taine and other characters in *Pharos*, even though they'd already discussed it via e-mail. Then she brought up the lighthouse again. June had recommended softball questions as a way to relax him before going for the jugular.

Coombs rattled off the answers about studying mythology, and when he'd first seen the Monomoy Point Lighthouse. "It just spoke to me, Tilda. I knew that it was exactly what I needed in the comic."

"It is beautiful," Tilda said. "You know, we've mostly spoken about the writing in *Pharos*. My bias, of course, since I'm a writer myself. What about the art? How did you learn to draw like that?" That was another one of June's suggestions.

"Self-taught," he said promptly. "I was always doo-dling as a boy. I can't tell you how many times my teachers got annoyed at me."

"I can imagine." Then, as if it had just occurred to her, she said, "Do you think you could draw something for me? Maybe a picture of Dylan, or the lighthouse?"

"Oh, I'm sorry, you didn't tell me that you wanted me to bring my sketch pad, so—"

"I have one right here." She handed over a brand-new pad and pencil. "According to your reply to the reader letters in the last issue of *Pharos*, those are the brands you like to work with."

"Wow, that's some attention to detail," he said, his smile a bit strained. "But I'm really rusty—just haven't got the time to draw anymore. I don't think I've picked up a drawing pencil in years."

"Understood," Tilda said. "This isn't for publication, anyway, just for a big fan. Please?"

Coombs swallowed, but had a go at it. Tilda busied herself with her papers, pretending she didn't see him referring to the stack of *Pharos* comic books on the table.

After fifteen minutes of what must have been pure torture for the man, he said, "Wow, I'm even rustier than I thought. This is embarrassing."

"Let's have a look," Tilda said.

"Honestly, I hate for anybody to see this." He tried to close the pad, but Hoover reached over him to take it and hand it to Tilda.

She stared at the so-called sketch for a full minute before finally saying, "You have got to be kidding me. I've seen infants do a better job with anatomy than this."

"Did I mention that I was in a car accident some years back? I lost a lot of dexterity in my drawing hand. I can still write—I'll have no problem signing autographs—but drawing is another story."

Tilda pointedly poised her pen over her pad. "Where were you treated? Who was your doctor?"

"Actually, I was overseas at the time."

"Where?"

"Mexico?" he said.

Tilda decided there was no need to bring in her big gun, the mystery of the corrected panel. She just looked at Coombs, waiting for him to break. Hoover told her later that he had timed it, and that it took exactly two minutes and twenty-seven seconds.

That's when Coombs said, "Okay, you got me. I'm not really Leviathan."

"No kidding."

"Hey, you can't blame a guy for trying. My nephew goes to those comic book shows all the time, and told me how much he pays for an autograph from some fat boy in a Spider-Man T-shirt. He's the one who told me how you were looking for this Leviathan guy and I got the idea to fake it. I figured it might be a good gig—I could go to those shows, sign some autographs, pose for pictures, make some extra cash. My nephew helped me study up so I could answer your questions."

"Did it never occur to you that you'd have to prove you can draw?"

"At first I didn't realize that the same guy wrote and drew *Pharos*. With most comics, it's different guys, right? By the time I found out I was supposed to be an artist, we'd gone back and forth by e-mail half a dozen times. I thought I had you fooled."

"You were fairly convincing," Tilda had to admit.

"Look, you still need a Leviathan for this article, right? Rather than get you in trouble, why don't we just say I'm him? Who's going to know? I'll even cut you in for a percentage of the profits when I start hitting the comic book shows." He nodded at Hoover. "The big guy, too. Hell, he can be my roadie. It's a win-win proposition. What do you say?"

"Forget it. For one, I don't roll that way. For another, I said you were fairly convincing—I never said you had me convinced. I've dealt with over a dozen people claiming to be Leviathan. You're just one of the crowd, and with you eliminated, I'm that much closer to the real person."

Coombs shrugged. "Nothing ventured, nothing gained." He stood and offered his hand again, but this time Tilda wasn't inclined to shake. Maybe he hadn't lost anything, but he'd sure wasted a lot of her time.

Hoover tapped him on the shoulder, and escorted him out of the room. Assuming he kept to the plan, he'd be sticking with Coombs until he drove out of the parking lot.

"One down," Tilda said to the empty room, "two to go."

# Chapter 36

South Monomoy Island, home of the Monomoy Point Light-house, may soon be a tourist destination. The lighthouse, which was in operation from 1823 to 1923, is the inspiration for the mystic fortress of Dylan O'Taine in the comic book *Pharos*, and is featured in the forthcoming movie of the same name.

—"MASSACHUSETTS'S MYSTICAL LIGHTHOUSE" BY
TILDA HARPER, *YANKEE MAGAZINE*

TILDA'S next interview wasn't scheduled until the next day, leaving her at loose ends, so she took a chance and called Joni and Edwina to see if they were available that evening. It turned out they had nothing pressing planned, and they invited Tilda to join them for dinner and conversation.

Afterward, Tilda was convinced that all interviews should be conducted in plush hotel suites while eating takeout Chinese food and guzzling beer. She'd rarely had subjects get so open—the only downside was having to monitor her own beer consumption to ensure her notes would be legible the next day.

The two partners were both from New England, but came from such opposite backgrounds that it made them a nearly perfect match.

Joni's family was artsy and despite encouraging her to do anything she wanted with herself, as long as it was creative and life-affirming, they were somewhat non-plussed when she dove into the startlingly commercial world of moviemaking.

Edwina was from New England blue blood stock, and her family had carefully planned out her life from kin-dergarten all the way to achieving partner in the right law firm. They were flabbergasted when, after a chance meeting with John Laryea, she ended up moving in with him—in California, of all places. And even she herself was surprised to find out how much she liked the cre-ativity of Hollywood. The relationship with John didn't last, but her love of moviemaking did.

Ironically, both partners had spent their summers on the Cape when growing up, but since Joni's folks were immersed in the arts community of Provincetown while Edwina's family had a summer home in Chatham, they'd never have met without Laryea. He introduced them just about the time his relationship with Edwina was ending— he'd dated Joni two years earlier.

The women had been working together ever since, often with Dolores as screenwriter, and their reputation was growing steadily. After several movies, they had plenty of good stories, too.

Even though Tilda had officially handed off Fos-ter's murder to Dom and Nick, she did sneak in a few questions about how the women got along with Laryea. But even under the influence of their third beers, nei-ther woman showed anything but affection for him. It was somewhat amused affection, as neither of them was blind to his faults, but still sincere. She noticed that neither of them made even a veiled reference to his height, or lack thereof, and that said a lot about their relationships right there.

As the evening wore on, Tilda gave up on taking notes. For one, she no longer trusted her handwriting. For another, the reminiscences about Laryea were getting too raunchy for any of the markets she was likely to sell to.

Tilda finally bagged on them at midnight, wanting to make sure she got a full night's sleep before the next day's meetings.

# Chapter 37

Ceto, who commands the Asrai, is the nastiest of Dylan O'Taine's enemies. The Asrai themselves are transparent, but Ceto can take on the aspect of any person who ever died in the ocean. When O'Taine reveals her actual hideous appearance, she swears vengeance.

—*TEENAGE MUTANT NINJA ARTISTS:*
*THE BEST OF INDIE COMICS* BY JERRY FRAZEE

ANDREW Kiel showed up at a few minutes after ten, dressed neatly in jeans and a button-down denim shirt. According to his e-mails, he worked for a software company in Cambridge that developed products for managing online relationships through the use of asynchronous electronic messages. Tilda had made a note to remind herself to avoid ever asking about that work.

They introduced themselves and shook hands, and Tilda was about to sit down when Kiel offered his hand to Hoover and said, "And you are?"

"Carmine Hoover," he said, surprised. "Tolomeo Personal Protection."

"Is there some danger I should be aware of?"

"Just a precaution," Tilda said, figuring that was vague enough to cover contingencies. "Won't you have a seat?"

"Certainly. I can't tell you how exciting this is for

me. My work on *Pharos* was so long ago, and normally I'm not one for looking back, but this is different. The movie deal and all. Who would have thought this would happen?"

"I write about Hollywood, but don't ever ask me to explain how it all works."

He laughed. "What can I do for you? I'm guessing you want to make sure that I'm really Leviathan."

"Why do you say that?"

"The waves of requests for information, the timing . . . I don't blame you for being suspicious. There are plenty of people who wouldn't hesitate to claim another person's creative work. I find that sad, don't you?"

Kiel was the first one to acknowledge the possibility of other pretenders to the *Pharos* throne, and Tilda honestly didn't know if that made her trust him more or less. She wished she'd made June come back for the interviews.

Since it was too late for that, she settled for her sister's recommended protocol. That meant starting in on the easy questions, all of which Kiel answered while giving the impression that he was patiently humoring her. But when she brought up the Monomoy Point Lighthouse, he said, "Didn't we go over this in e-mail?"

"E-mail isn't the same as real-life conversation."

He raised an eyebrow as if disputing that, but didn't object further.

"But moving on from our e-mail interactions, I realized in retrospect that I only asked about the writing of *Pharos*, not the drawing."

"It's an understandable bias, since you're just a writer.

Most people aren't used to creative artists who work in more than one medium." He hesitated. "I'm sorry, but perhaps I shouldn't have assumed that you don't have any other talent."

She bared her teeth and said, "Actually, my art teacher said I made the best egg carton dragons she'd ever seen, but it's been a while since I've devoted any time to the form. Can you tell me where you learned to draw?"

"Rhode Island School of Design. Unfortunately I never graduated. I had a run-in with a professor who didn't think that comic book art was a worthy subject, and when he made it clear that he wasn't going to pass me, I dropped out." He shrugged. "I probably should have tried for some sort of compromise, but at the time I was younger and more hot-blooded. As an artist, I felt very strongly about following my muse."

"How long did you attend?"

"Nearly three years, and for most of that time, I thrived. That much talent concentrated in one place . . . It was one of the few places I'd felt completely comfortable with myself. We were all so focused on the work, but we partied just as hard." He smiled. "You know, I was the one who first came up with Scrotie."

"Scrotie?"

"Our unofficial school mascot. Short for scrotum."

"You mean somebody dresses up as a pair of balls—"

"As a penis, actually, not just the scrotum."

"So he dresses up as a penis and prances around basketball games?"

"I think official college history says he didn't appear until 2001, but I know I came up with a couple of designs for the costume back when I was a student. I dropped out before I had a chance to build them."

Tilda looked at her pad, trying extremely hard not to picture Kiel in a penis costume. "I've been wondering why you never drew comics after *Pharos*."

"Because of this." He held up his hand, and there was a noticeable tremor.

"Parkinson's?"

"Drugs. After I dropped out, which was around the time *Pharos* wrapped up, I went wild for a few years. My family cut me off, so I was living hand-to-mouth, crashing at friends' apartments and indulging in too many recreational chemicals. One day I woke up and could barely snap my jeans because of my hands shaking. I went into rehab that same day. But even when I got clean, the shaking never went away. The doctors say I've got an underlying genetic condition, and the drugs accelerated a process that might not have shown up for years otherwise. They don't think it's fatal, but they don't really know. There's not enough data." He smiled ruefully. "It's so rare, it doesn't even have a name yet— my doctor wants to call it Kiel's Syndrome, but all those decisions are political, so it may not happen."

"So you can't draw anymore?"

"I still dabble, but of course I'm not as sharp as I once was. I could probably manage a halfway decent Dylan O'Taine if that's what you're asking."

"I was hoping to score a sketch," she admitted, "but if you're not up to it . . ."

"I can only try. No doubt you brought along a pad and pencil for the purpose."

The guy was definitely getting on her nerves, but she handed him a fresh pad and drawing pencil.

Kiel fumbled a bit, but eventually produced a rough drawing of O'Taine in front of the lighthouse that was reasonably faithful to the artwork in the comic. The signature was good, too, though Leviathan had such a stylized signature that it was more logo than handwriting, and easy to fake.

"For you," he said, writing *To Tilda, who Doubted* on the top of the page. "At least I hope the doubt is past tense. Or do you have more tests for me?"

"Just one last question," Tilda asked, and she couldn't have said if she expected him to know the answer or not. His answers had been fine, but she just didn't like him. That didn't necessarily mean anything, but she hated the idea of a comic she liked as much as *Pharos* being created by a guy she disliked so thoroughly.

"I've been in contact with Marc Fitzwilliam—," she said.

"My old editor from Regal?"

"That's right. He sent me copies of the letters you two exchanged, and there are a couple of comments I was curious about. At one point he asked for a change to one of the panels, and though he didn't say in his letter what the problem was, he was pretty amused about it. Unfortunately he doesn't remember what the change was."

"And?"

"I thought you might know." She pulled out the graphic novel of *Pharos* and pointed to the pertinent panel. "It's this one here, with O'Taine on top of the sea horse."

"Good God! You don't really expect me to remember,

do you? It was twenty years ago. If remembering one little edit is your criteria for judging my authenticity, I may as well leave right now." He stood up and glared at her.

Out of the corner of her eye, Tilda saw Hoover moving closer, and didn't react. Kiel must have seen him, too, because he held up his hands as if in surrender and sat back down.

"Sorry, but I don't have a lot of patience for playing games."

"No game," Tilda said. "If you don't know, you don't."

"Let me explain something about myself that might make it clear to you. When I finish a project, I'm done. I move on. That makes working with an editor extremely difficult for me. All the nitpicky changes Fitzwilliam asked for were like exhuming a corpse and dissecting it, only to sew it back together like Frankenstein's monster. I did it, but I hated every minute. Is it any wonder the details didn't stay in my mind?"

"I suppose not."

"I've already told you about my days as a druggie. My body wasn't the only thing to suffer—my memory was affected, too."

"I see," Tilda said, wondering how much longer a man who claimed he didn't like playing games was going to keep playing this one.

"If I had the page itself here, I could rip the corrected panel off to show what I'd originally drawn, which was almost certainly superior to whatever inane change Fitzwilliam required. But I don't have the art anymore."

"Actually—"

"I know, you were going to ask about the pages,

weren't you? As if my having them would prove anything! The fact is I don't have any of that work anymore—nobody does. I burned it."

"Excuse me?"

"When I was living on the streets, the last thing I wanted was to drag those things along with me. So I burned them in a metal drum to keep me and a trio of other street people warm one night. Now I suppose you'll want the names of the homeless men so you can verify my story."

"I'll pass." She reached into the bottom of the pile of things on the table, and pulled out the mounted page she'd borrowed back from Joni. "As it turns out, I've got that page right here."

"That's not possible." Kiel reached for it, but Tilda drew it back and Hoover stood right at his elbow. "It's a counterfeit."

Tilda just looked at him.

"Or perhaps it's an early draft. That's probably what happened. Rather than endure replacing a single panel to make Fitzwilliam happy, I redrew the entire page. I gave that one to a girlfriend. The real one was the one I burned with the rest of the pages."

"I can lay my hands on nine more original pages," Tilda said. "Did you give those to your girlfriend, too?"

"You're insane!" Kiel snarled, standing so abruptly he knocked his chair over. "No, I know what this is. It's some sort of con game. Well, Tilda—if that's your name—I don't know what you're trying to pull, but you'll be hearing from my lawyer. I'm not going to put up with this. Do you know who my family is?"

"I thought your family cut you off?"

Kiel grabbed the pad Tilda had lent him and for a second it looked as if he was going to throw it at her, but he petulantly threw it to the floor, and she wouldn't have been surprised if he'd jumped up and down on it a few times to complete the toddler imitation. Instead he stomped from the room, pausing just long enough to point a finger at her and say, "You watch your back!"

Hoover was right behind him, talking into his mouthpiece as he went, so she wasn't surprised when Nick rushed into the room a few minutes later.

"He's gone," he said, "and we've sent a car after him to make sure he leaves the Cape. Are you okay?"

"I'm fine."

"I hear that guy went apeshit."

"Please. The guy's an amateur. I was there when somebody tried to pull off William Shatner's toupee. Now *that* man knows how to throw a tantrum!"

# Chapter 38

The Blue Men of the Minch preyed on unwary sailors by
trapping their ships in a magic whirlpool. Then the Chieftain
challenged the ship captains to a battle of wits. If the captain
won, the ship went free—if not, the whirlpool swallowed it.
—*TEENAGE MUTANT NINJA ARTISTS:*
*THE BEST OF INDIE COMICS* BY JERRY FRAZEE

AFTER Kiel's outburst, Tilda was happy to take a lunch
break before the last meeting. Already a flood of fiery,
profane spam had begun to arrive from Kiel and from
e-mail addresses supposedly belonging to Kiel's fans,
but which she suspected were from the loser himself.
Though she didn't think he'd do anything but blow
smoke, she carefully saved all of them while deciding if
she wanted to go after him for harassment. It might be
educational. The man's use of invective was so imagina-
tive that it deserved to be shared in open court.

Her welcoming smile when Bruce Williford walked
in was completely sincere. Not only was he the last Leviathan standing, but he looked the part of a comic book
artist who'd given up the life. He was of medium height,
with reddish brown hair, a deceptively boyish face, and a
shape that would be described as cuddly rather than buff.

She wasn't quite as happy to see the woman with him, since she didn't remember inviting anybody else.

"Bruce?" she said.

"You must be Tilda," he said. She thought he sounded nervous, and this was confirmed by the dampness of his handshake. "This is my fiancée, Sibyl Chenault."

Sibyl was a few years younger and not quite as cuddly looking as Bruce. Though she was cute enough, it was the almost white blonde hair that fell to her waist that really stood out.

"Won't you sit down?" Tilda said. "It's a real honor to meet Leviathan."

Sibyl beamed, but Bruce looked embarrassed as Hoover brought over another chair, then returned to his post.

Even though Tilda was sure Bruce was the guy, she still wanted to go through the protocol. So she started on the warm-up questions. The answers were prompt, thorough, and as far as she knew, correct. They just weren't from Bruce.

Tilda said, "You used a variety of mythological sources for *Pharos*. Do you have an academic background in folklore?"

"Bruce just loves studying different mythologies," Sibyl said. "You wouldn't believe the research library he has. After we get married, we're going to have to dedicate a whole room to the nonfiction books."

Bruce nodded.

Tilda said, "Since you're so close, will you be taking a trip to see the lighthouse on which you modeled Dylan O'Taine's?"

"No, we won't have time," Sibyl said. "It takes an hour to get to South Monomoy Island, and it can get pretty cold this time of year. We're planning to go when we come back in the spring for our honeymoon."

Bruce shook his head to the first part, and nodded to the second.

"In our e-mails, I mostly asked about the writing in *Pharos*. What about the art? Did you study formally?"

"Oh, no," Sibyl assured her. "Bruce is completely self-taught. Isn't it wonderful?" She looked adoringly at him.

Bruce looked modestly at his feet.

"Bruce, do you think you could draw something for me? Maybe a picture of Dylan O'Taine, or the lighthouse? If you don't have a sketch pad—"

"Oh, we always carry a pad." Sibyl pulled out a pad just like the ones Tilda had bought, albeit more battered, and a zippered pouch from which she produced a pencil. "Draw Dylan, Bruce."

He, of course, nodded. Then he took only a moment or two to consider before he drew Dylan O'Taine in his study. But instead of one of studying one of his spell books, O'Taine was reading a copy of *Entertain Me!* with Melusine on the cover. Almost as an afterthought, Bruce added the stylized signature at the bottom.

"That's amazing!" Tilda said. Not only was it cute as hell, but it was clearly Leviathan's style. "Can I keep it?"

"Sure," he said, and tore it from the spiral binding to hand it to her.

Sibyl patted his arm proudly, but Bruce still looked embarrassed about the whole thing. Tilda didn't know how the poor guy was going to react to the limelight he was about to be thrust into, but she figured that Sibyl could handle it.

Now that she was sure he was Leviathan, she went on to ask Bruce more questions. At least she tried to, and did look directly at him, but Sibyl answered every time. Tilda figured she could either have Hoover drag the woman out by the scruff of her neck, or go with the flow. She went with the flow.

"Why did you quit drawing comics after *Pharos* was cancelled?" she asked.

"Bruce's father died just as the last issue came out, and he had to quit college to help his mother. Her health was pretty bad, too, and he spent most of the next few years caring for her. He just didn't have the time or energy for art."

"Why didn't you ever come forward as Leviathan?"

"I guess you can see how shy Bruce is. Besides, he didn't think anybody would care. Isn't that crazy? It wasn't until he got involved in our group—we do Leviathan fan fiction and fan art—that he realized how much people still love his work."

"Didn't the news about the *Pharos* movie convince him that there was still interest?" She realized she'd forgotten to aim the question at Bruce, but nobody else seemed to notice.

"Sure, but he didn't know who to talk to—it's not like he's had any contact with the Hollywood people, and he's sure not getting any of the money." Sibyl sniffed indignantly. "And he wasn't sure anybody would believe him, after all those years. As if anybody else could fake his talent." She patted his arm again. "I had to talk him into answering your e-mail on the *Pharos* board."

It all made perfect sense to Tilda, and with what she'd already gotten via e-mail, it was going to make a terrific article. She couldn't wait to introduce Bruce to Joni so they could talk about the *Pharos* script. There was always the chance that Bruce, or even worse Sibyl, wouldn't like it, but Tilda didn't think it was likely.

"There's just one last thing," she said. "Marc Fitzwilliam from Regal Comics—"

"That sleaze? You know Bruce never got a cent from all the reprints of *Pharos*? And Fitzwilliam kept all the original pages, too! Bruce doesn't have a single one. Fitzwilliam probably sold them."

"Really?" Tilda said, trying to sound noncommittal as she made a mental note to check on that. Fitzwilliam had told her that Leviathan kept all the art, and she'd assumed that Leviathan had sold the pages himself. Of course, that had been on the phone, not in person, and June had warned her about how hard it was to judge lies that way. "If it makes you feel better, Marc isn't getting any of the movie money either."

"Good!"

"I spoke to him about the editing process, and he sent me a copy of a letter in which you discussed having to redraw some of the panels." She pulled out the graphic novel, opened it to the pertinent page, and handed it to Bruce. Sibyl actually let him take it. "It's that bottom right panel, with O'Taine on top of the sea horse. Fitzwilliam's letter to you said, 'You better look at that one again—ha ha ha,' and your response was, 'I cannot believe I didn't see that. Ha ha ha.' I'm dying to find out what was so funny."

"Doesn't Fitzwilliam know?" Bruce asked for himself, to Tilda's surprise.

She shook her head.

He looked at the page for a minute, then said, "Oh, yeah now I remember. You see how O'Taine is holding the Horn of Panlong? It's kind of tucked under his left arm, which is wounded. I originally had him holding it in his left hand, so he could hold on to the sea horse with his right hand. But since he was wounded, the left hand was in his lap. With the Horn kind of sticking out from between his legs, it looked like . . . You know. He was playing with himself or something."

Sibyl let out a little gasp, and then started giggling. "You never told me about that."

He shrugged, but for once, didn't look embarrassed. Instead he looked proud of himself, and Tilda didn't blame him. He'd come up with a totally convincing lie on the spur of the moment.

"Really?" she said. "I can see why you didn't want O'Taine playing with himself. What I don't understand is why you're playing with me."

"What's that supposed to mean?" Sibyl asked.

Tilda pulled out the actual page and the panel Patricia had removed. "I've got the artwork right here. We brought in an art conservator to help us out." She held up the piece Patricia had so carefully removed. "Here's the panel that was used." Then she held up the actual page. "And here's the page with the original panel."

Hoover moved up, just in case Bruce or Sibyl tried to rip the thing out of Tilda's hands, but the couple barely moved. They just stared at the page.

The panel in the comic book showed a wounded Dylan O'Taine astride a giant sea horse, about to ride into battle. The original drawing had him behind the sea horse, hunched over as he dragged himself onto the saddle, and the expressions on both O'Taine's and the sea horse's faces made for a very different interpretation of what was going on.

Tilda had laughed like an idiot the first time she saw it, but neither Bruce nor Sibyl seemed to find it amusing.

"I don't understand," Sibyl said. "Bruce, were you thinking of a different page?"

He didn't answer.

"I mean, if you've just forgotten, just say so. It's been a long time."

Bruce still didn't answer.

"It doesn't make sense." She looked at Tilda. "What are you trying to do?"

"All I'm trying to do is find Leviathan."

"But you've found him! Bruce is Leviathan. Tell her, Bruce."

"I'm sorry, Sibyl," he said in a low voice.

"There's nothing for you to be sorry about. You just forgot what was under that panel, or mixed it up with another one."

"No, that's not it. I lied, Sibyl. I'm not Leviathan."

"Of course you are. That's how we got together. It's been our secret, but now we can tell everybody. You're Leviathan. I'm going to marry Leviathan."

"I'm not Leviathan," he repeated.

"Then who are you?"

"I'm Bruce Williford. That's all I am. But I love you, Sibyl." He reached toward her, but she hopped out of her chair.

"Don't touch me! You lied to me! You've been lying to me all along."

"Not about everything. I do love you, and I want to marry you."

"Go to hell!" She grabbed up her bag and stormed out of the room.

Bruce stared after her miserably, and Tilda was afraid he was going to break down, but he took a couple of choking breaths and held it together. "I'm sorry," he said, not looking at her. "I didn't think it would go this far."

Tilda couldn't think of a solitary thing to say, so she just nodded. Hoover started to step forward, but she stopped him with a look. She could tell that Bruce wasn't going to get violent.

He just picked up his pad and pencil and slumped out of the room.

"Shit," Hoover said.

"Yeah."

"You okay?"

"Nope."

"I better go make sure they're not causing any trouble."

"I think I'll just stay here and hate on myself for a while."

"Hey, don't beat yourself up. You know?"

"Yeah, I know."

He left, and she reflected that she knew too damn much. She knew that she'd ruined a marriage before it even happened, and she knew that she hadn't found Leviathan and had no idea where else to look.

# Chapter 39

**Episode 6**
In a retelling of *Cyrano de Bergerac*, Sid and Marty help
Posit win the love of a glamorous lady alien by making it look
as if he's the one singing their love songs. When the deception
is revealed, the lady at first spurns Posit, but is won over by
his skill at drumming.
—*SATURDAY MORNING SPREE* BY CHARLES M. LUCE

TILDA expected Bruce and Sibyl to be long gone by the
time she finished kicking the wall and packing up, but
when she left the function room, she saw the two of
them in the lobby.

"At least let me take you home," Bruce was saying.

"Go away, Bruce," Sibyl said with great finality.

There was nothing the guy could do but turn away
and trudge out the door. Sibyl maintained her impla-
cable air until he was out of sight, then started sobbing.

Tilda rolled her eyes and sighed heavily, then went
to the bathroom, grabbed a handful of tissues out of the
holder, and brought it out to thrust at the crying woman.

"Thanks," Sibyl sniffed, then spent another five minutes wiping her eyes and blowing her nose.

When Tilda thought she was done, she asked, "I hate
to ask this, but how are you going to get home?"

"I don't know!" Sibyl wailed, and the tears flowed freely once more.

Tilda took another trip to the bathroom for another wad of tissues. Then while Sibyl sniffled, she went just out of earshot to use her cell phone. When she returned to Sibyl, who was at least temporarily back in control of herself, she said, "Look, one of the security guys has to go back to Boston tonight. He'll take you along, if you want."

"Really? That would be great. I was afraid that I'd have to call my mother, and I don't think I could handle that right now. She never liked Bruce."

"The only problem is that he's busy for another couple of hours, so you'll have to wait around."

"That's okay." Sibyl looked around the lobby as if gauging its comfort level.

Tilda had every intention of going her own way, but made the mistake of looking at Sibyl again. That reminded her of the time she broke up with a boyfriend on Valentine's Day, and how a guy she barely knew had taken pity on her and comforted her with ice cream. She and Cooper had been fast friends ever since. She owed it to what Dylan O'Taine would call the Cosmic Balance to return the favor.

She said, "Look, the bar here makes a pretty good cosmo. Let's go get a buzz on."

With most of the film crew out prepping the next day's location, the bar was nearly empty, and the bartender was happy to bring them cosmos and a bowl of pretzels.

Of course, Tilda knew she'd have to sit through the

tale of Sibyl's and Bruce's ill-fated love affair, but as long as the waiter kept the drinks coming, she figured she could interject the right questions and maintain the correct facial expressions.

"I should have known he was lying!" Sibyl said. "He only pretended to be Leviathan because he knew I was a huge fan of *Pharos*."

"Then you knew each other already?"

She nodded. "A bunch of us from a comics fanfic board got together at Boskone a few years ago. Bruce said he really liked my stories, but now I don't know whether to believe him or not."

Worried that the tears were about to return, Tilda asked, "Did he tell you right away that he was Leviathan?"

"No, not for a long time. We saw each other several times at cons before he said anything about it. But when we were at Arisia the next year, he asked if he could talk to me alone over dinner. That's when he pulled out his sketchbooks and told me." She almost smiled as she said, "He said that if *Pharos* hadn't been cancelled, my stories were just the kind of thing he'd have wanted to do. But I suppose he was making that up, too. He just wanted to get into my pants."

The next round arrived, and Tilda gave her drink a moment's attention before saying, "He has Leviathan's style down cold. I wonder how many other girls he used that story on."

"Bruce would never have done that," Sibyl said, sounding shocked.

"Seriously? There are a lot of *Pharos* fans—he could have used those sketches to get some serious booty."

"Not Bruce!"

"But once he bagged you, he moved on, right?"

"Of course not! We've been . . . We dated for almost three years."

"And he treated you well?"

"Oh, yeah, we get along great."

Tilda noticed Sibyl had switched back to present tense. "Is he good in bed?"

"Tilda!" Sibyl said. Then she giggled, no doubt thanks to her second cosmo, and said, "Yeah, he really is."

"A nice-looking guy, treats you well, good in the sack . . . But you never considered dating him before he told you he was Leviathan?"

"Not really. I mean, he was nice and all, but I just never thought about him in that way."

The third set of drinks arrived just as Tilda came up with a plan. "I wonder how long it took him to learn how to draw like Leviathan. I'm no artist, but I wouldn't think it would be an easy style to master."

"He knew exactly what he was doing," Sibyl said with an indignant sniff.

"He must have been pretty motivated to put in all that time just to get your attention. It's not like he was desperate or anything. Nice-looking, knows how to treat a woman, good in bed . . . Yet he did that just to get to you. It's kind of flattering."

"I hadn't thought of it that way," Sibyl said, stirring her cosmo.

"Not that he was right to lie, of course, but tell me the truth. If he'd shown you his drawings without saying he was Leviathan, just said he was a *Pharos* fan, would you have been interested in him?"

"I'll never know now, will I?" Sibyl said, but she wouldn't meet Tilda's eyes.

"But you said you'd known him awhile, right? Maybe he thought that this was the only way he could get you to date him. And if he hadn't, you wouldn't have realized what a great guy he is."

"Yeah, real great. For a phony."

"But now that you know—" Then Tilda waved her hand, as if brushing the idea aside. "No, you can never trust him again. I get that."

"Never!" Sibyl said.

They sipped in silence for a few minutes, then Tilda went for broke. "You know, since you're not going to be seeing Bruce anymore anyway, would you mind if I called him?"

"Are you serious?"

"I'm between boyfriends, and I already know he's not Leviathan, so that's not going to bother me. And if he's that good in bed . . ." Tilda looked at Sibyl. "You don't care, do you? I mean, you said you were through with him."

"I am. Definitely."

"Then you don't mind?"

Sibyl opened her mouth, then closed it, then opened it again to say, "Hell yes, I mind! I love that idiot!"

"But you said—"

"I know what I said, and I know exactly what you're doing. You're saying that I'm a moron for not noticing what a great guy he was and making him come up with this whole Leviathan thing to get my attention, and I'd be an even bigger moron to let him go now."

"I just hate to see a good guy go to waste," Tilda said.

"Well you can just forget about him going to waste. Bruce is *my* good guy." Sibyl pulled a cell phone out of her purse, and pressed the first number on her speed dial. "Bruce," she said, "it's me. I've changed my mind. I'd really like you to take me home. . . . Yes, you will have to make it up to me, but maybe I've got some things to make up to you, too. . . . Okay, I'll meet you outside."

"How far did he get?" Tilda asked.

"He's in the parking lot," Sibyl said with a happy grin. "He said he was too upset to drive back to Boston."

"Sibyl, I can be a lousy judge of my own relationships, but I really think he's a keeper."

"I think you're right." The bartender, sensing they'd come to the end of their debauchery, slipped a check onto the table, and Sibyl reached for her wallet.

"Nope, this is on me," Tilda said. "You go get your guy."

"Thanks, Tilda."

"You can thank my friend Cooper if you ever meet him."

She looked confused, but just nodded and ran out.

Tilda considered getting another cosmo, but figured being a professional failure was painful enough. There was no reason to add a hangover to the mix.

# Chapter 40

"It's no secret that Quasit was inspired by Posit," Wilder said. "I started out using Posit, but the studio objected. I hear Marvel Comics did the same thing to Sonic Man, who started out as Spider-Man. I wasn't trying to steal the character—I just have such great memories of my time on *The Blastoffs*."
—"Hey Kids! It's Cartoon Time!"
by Tilda Harper, *Entertain Me!*

TILDA went upstairs to her room and called around in search of sympathy, but her luck continued to suck. June was at an open house at the kids' school, Cooper was at a party, and Nick was busy getting ready for tomorrow's shoot. If that weren't depressing enough, he said that Dom and he had made no progress in clearing Pete Ellis of the hit-and-run. Maybe if it had happened during the summer, when the Cape was busier, there might have been another witness around, but all they had was Tilda, who hadn't seen enough to help.

She was tempted to hide in her room, but she was tired of room service. In fact, she was tired of the hotel. It was time to get out and go somewhere else, anywhere else. The clerk at the front desk gave her directions to the Cape Cod Mall in Hyannis, which was enough like any other mall that she could forget she was even on the

Cape. She window-shopped, ate at the food court, and then wasted time and cash at the arcade. By the time she got back to the inn, she'd managed to nearly wipe out what a debacle the day had been, and was willing to stay absentminded for the rest of the evening.

Unfortunately, her luck still hadn't improved. Hugh Wilder was sitting on a bench in the lobby, and when he saw her, came right over.

"Tilda," he said, "I've been looking for you. Can we talk for a minute?"

"Sure." Tilda wondered what Wilder was going to want her to write about. Everything I Need to Know I Learned from Watching *The Blastoffs*? Chicken Soup for *Blastoffs* Fans? Ten Things about The Blastoff Brothers That Nobody Gives a Crap About? Since she was betting on the last one, she didn't want to invite him to her room because that would make it tricky to get rid of him if she got bored, so she said, "Let's see if there's a seat in the bar."

They found an empty booth and ordered sodas. Once they'd been served, Wilder said, "I've had something on my conscience, and it's been bothering me."

"Oh?"

"You know how I told you those stories about life on the set of *The Blastoffs*? How it was one big happy family, and how the kids were such good kids? The fact is, I haven't been completely honest with you."

"Really?" Was she finally going to get some dirt about Laryea?

"You know young men can get a little wild. Especially in Hollywood. Good-looking, a little money in their pockets . . . I'm sure you've heard all the stories about Britney Spears and Lindsay Lohan, so you know what can happen when young people aren't supervised properly. The fact is, there was some of that going on on the set. The producers didn't want a scandal, so they told us to just pretend we didn't see the empty bottles, or smell the wacky tobaccy, or hear the noises coming from the dressing room."

"So Laryea was a bit of a party animal when he was young?" Tilda asked, not particularly shocked. But what Wilder said next did shock her.

"Oh, no, not John. He was always a good kid. We never had a minute's worry with John. It was the other guy. Spencer Marshall. He was a born troublemaker."

"Marshall was a troublemaker?" Tilda said, not sure she'd heard him right.

"From day one. I tried to stay away from him myself, because he tended to blame other people for his mistakes. If he missed a line, it was because somebody had given him the wrong script. If he missed his mark, it was because somebody pushed him or got in his way. It was never his fault."

"Really?"

"Plus he had a temper, and a mean streak, too. There was an incident with a girl on the set. I never did hear the details, but if the rumors were true, he did a lot more than lose his temper with her."

"He always seemed so nice on the show."

"He did a good job on camera, I'll give him that. But once the lights went out? It was like night and day. After a while I started to wonder if there was something wrong with the boy. Psychologically, I mean. You know how some kids get off on playing with fire? Well Marshall had this lighter he carried everywhere, and was always flicking it open and staring at the flame. Kind of creepy." He paused as if deciding how much more to say. "And there were incidents on the set."

"Like with the girl?"

"Like with fires. Just small ones, more smoke than anything else. But it seemed like there were a lot more than there should have been."

"I never heard word one of this." Admittedly she hadn't spent a lot of time reading up on Marshall on the Web, but nothing she'd seen had even hinted at this. "Why didn't you tell me this before?"

"It was a long time ago, and it's not like he was ever a big star. After the show ended, people pretty much forgot about him."

"Then why are you telling me now?"

"A couple of reasons. First off I've been feeling guilty about deceiving you the way I have been. I meant well—I don't like to speak ill of anybody, especially somebody who's not around."

"You said there were two reasons."

"I did. The fact is, I may have seen—I think— Look, I better not say any more until I make sure of my facts."

"Come on, you can't leave me hanging after dropping a bombshell like that."

But the older man shook his head. "No, it just wouldn't be right. You know what Posit used to say: 'Gossip travels faster than light—don't repeat it unless you know that it's right.'"

Tilda pushed a little, but could see that there was no

use. He'd told her as much as he was going to, and after a minute or two more, he came up with an excuse to leave.

She was just as glad. She needed a few minutes to try to digest what Wilder had told her. Could she have been that far off in her reading of Pete? Sure, she knew he'd been a drinker, but he'd started that long after *The Blast-offs* blasted off the air. Of course, the only way she knew that was because that's what he'd told her. A reporter should know better than to accept an unconfirmed story. Then there was the other stuff, the temper and the mean streak.

Wilder hadn't told her why he'd decided to spill his guts all of a sudden, but Tilda knew what the reason must be. He knew Pete Ellis was Spencer Marshall, and that Pete was there on the Cape. Could he have seen something in Pete's behavior to remind him of those earlier, nastier times? She hadn't seen anything like that, and she knew Dom hadn't either. Then again, Pete was an actor, and what had June called them? Professional liars. Tilda had recently been fooled by that actor from the *Power Pets*, so obviously her instincts weren't perfect. As for Dom, his record was solid, but was he that good?

She ran her fingers through her hair. The man Wilder had described sounded nothing like the Pete she knew— what he sounded like was the kind of man who could have gone out driving while drunk, hit somebody, and then denied it. It also sounded like the kind of man who would have gotten mad about Tilda identifying the limo, and decided to get back at her, maybe with a knife.

No, it didn't make sense. Pete couldn't have gotten

to the cottage ahead of her the night it was broken into.
Except . . . Now that she thought about it, she remembered that she'd initially gone to the wrong cottage. How
long had she spent trying to get that door open before
realizing it was the wrong one? Long enough for Pete to
slip past her and get into her cottage?

No, she told herself, he would have had no reason to
go to her cottage. It was like she'd told Nick. He could
have done anything to her he wanted on the beach.
Unless he was worried about a boater or somebody else,
whereas at her cottage, he could be assured of privacy.

Tilda couldn't imagine a worse day. She hadn't found
Leviathan, and she might have been helping a killer.
Was it any surprise that she couldn't even sleep well that
night?

# Chapter 41

Anxiety is the handmaiden of creativity.

—CHUCK JONES

THE next day was the last shooting day on the Cape, and Tilda really tried to get excited about seeing the big special effects bonanza on the beach, with Dylan O'Taine sending bolts of mystical energy from atop the lighthouse.

Of course, they weren't actually filming at the Monomoy Point Lighthouse—Tilda shuddered to think of the lawsuits that would result if they chipped the first bit of paint off that place. Instead, Laryea would be perched on a mocked-up tower. The bottom would just be bare scaffolding holding up a set that duplicated the lantern room of the real lighthouse.

But after all that she hadn't managed to accomplish, it was hard for Tilda to muster enthusiasm for doing much of anything. It was only the text message from her roommate Dianne reminding her that her share of the rent was due that motivated her into her car to drive over to the shooting location.

From the number of cars parked haphazardly up and down the beach, Tilda decided she must have been the last person on the Cape to arrive, and it took forever to find a place to park. Then when she pulled out her camera to check the charge, she remembered that her last memory card was already full from the day she'd spent following the second-unit crew around. "Proving once again what a consummate professional I am," she muttered to herself.

She checked her watch and saw that she had some free time before the big booms and flashes, so she pulled out her laptop and the necessary gadgetry to download all the photos onto the computer's hard disk so she could erase the memory card for reuse. Once that was done, she figured she might as well go ahead and copy the files onto a thumb drive for backup.

She was reasonably sure she was just being cautious and not just moping in her car. And if she still didn't get up and moving once all the files were in order and her camera was ready for action, it was because she wanted to take a quick look at some of the photos she'd taken to make sure that she had plenty of shots to choose from. It wasn't because she didn't want to have to see Joni and admit that she'd had no luck finding Leviathan. The fact that she was playing The Cure on her iPod during all the administrative activity was just a coincidence.

At least she had some decent pictures. Laryea did look quite impressive in his costume, and there were some great shots of him talking earnestly with Joni, as if discussing important business. There were, however, no pictures of him standing next to anybody taller, despite the best efforts of Wilder and the Photo-Operative to get shots of themselves with him.

She did have plenty of pictures of Wilder with various people at the inn: hamming it up with Nick, chatting with Hoover, posing proudly with a gaggle of female PAs. In one shot, Wilder was standing next to some techie who'd dredged up a T-shirt with the Blastoff brothers and Posit on the front.

Tilda stopped at that last photo for a minute, looking at the design on the T-shirt. Something looked wrong, but she couldn't put her finger on it. On a whim, she opened up a Web browser and went to IMDb. The T-shirt design was based on the publicity still of the Blastoffs and Posit she'd looked at before, when trying to decide if Pete was Spencer Marshall, and she enlarged it as much as her laptop screen would allow. It was a promotional shot of the cheesy spaceship interior, with Laryea and Pete in their shiny Blastoff costumes and Posit standing between them.

Laryea was easily recognizable. His face hadn't changed much, just gained character. He was an inch or two shorter than Pete, so Tilda figured he hadn't started wearing lifts yet. And both Blastoffs were taller than Posit.

Which made no sense.

Tilda knew she didn't have a picture of Wilder with Laryea, but she remembered taking one of Wilder and Pete. She flipped through pictures until she found the one she'd snapped right after interviewing Wilder, while he and Pete were talking in the parking lot at the inn. It showed clearly that Wilder was two or three inches taller than Pete.

How was that possible? Wilder had been a grown

man when *The Blastoffs* was on the air. So how could Pete have been taller than Wilder then, and shorter than him now? Even in the Posit costume, which would have added an inch or two, Wilder was still shorter than Pete.

There were no lifts on earth that could make the Wilder from twenty years ago taller than Pete, yet now he was definitely taller.

Tilda looked back at the publicity still on the Web. Could it have been taken with somebody else in the Posit costume, maybe before Wilder was cast?

A quick trip to YouTube scotched that idea. There were quite a few clips from *The Blastoffs* posted, including several complete episodes, and the Posit in the show was shorter than the Blastoff brothers. There was no way around it. Wilder couldn't have been Posit.

Tilda's heart was racing nearly as fast as her thoughts as she tried to put the pieces together. How had Laryea not noticed? Hell, she knew the answer to that. He never noticed anybody! If he hadn't recognized Pete, why would he have recognized a man who'd spent most of his time on set in an alien suit?

Tilda knew she didn't have it all yet—there were a dozen details that needed explaining—but she did know that there was a man running around pretending to be somebody he wasn't, and she'd just seen how the wannabe Leviathans had acted when called out. How much angrier would somebody who'd been faking it for years be? Angry enough to kill?

One man was already dead. If Laryea had been the target, he was still in danger, and right now, there was a cache of explosives about to go off under his feet.

She grabbed her cell phone and dialed Dom's number, but it went straight to voice mail. "Damn it!" Then she tried Nick, but got voice mail again. Angrily she pressed redial. "Damn it, Nick. Answer your freaking phone!"

Only then did she remember Joni's ruling that all cell phones be turned off during shooting. Obviously neither Nick nor Dom had forgotten.

Damn it! She checked her watch. It was nearly time for the big battle. Even if she called the cops, they couldn't get there fast enough, assuming that she could convince them she was right. Leaving everything but her keys and phone behind, Tilda jumped out of the car and started running toward the scaffolding the film crew had erected to fill in for the lighthouse.

The farther she got, the thicker the crowds she was pushing her way through. She knew she wasn't making any friends, but there was no help for it. Finally she made it to the restricted area, and lifted the rope marking it to duck under. One of Dom's security guys appeared, but she'd seen him before. "Joe," she said, reading the name from his shirt, "where's Nick?"

He pointed toward the faux Pharos, just visible from there.

"Get on the radio and tell them to stop the shoot! Don't let them set off those explosives!"

Without waiting to see if he'd obeyed, she took off. With all the techs and publicity people and caterers and who knew what else, there wasn't much more room to maneuver inside the rope than there had been outside, and there was an obscene amount of equipment to dodge around as well.

Finally she reached yet another rope barrier, this one surrounding the lighthouse set. But Hoover was at this one, and he wouldn't let her slip underneath. Instead he grabbed her around the waist and pulled her back.

"They're about to go live," he said. "You can't go in."

"You've got to stop them!"

But before she could even try to convince him that something terrible was going to happen, she heard the warning horn, and knew it was too late. There was a sharp crack, a series of loud pops like firecrackers on steroids, and then . . . Nothing. Nothing at all.

A minute later, she heard the cussing from above. Dylan O'Taine, keeper of the mystic lighthouse Pharos, was not a happy man.

# Chapter 42

A hunch is creativity trying to tell you something.
                                        —FRANK CAPRA


THERE was a wave of confusion as people tried to figure out what had happened. A few minutes later Nick finally made it over to where Hoover was still keeping Tilda out of trouble, and said, "What in hell is going on? I got a message that you wanted me to abort the shoot."

She couldn't even meet his eyes, she was so humiliated. "I thought he was going to try to kill Laryea."

"Who was?"

"Posit. I mean, Hugh Wilder, who wasn't Posit at all. He's an imposter, and he must be the one who tried to kill Laryea."

"What?"

"Wilder is too tall to be Posit. So he was trying to kill Laryea because—" She stopped, unable to think of any reason for Wilder to kill the man who hadn't even noticed he was a phony. "Shit, I don't even know what I'm saying, Nick. What happened with the explosives?"

"That's what we're trying to find out. There were supposed to be some serious blasts, but all they got was a fizzle. Joni is furious because she lost the light and they're going to have to try again tomorrow or fake it in the studio, either of which will cost a fortune. The special effects guys are going nuts trying to figure out what went wrong. Dad is making sure security didn't screw up. And of course Laryea . . ."

At that moment, the man himself stomped by as best he could in the sand, cursing like the proverbial sailor. Sebastian was trying to keep up with him while offering comfort and a water bottle, both of which Laryea ignored.

"I am not going to stand around while they figure out which asshole to fire," Laryea said. "I am going back to the effing hotel, where I better find my dinner waiting, and I am going to take off this effing costume, and I am going to call my agent." He pointed at Nick. "You. Where's my driver?"

"I'll find him right now, sir."

"Forget that. You can drive me."

Nick swallowed a sigh and said, "Right away." He gave Hoover a nod. "Tell Dad where I've gone."

The limo that Laryea had been using ever since the other one was impounded was parked close by, and Nick followed Laryea and Sebastian toward it.

Tilda couldn't figure out where her logic had gone wrong. She was sure that Wilder had killed Foster in an effort to get at Laryea, and this would have been the perfect opportunity to try again. But there had been no bomb. There hadn't even been the planned pyrotechnics.

Beside her, Hoover picked up his radio when it crackled, and she heard Dom's voice saying, "It looks like somebody ran off with most of the explosives."

Missing explosives? Nick was opening the car door for Laryea and Sebastian. Hadn't Wilder said something about explosives? No, fires. He'd said Pete liked to set fires.

Except that she no longer believed anything the old man said. He'd probably been lying to try to set Pete up, just like he'd tried to blame Foster's death on him. Laryea and Sebastian were in the limo now, and Nick had just shut the door.

Wilder must have been meaning to blame Pete when the explosion went off and killed Laryea. Except it didn't go off.

Nick had opened the front door and was reaching behind the sun visor to pull out the keys. Suddenly Tilda knew where the missing explosives were.

"Nick!" she screamed, and slipped away from Hoover to run for the limo. "Don't start the car! Get away from the car! There's a bomb!"

People scattered when they heard the word *bomb*, but Nick just froze.

She reached him and grabbed his arm. "The stolen explosives!" she said, trying to talk and breathe at the same time. "There's a bomb in the limo."

She expected questions, even disbelief, but instead he left the front door open and went to open the back door.

"Mr. Laryea, Sebastian, I think you should get out of the limo. We have reason to believe there is a bomb on board."

"This is absurd," Sebastian sputtered. "If you don't get in the car this minute, I will have you fired. In fact, I will make sure that neither you nor your father ever works again!"

Nick didn't argue with him. He just grabbed the smaller man by the front of his shirt and dragged him out of the limo. While Sebastian was squirming and arguing, Tilda leaned into the limo and in a very quiet voice said, "Mr. Laryea, if you do not get out of this limo, I am going to pull out my phone and I am going to tweet to the world that you have been lying about your height. I will tweet about the lifts in your shoes and the elevator boots you're wearing in the movie. I will then go to Facebook and post it there. How long do you think it would take to go viral? How long do you think it would take Perez Hilton to hear about it?"

Despite the amount of makeup Laryea was wearing, he blanched, and without saying a word, climbed out of the limo.

Hoover showed up, and he and Nick kept everybody clear while Nick called his father and the cops, who in turn called for experts that quickly verified that the limo had been rigged to explode as soon as Nick turned the key. Given the amount of explosives involved, not only would everyone in the limo have been killed, it was likely that a fair percentage of the film crew would have died, too, or at least been badly injured.

It was after the bomb squad had sent everybody to a safe distance that Tilda saw Hugh Wilder hovering in the crowd. She didn't quite see red, even if that was the cliché, but she heard a roaring in her ears that could not be denied.

She pointed at him. "You, Wilder. Get your ass over here!"

The old man stared at her. "What . . . ?"

Tilda went to him instead. If she'd been thinking straight, she might have considered the idea that approaching a murderer directly was not the brightest thing she'd ever done. But she wasn't thinking straight. She wasn't thinking at all.

"You son of a bitch! You cowardly, lying sack of shit! How many more people were you planning to kill?"

"I don't know what you're talking about."

"The hell you don't. I know damned well that you were the one driving the limo that killed Foster, not Pete Ellis. And you were the one who broke into my cottage to come after me, and I know you were planning to stab a lot more than my pillow."

"I didn't—"

"The only reason you didn't is because I got lucky. But did you stop there? No, you stole explosives from the set, didn't you? And you put a freaking bomb in the limo! I heard what the police said. You'd have killed everybody in the limo, and God knows how many more people."

"No, I—"

"And was it for money or revenge or something that was even worth killing over? No, it was so you could keep playing dress-up in a freaking fur suit!"

"I'm not—"

"And it's not even your suit! You're not Posit—you never were Posit."

The accusations of murder had confused Wilder, but it was Tilda's revealing his deception over the TV role that really got to him. Fat tears started rolling down his face. "No, no! That's not true. I was Posit. Of course I was Posit."

She scoffed. "The man who played Posit was a foot shorter than you are."

"I am Posit. I am!"

"What you are is a murderer."

"I had to—" He stopped himself. "I didn't mean to kill Foster. It was just that Spencer knew—I mean, Pete. He knew! He knew, and he would have told, and they would have taken Posit away from me. I couldn't let him take Posit away from me."

"What about me? How was I going to take Posit away from you?"

"I was just trying to scare you," he said. "Everybody but you believed Pete was driving the limo, and I thought that if I scared you, you'd believe it, too."

"Yeah, like I believe you were just going to scare me. If I was dead, you could be sure I wouldn't help Pete, couldn't you?"

"No, no. I didn't want to hurt anybody."

"Then what about the bomb? Were you planning to blame that on Pete, too? That's why you told me all that crap about him setting fires when he was a kid, isn't it? So it would look as if he'd set the bomb, not you."

"I meant to be here to stop anybody from getting into the limo—I didn't think John would want to leave so early. I was going to save everybody. But I had to stop and sign autographs for the kids. I do everything for the kids. The kids love Posit—they love me."

"You think they'll love you now, when they know you killed one man, and tried to kill more?"

"I didn't want anybody to get hurt," he insisted. "Posit never hurts people."

Tilda knew damned well that Wilder was lying—he'd had no intention of saving anybody. The awful thing was, she didn't know if he was lying to her or to himself. "You're not Posit," she said again.

Wilder kept blubbering, and the cops took him away, treating him far more gently than he deserved in Tilda's opinion. She knew she should have felt some pity for him, but she just didn't have it in her.

Later on, both Dom and Nick would applaud her brilliance in going after Wilder to make him crack in public that way. Otherwise, it would have been hard to catch him. There really hadn't been much in the way of physical evidence. Wilder hadn't been seen in the limo, and he hadn't left any prints. The same went for the knife attack on Tilda's pillow: no witnesses, no prints, no helpful DNA or security camera tapes. Maybe they would have found something on the stolen explosives, but since the best way to get rid of a bomb was to detonate it, any useful evidence wasn't likely to be around long.

Tilda just nodded and pretended that getting Wilder to implicate himself had been part of her master plan. But this time, she was the imposter. The real story was that after seeing Nick come within seconds of blowing himself to hell, she'd nearly been mad enough to kill.

# Chapter 43

**Episode 8**
Sid and Marty, tired of being mobbed by fans, use elaborate disguises and tricks to avoid them. Then they run into a trio of orphans crying because they can't go to the Blastoffs' only concert on their planet, and realize how important their fans are. As Posit puts it, "The fans need us, and we need them!"
—*SATURDAY MORNING SPREE* BY CHARLES M. LUCE

THERE was even more confusion after that: sessions with the police, explanations to Dom and Nick, more explanations to Joni and Edwina, calls to June and Cooper, reporter dodging, and articles sent to *Entertain Me!* There were probably meals scattered in there, too, but she really wasn't sure. She did know she was too tired to be hungry by the time she made her way up to her suite at the inn, and was about to throw herself down onto the bed, clothes and all, when there was a knock on the door.

It was Pete Ellis.

She'd have blown off anybody else, but him she wanted to talk to, so she let him in.

"Hey," she said. "Where've you been hiding?"

"You mean while Hugh Wilder was trying to blow up John? I didn't know anything about it until afterward. I was lying low like my lawyer told me to."

"Accepting the inevitable?"

"Except it wasn't inevitable, thanks to you."

"It took me long enough to figure it out."

"You mean about Wilder not having been Posit? I just spent time with the cops talking about that."

"You already knew, didn't you?"

He nodded.

"Since when?"

"Ever since that day we got to the Cape. As soon as I saw him, I knew it wasn't Posit."

Now that he said that, Tilda thought she remembered Pete starting to say something about it not being Posit, but she'd interrupted him. "Why in the hell didn't you tell me?"

"I didn't think it mattered. I knew the real Posit died years ago in a car crash, so if Wilder could make a few bucks, who was I to screw it up? You said yourself he was a good guy, so . . ."

"Yeah, he sure had me fooled." She'd leave people judging to Dom from that point on. "Who is he, really?"

"He really is Hugh Wilder, and he really did work on the show—he just wasn't Posit," Pete said. "He mostly coordinated stunts."

"Including stuff with explosives?"

"Yeah, some. We didn't have a big special effects budget, but he helped with the rocket ship blasting off and did some flashy stuff with the band. And when we needed a body to wear alien costumes, he did that, too. He played the tie-dye gorilla queen and that shooty dog thing that helped win a revolution."

"I don't even remember them. Posit is the one everybody

remembers." Then, realizing who she was talking to, she added, "Of the aliens, that is."

But Pete was grinning. "I know nobody remembers me. They wouldn't remember John either if he hadn't hit it big."

"So why is it you knew it wasn't the real Posit right away, and Laryea never did figure it out?"

"Because John's kind of a jerk. No, that's not fair. He was just really focused on his career, even then, and he would never have wasted any time talking to a dude in a fur suit. Hell, he barely spoke to me."

"I thought he was avoiding Wilder because of—" She stopped, because she wasn't sure if Pete knew about Laryea's height issues. "I mean, I guess he was avoiding Wilder because he didn't remember him and didn't want the guy to realize it."

"That makes as much sense as anything. Not that any of it really makes sense. I mean, why did he want to kill John? Or Foster? Which one was he after anyway?"

"Neither. He was after you."

"Say what?"

"You knew he wasn't really Posit, right? That means you were a threat. You could have totally destroyed his world."

"But I told him I wasn't going to tell anybody. I'd keep his secret, and he'd keep mine."

"You could have changed your mind. You could have been lying. You might have told somebody, someday."

"But I wouldn't have—"

"Pete, whether or not you really were a threat, Wilder *thought* you were." Tilda was reminded of her roommate's guinea pigs and how they'd reacted to the bag of food pellets being left on top of their cage as if it were a predator. "He decided he had to get rid of you somehow, and he must have known that you were going to be drinking that night."

Pete looked abashed. "I ran into him in the store where I went to buy beer. So yeah, he knew I was going on a bender."

"So all he had to do was wait for you to pass out, then steal the limo."

"How did he know that Foster and Laryea were going to be walking along that road?"

"I don't know that he did. I don't think he cared who he hit. It could just as easily have been me." In fact, Tilda realized, it nearly had been her. If she hadn't been so gun-shy about cars that she'd gone away from the road when she heard the limo approaching, he probably would have hit her instead. "He didn't need to kill anybody—he was telling the truth when he said he didn't mean for Foster to die. He just wanted to hit somebody so you'd get in trouble. Best case scenario, you'd go to jail. Worst case, you'd be fired. He didn't count on Dom believing you."

"Not Dom. It was you who believed me when nobody else did."

"Which is why Wilder came after me. I don't know if he meant to kill me or scare me off, but either way I'd be out of his way. Come to think of it . . . Did you see him that night?"

Pete thought about it. "Yeah, I did. He was at the inn, and might have heard me tell Nick I was going to take a walk."

"So he was probably planning to frame you for the attack on me, too. I mean, I was your only alibi, and if I was dead . . ."

"Jesus, Tilda. The guy's a psycho!"

"That's what my sister the psychologist said, too."

"I don't know how I can ever thank you."

"I told you—being nosy is my job. But if you really want to thank me . . ."

"You know I do."

"Can you drive me to my sister's house some night in the limo? Just so I can see her face."

He laughed. "Sure thing. Though I'm surprised you didn't ask for an interview about *The Blastoffs*, now that it's all out in the open."

"I'm sorry about that, Pete. I had to tell the cops what I knew."

"Of course you did—I'm not blaming you. I guess it was time. I'm not saying I won't be quoting the Serenity Prayer a lot over the next few days, but I'll be okay. When things calm down, I'd be glad to sit down for an interview."

"I'd like that. It will be a great story, Pete, and I don't think anybody will laugh at you."

After he was gone, Tilda finally got to bed, but lay there awake for a while thinking about Hugh Wilder and why he'd felt the need to lie. At first, it had been for the attention, and then to get the job on the cartoon show. But the real irony was that he'd killed a man, and had been willing to kill more, just so people would love him.

# Chapter 44

**wrap** *n* Refers to the completion of film shooting (either for the day or for the entire production or project); in the early days of cinema, the cameraman would say after filming: "Wind, reel, and print"—abbreviated as WRAP. An entirely completed film is termed *in the can*.

—TIM DIRKS, WWW.FILMSITE.ORG

THE next day, they filmed the explosives scene for real. Security was incredibly tight, but a special vantage point was provided for Tilda, so she got great pictures and a plate of nachos while she waited.

Laryea, despite his earlier scare, was in fine form, and Tilda heard Joni tell Edwina that maybe actually having been in danger had improved his portrayal of a man in battle. Or maybe he just wanted to get it right so he could get out of Glenham. Whatever it was, his performance was spot-on. After Joni yelled, "Print it!" there were cheers from the crew, and Laryea bowed happily.

There was a clambake on the beach that afternoon to celebrate the end of the shoot. From what Tilda knew of moviemaking, usually a shindig like that would have been thrown after the whole movie had been shot, not just one location's worth, but this was a special case. As Nick put it, they were celebrating their survival.

It was a little chilly to eat outside, but nobody seemed to mind, especially not when Joni and Edwina handed out *Pharos* jackets to everybody, including Tilda and the security team. Nick and Dom were keeping an eye out so the rest of the guys could relax, but Pete was there, looking serene and happily sober.

Since everybody was going to be leaving town the next day, the party ended early in the evening and Tilda headed back to her room to pack. It was surprising how quickly she'd spread her belongings all throughout the suite, and she realized she still had the page from *Pharos* that she'd used to eliminate the wannabes. So she went down the hall to Joni's suite, but it was Edwina who answered her knock.

"Joni's on a video conference downstairs," she explained.

"I just wanted to return this," Tilda said.

"Add it to the pile."

Tilda went to put it on top of a stack of artwork that included the storyboards used on the shoot. The one on top was the one Edwina herself had drawn at the last minute, and Tilda noticed that she'd done an excellent job of drawing the lighthouse. She picked it up to look at it more closely, impressed by how close the style matched the comic book's look. Then suddenly she wasn't so impressed.

"I hear you didn't have any luck finding Leviathan," Edwina said.

"I wouldn't say that, exactly."

"I thought all the wannabes were fakes."

"They were, but you're not."

"I beg your pardon?"

Tilda looked her right in the eye. "You're Leviathan."

# Chapter 45

When I was a child I was a dreamer. I read comic books, and I was the hero of the comic book. I saw movies, and I was the hero in the movie. So every dream I have ever dreamed has come true a hundred times.

—ELVIS PRESLEY

TILDA would have given fifty-fifty odds of whether or not Edwina would cop to it, but the producer seemed resigned to the discovery.

"And I thought I'd covered my tracks fairly thoroughly," she said.

"You did," Tilda said. "In fact, you covered them a bit too well, which should have been a clue. None of the wannabes struck me as being that careful, but a lawyer like you—"

"Actually, I was only prelaw when I drew *Pharos*. But I suppose the instincts were already there. I was very good at hiding things."

"Including yourself?"

"Especially myself. Growing up in my family meant there were certain expectations. I was to go to a good prep school, attend a prestigious college, and enter a certain kind of profession: business, medicine, or law. I did what the family wanted, too—played the right sports, had the right friends, and so on.

"But I also had some friends I didn't invite to have dinner with my parents, and they're the ones who got me hooked on comic books. I read my way through a couple of friends' collections, then started buying my own. I couldn't collect, of course, because it would have been noticed, so I'd buy the titles I wanted, read them two or three times, then pass them on to friends."

"And reading led to writing?"

"And drawing. I'd had a lot of art classes along the way—having an appreciation for fine art fit into my family's plan. So I took all those lessons in sketching and oil painting and applied them to comic books."

"*Pharos* always did have a more formal feel than most comics."

"My friends thought I was good enough to get published, but I couldn't do that. It would totally ruin my chances of getting into a good law firm, let alone making partner."

"But if you didn't want to be a lawyer . . ."

"I *did* want to be a lawyer. It just wasn't enough. I wanted the comics, too."

"Like a superhero with a secret identity?"

Edwina smiled. "Anyway, I drew a couple of Batman and X-Men pastiches purely for my entertainment. Nothing I could have sold of course—there was no way DC or Marvel would have let me mess with their biggest properties. Then some of my friends went to a comics convention in North Carolina, and told me about meeting Marc Fitzwilliam, who was just starting Regal. He handed out business cards, looking for talent, and a couple of my friends had decided they were going to submit ideas for a title."

"Did he buy any of them?"

"No, they were dreadful. But seeing them go through the process taught me the mechanics of submitting: the kind of paper to use, what to put in a proposal, and so on. And I started working on *Pharos* in secret."

"You didn't tell your comic book friends?"

"I didn't tell anyone. I couldn't risk word getting back to my family. And I knew I had to come up with something different so my friends wouldn't recognize my style. Since I'd only done superhero stuff before, I tried something supernatural. I worked up the first issue and submitted to Fitzwilliam, telling him we'd met at the con. Since he'd handed out business cards like a lawyer drumming up business, I figured he'd never know if he'd really spoken to me or not. When he accepted the book, I told him something mysterious about having to keep my identity secret, and he went along."

"No wonder. He said the book was the best thing ever submitted to him."

"Really?" She smiled again. "Of course, the whole idea of a secret creator appealed to him, too. Anyway, I set up a separate bank account, and for a little over a year, I got to be a comic book writer."

"And when *Pharos* was cancelled?"

"In a way, it was almost a relief. I loved doing it, but I was in law school by then, and I didn't have the time to do it properly anymore. Fitzwilliam wanted me to try to come up with another character, but I told him it was time to let Leviathan disappear."

"But he didn't. Or she didn't."

"No, and that was the amazing part. When Fitzwilliam sold Regal to MasterWork, they brought out the issues again."

"That reminds me. How could a lawyer, or even a pre-law student, sign away all those rights?"

She looked embarrassed. "I wasn't up to speed on intellectual property law, and of course Fitzwilliam didn't know what he was doing, either. He swore that he was using an industry standard contract, and I did enough research to see that it was pretty close to what Marvel and DC were doing. What I didn't know is that smaller companies usually let creators keep the characters." Defensively, she added, "It's not like I could ask anybody for advice."

"I suppose not."

"And I didn't care about the money. My family had money. The comic book royalties would have been chicken feed in comparison. I just wanted to have the books out there."

"If it were today, you could have put it out on the Web."

"I might very well have done that."

"So why did you end up buying the rights back?"

"I didn't. Joni did. I've never told anybody about being Leviathan, not until now, but I did show the book to people. I wanted to know what they thought of it."

"What if they didn't like it?"

"They all liked it," she said with a sniff. "Only Joni

didn't just like it—she loved it. Which is why I 'found' those original pages for her."

"I should have caught on to that sooner," Tilda said. "Fitzwilliam said he didn't have them, and I'd been told that they'd never been seen at art shows or made available on eBay. Yet Joni had a bunch. I take it you've got the rest."

"I have a couple of framed covers at my house, but the rest are in storage. I couldn't show them or sell them without risking somebody figuring out who I was, and I didn't want to sell them anyway. Giving them to Joni was different. I think it was having the pages that convinced her that *Pharos* would make a terrific movie."

"You mean that wasn't your doing?"

"It honestly wasn't, but I loved the idea. So I went about acquiring the rights, and we got the ball rolling."

"Why didn't you tell her you were Leviathan? Why don't you tell her now? You can't still be trying to live up to your family's expectations."

"I just never found the right time. Not to mention the fact that it would have been harder for us to get funding if we said, 'This is my comic book—let's make it a movie.' And I was afraid Dolores wouldn't be as willing to write the script—she would have been worried I'd be offended when she made changes."

"All good reasons. And I don't believe any of them."

Edwina bent her head and fiddled with a pen, looking tentative for the first time since Tilda had met her. Finally she said, "I was afraid Joni wouldn't believe me. She's the creative one—I'm the businessperson."

"So now you're living up to her expectations?"

"Something like that. Are you going to tell her?"

"God, no."

"What about the article you were going to write?"

Tilda considered it. "I could still write it, if you'd cooperate. No picture, or only a fuzzed out one, and you can answer questions about the comic and the adaptation without saying anything about yourself. Joni won't even have to know if you don't want her to."

"How will people know it's really Leviathan after all the wannabes?"

"I'll make that part of the story, including how I figured out why none of them were you. Besides, I do have a certain reputation in this field." As she said it, Tilda was pleased to realize that she was right. She *did* have a good reputation.

"Can I sleep on it?"

"Sure, but only on one condition."

"What's that?"

"Can I have that storyboard you drew?"

Edwina smiled broadly, then used the pen in her hand to add the Leviathan signature. "How's that?"

"Perfect." Maybe she wouldn't be able to display it, but it was enough to have a genuine piece of art from Leviathan.

# Chapter 46

The announcement that *The Blastoffs* had not been renewed for a second season came as filming was winding down on the eighteenth and final episode, so there was no opportunity to officially end the show. The most they could manage was a musical number of the theme song "Blasting Off!", followed by the cast and crew waving farewell.

—*Saturday Morning Spree* by Charles M. Luce

TILDA checked out of her room around ten the next morning, though she wasn't quite ready to leave. She was taking a load of luggage out to her car when she saw Greg Dickson sitting disconsolately on the hotel veranda. She ignored him when she walked by the first time, but on the trip back, she relented. If he hadn't made such a pest of himself, she might not have realized Laryea's real height, and if he hadn't posted that photo of himself and Wilder on his website, she might not have figured out that the guy wasn't really Posit. So maybe she ought to throw him a bone.

"Hey," she said.

"Hey. Look, I want to apologize about what I said the other day. It was totally uncalled for and unprofessional, and I can't believe I said it."

"I can't say that I expected professional behavior from you."

He winced, but didn't object.

"On a personal level," she added, "it was definitely uncalled for and I can't believe you said it, either. Still, I know how frustrating it is to try to get a story or picture and not be able to. If you still want Laryea's picture—"

"You know I do!"

"Then I've got a suggestion."

She raided the first aid kit in her car and borrowed more supplies from the inn to perform a little special effects magic. Then she consulted Nick to find out that Laryea was in the dining room, and got him to agree to let Dickson sit on a couch in the lobby.

After a few minutes' wait, Laryea and Sebastian came out of the dining room and headed for the elevator.

"Mr. Laryea!" Dickson said loudly. "Do you have time for a picture before you go?"

Laryea turned toward him as Sebastian moved into defense mode, ready to block Dickson until his boss could escape.

Following Tilda's instructions, Dickson said, "I'm sorry I can't get up, but with my foot . . ." He gestured at his right foot, which was wrapped in three packages' worth of ACE bandages.

Tilda hoped neither Laryea nor Sebastian knew enough about medicine to recognize what a lousy job she'd done, but everything she knew about medicine came from watching reruns of *House* and *Doogie Howser, MD*.

Laryea flashed his multimillion-dollar smile. "Of course, I'd be happy to. Sebastian, would you mind?"

Sebastian accepted the camera from Dickson, and took a picture of Laryea standing next to the seated Dickson. The camera was returned, hands were shaken, and everybody was happy.

As soon as the elevator door shut behind Laryea and Sebastian, Dickson started unwrapping his foot. "Tilda, that was brilliant! What made you think of it?"

"I read that Laryea was briefly confined to a wheelchair, so I thought an injury might get his attention." Of course, it wasn't the real reason, but it was semitruthful. In one of the episodes of *The Blastoffs*, Laryea's character got a laser burn or some such and had to zoom around in a space wheelchair. Tilda seemed to recall that it was rocket powered.

"Well, I owe you one."

"Yes, you do, and I always collect on owed favors."

# Chapter 47

Though there is a satisfying climax at the end of *Pharos*, there is also a sense that while Dylan O'Taine may be bruised, he has not been defeated. The last panel, with O'Taine standing at the top of the lighthouse to look out to sea, convinces the reader that he is still there, guarding the border between the ocean and the walking world.

—*TEENAGE MUTANT NINJA ARTISTS: THE BEST OF INDIE COMICS* BY JERRY FRAZEE

TILDA made the rounds, saying good-bye to people and exchanging e-mail addresses and phone numbers. Eventually she caught up with Nick, who was staring out the window, watching the ocean. It was a gray, windy day, making for a gloomy sight. Nick's expression matched the weather perfectly.

"Dude, what's the matter? We caught the bad guy and confirmed that when it comes to judging people, your father is still undefeated. You should be planning your victory trip to Disney World."

"Yeah, I know. That's all good, but . . . I just got a text from Cynthia. She dumped me. She dumped me in a freaking text message."

"Wow," Tilda said in a monotone. "What a bitch. Who would ever do something that cold?"

When Nick glared at her, she couldn't stop the giggles. That made him glare more ferociously, and of course, that made her laugh even harder. A minute later he gave up the fight and joined in.

"Okay, it was karma biting me in the ass," he said.

"Yes it was, but I'm still sorry it didn't work out. I hate to see a friend get his heart broken."

"Well, I can't say my heart is broken."

"I thought you and she were pretty serious."

"I thought so, too, when we were together, but distance didn't make the heart grow fonder."

"Shall I spout the usual platitudes? She wasn't good enough for you. There are plenty of other fish in the sea. Who wants to be tied down anyway, unless it's with leather straps?"

"I don't think I recognize that last one."

"Really? It's very common in these parts."

"Seriously though, maybe it's for the best. The fact is, I've really enjoyed spending time with you these past couple of weeks. Do you think maybe we could take up where we left off?"

"What do I look like? Rebound Rita?"

"Sorry, I didn't mean it like that. Could I call you? Maybe in a week or two?"

"If anybody is going to do any calling, it'll be me."

"Fair enough. But I hope you do call." He grinned. "It would make Pop extremely happy."

Speaking of whom, Dom appeared on the other side of the lobby and called to Nick. Nick hesitated, then leaned over to give Tilda the briefest of kisses before going to join his father. She watched him walk away, which was a striking reminder of his shapeliness from that angle. In fact, she was pretty sure he was strutting just a bit, to make sure she noticed.

"Asshole," she said affectionately. "You probably think I'm going to call you as soon as I get home." She'd show him. She'd wait until the next day.

It was time for her to head back to Malden—the guinea pigs, dogs, cats, and other assorted pets that inhabited her house must be missing her terribly. Well, maybe not the snake.

One of the Tolomeo limos was parked outside, with Pete standing at attention by the door.

"Isn't this where we came in?" she asked him.

"I think so. I'm taking Laryea back to the airport."

"Drive safely."

"I always do."

Sebastian came out, leading a phalanx of bellmen, and officiously supervised as they loaded the luggage. Then Laryea himself came up to Tilda.

"I haven't thanked you for what you did." He went for the air-kiss, but when his mouth was right by her ear, he added, "and for what you haven't done."

"John, it has been a pleasure meeting a *big* star like you."

He smiled.

"You know," she said, "most of the time I write about people who used to be famous, folks that are long out of the spotlight. So I just want to say that I hope I never have a reason to interview you again."

"Thank you, but if you ever need anything, call me. Better yet, call Sebastian. I know how fond he is of you."

Sebastian narrowed his eyes, but did nod before climbing into the back of the limo. Laryea started to get in, too. Then he stopped, and for the first time Tilda could remember, really looked at Pete. Then he opened the door to the front seat and said, "I'd like to ride up here with you, if that's okay."

"Whatever you want," Pete said, and closed the back door on Sebastian's indignation.

Laryea got inside, but before he shut the door, Tilda heard him say, "Are we ready to blast off?"

"Blasting off, bro!" Pete replied.

And the Blastoff brothers took off once again.